BORDERLANDS
DEBT OR ALIVE

ANTHONY BURCH

TITAN BOOKS

BORDERLANDS®: DEBT OR ALIVE

Print edition ISBN: 9781803363530
E-book edition ISBN: 9781803363639

Published by Titan Books
A division of Titan Publishing Group Ltd
144 Southwark Street, London SE1 0UP
www.titanbooks.com

First edition: June 2024
10 9 8 7 6 5 4 3 2 1

This is a work of fiction. All of the characters, organizations, and events portrayed in this novel are either products of the author's imagination or are used fictitiously. Any resemblance to actual persons, living or dead (except for satirical purposes), is entirely coincidental.

A CIP catalogue record for this title is available from the British Library.

Printed and bound by CPI (UK) Ltd, Croydon, CR0 4YY.

Dedicated to my spouse Lauren.

PROLOGUE

It was a bright sunny day on Pandora and Fiona was about to get her face blasted in.

"Hold on," the young girl said into the rusted barrel of a Jakobs revolver. "You just had some lint. In your pants pocket."

The man at the other end of the pistol squinted at her with his one remaining eye. The other, a cyber-prosthetic, whirred and extended toward her face in curiosity. His grip on the gun was solid and unwavering.

"And you decided to take my wallet with it?" he asked.

Fiona shrugged. "Big piece of lint."

"How old are you?" he asked in an accent as smooth as Pandora was rough.

"How should I know? Leggo my wrist," she complained, struggling against his viselike grip.

"You don't know how old you are? So, no family, then."

"I wouldn't say that."

Fiona's eyes flicked involuntarily over his shoulder to the pipsqueak perched on a nearby rooftop, awkwardly clutching a sniper rifle as big as her body.

Sasha thrust a thumb into the air. She had a shot. A single nod from Fiona and the One-Eyed Man would turn into (depending on Sasha's aim) the No-Eyed Man, the Two-Eyed Man, or Still The One-Eyed Man But With A Sucking Chest Wound.

The man's expression changed from mild amusement to genuine interest. He let go of Fiona's wrist, grabbed her by the scruff of her shirt, and whirled, hauling her up into the air and directly into Sasha's line of fire.

"Please tell your friend with the rifle to hold her trigger finger, unless she wishes to have one less…" He squinted at Fiona's face, then at the shocked sniper on the rooftop behind her. The orange rays from the Pandoran sun glinted off her scope. Even at distance, and even bathed in the evening light, the familial resemblance was obvious. "…sister?" he ventured.

Fiona nodded, her feet dangling uselessly above the ground. "Good guess. So, what now? We stay like this until your arm gets tired?"

"Perhaps. Answer me this, though. There are many fine marks in this bazaar. Why rob me?"

Fiona tried to shrug casually—not an easy thing to do when being held aloft by your neck at the wrong end of both a sniper rifle and a revolver.

"Your clothes are the closest thing to clean I've seen in a month. Some people, you rob 'em and they're ruined for life. You? You look like you could survive a little pickpocketing."

The man scowled and shook his head. "Terrible reason. Try again."

Fiona frowned. "You looked rich. Might have something worth selling."

"Getting warmer. Try again."

"Because we're hungry."

"And you'd do anything to fill your bellies, would you? Even rob a one-eyed man?"

"I don't know if I'd use the word 'rob.' I didn't mean to offend—"

The man cocked the revolver with a chunky click. "Be honest, now," he said. "With yourself as much as me. *Why* did you choose to rob me?"

Fiona stared into the man's eye and tried not to think of a very large, gold filigreed bullet entering her face. Tried not to think of what Sasha would do without her.

"Because your peripheral vision sucks. Because you walk with a limp and would have a hard time chasing me down. Because you smiled at the waterseller and nobody smiles on Pandora except for idiots and conmen."

The man held her gaze for a moment, then nodded.

"Tell your sister to leave the gun and come down," he said, holstering his gun. "We've got a lot to discuss."

"I'm not going to a second location with you."

"I'm not going to murder you, you idiot."

Fiona, after briefly flirting with the idea of signaling Sasha to blast the guy apart anyway, waved her sister off, then beckoned her to join them.

"Your instincts are good," the man said, setting her back down on the dry Pandoran dirt. "But your execution is terrible. A man with one eye has sharper hearing than a man with two. You should have made more noise to mask your approach, not less. And if my clean clothes and winning smile make me look like a fool, well… then I suppose they're doing their job, aren't they?"

Sasha approached the man from his front. She walked with her hands clasped behind her back, which was about as subtle as a T-shirt reading, I HAVE A GUN TUCKED INTO MY WAISTBAND AND WANT TO BE ABLE TO ACCESS IT QUICKLY.

"Take the gun out if you want," the man said. "You're not going to need it. Let's walk."

Sasha did. The small Tediore pistol looked massive in her hands. Her arms shook with the strength required to keep the weapon up, but she bit her lip and struggled to keep it level anyway.

As the three of them stepped away from the waterseller's stall, the man smiled again. Fiona typically wanted to put her fist through smiling faces, but there was something warm about the way the man's eyes crinkled. Something that, on any other planet, Fiona might have mistaken for authenticity.

"I'll admit, I look like an easy mark. That's the point. If you're going to be a proper villain, though, you'll need to see past the obvious. The bulge in my hip pocket should have told you 'personalized shield,' which should have told you 'prepared.' And after I caught you pickpocketing me, you—much like the unfortunate proprietor of that water stand—should have been watching the hand *without* the gun in it." He pulled a thin metal tube from his pants. A blue snowflake emblazoned on its side.

"Cryo-tubes typically go for a few thousand bucks at your typical waterseller's stand. But if your fingers are quick enough, and you've got a distraction—like, say, a young girl and her sister trying to rob you in broad daylight—you can get one for the low, low price of free."

Fiona and Sasha tried to look unimpressed. Neither had seen him pocket the cryo-tube from the waterseller, and Fiona had been inches from him while he'd done it.

"Now, I'm going to go sell this to a 'nadesmith. As you assisted with the theft, I'll cut you in to the tune of one percent."

"Ten," Sasha yelled, trying and failing to raise her gun menacingly.

"Two," the man calmly replied.

"We'll take it," Fiona said, signaling Sasha to fall silent. "But the next job we split fifty-fifty."

"The next job? Presumptuous of you."

Fiona put her hands on her hips. "No thief worth their skagspit works alone. I had your cashpurse out of your pocket before you caught me. So, we'll work with you."

"Fi," Sasha whispered. "You sure about this? He could be a... a serial killer. A pervert, or something. He's got a mustache."

"What's wrong with my mustache?"

"What's right with it?" Sasha countered.

Fiona waved her hand. "If he tries anything on me, you shoot him. If he tries anything on you, I'll shoot him. Sound fair?"

Sasha sighed.

The man crossed his arms. Leaned against a rusted road sign. The girls tried their best to act like they didn't care if he accepted their deal or not.

"Never had apprentices," he said.

"You still don't. We're partners."

He raised an eyebrow. "Whatever you say, child. But if we're going to work together, you need to know: That was the wrong answer you gave me, back there."

"How so?"

The man knelt before Fiona. She heard his cyber-prosthetic whirr as it once again focused on her. "You don't rob somebody because they look like an easy mark. You don't rob somebody 'cause they look like they can take it."

He thrust his pistol into her hands.

"You rob somebody because fuck 'em. There's only one rule to surviving on this planet, or any other: You always look out for number one. Doesn't matter what you have to do. Doesn't matter who you have to hurt. You take care of yourself. And...?"

He gestured at the smaller of the two girls, the unspoken question still on his lips. They'd nearly blown each other apart, but they didn't know one another's names yet.

The older girl hooked a thumb at her younger sister. "Sasha. And I'm Fiona."

"Nice to meet you," the man said. "I'm Felix. And anybody who isn't us can go straight to hell."

Many years later…

1
SASHA

Sasha died.

She and her sister were speeding through the innards of a large ancient alien Guardian in their jet-fueled caravan.[1] The Guardian protected a Vault—an alien cache of immeasurable wealth.

Sasha and Fiona were fans of immeasurable wealth, and so they'd decided to blow up the Guardian. They'd planted a hilariously powerful bomb inside the creature's teleportation gland and were boosting their way out of the monster's body when everything went wrong.

"Fiona, what's your status?" a panicked voice barked through Fiona's earpiece. The voice belonged to Rhys, a former executive who had helped Sasha and Fiona track down this Vault over the course of a few years with just as many betrayals. Rhys had wanted to buy a Vault Key. Sasha and Fiona tried to con him into buying a fake one. After that, several interested parties tried to kill all of them, which led directly to the trio becoming friends.

Sasha and Rhys had developed feelings for each other, much

---

1 As one does.

to Fiona's consternation. Sasha had never asked Fiona why she objected so much to the pairing, but it wasn't much of a secret: Sasha was intelligent and dependable, and Rhys once gave himself a papercut opening a box of cookies.

Sasha had initially felt that Rhys had half a brain cell on a good day, and about as much dependability as an outrider with a faulty brake line. Through their adventures together, however, and through seeing the lengths he'd go to protect his friends, those feelings had shifted.

"The charges are set," Fiona radioed to their allies outside.

Fiona weighed the detonator in her hand as Sasha watched in anticipation. Years of chasing leads and dodging bullets had all led to this. She clicked the detonator.

Nothing happened.

"Uhh, no," she said. "Shit. We're out of range. We're out of range! We have to stop."

Sasha shook her head as the caravan vibrated with speed around them. "We can't! The boost is going! We can't shut it off mid-burn." Sasha snatched the detonator from her sister's hand and gave it another click. *Maybe*, she thought, *she just didn't press the button hard enough*. Then she remembered Fiona had just spent the last half-hour dodging bullets and killing alien robots. Maybe Fiona deserved a little more credit.

"Dammit!" Sasha shouted at the lack of an explosion which followed.

"Fi," Rhys yelped over the radio. "We're commencing our attack!"

At that moment, Rhys and a handful of Sasha's other allies were strapped into the cockpit of a bipedal mecha, preparing to pound the Vault Guardian into submission once the sisters destroyed its ability to teleport.[2]

---

2 Long story.

"Are you almost out?" he asked. "Fiona? Come in!"

Fiona floundered, hurriedly trying to come up with a plan. Something about how the detonator was too far away from the bomb, that they'd have to wait for the boost to finish, then turn around and try the detonator again.

It was a bad plan, and Sasha knew it. Everyone would be dead by the time they could so much as turn the caravan around.

As Fiona struggled for a solution—Fiona always had a solution—Sasha crept to the caravan door. She yanked it open.

The sisters had saved one another's lives countless times. They never talked about it, but each of them privately kept a tally of who had saved their sister on more occasions. Today, Sasha was ready to come out on top. For good.

"Fiona," Sasha said, the wind nearly drowning out her voice. "It's okay."

Sasha winked.

Smiled.

Threw herself from the caravan.

She tumbled backward, deeper into the heart of the Vault Guardian, every bump and bruise bringing her closer into range of the charges. Sasha hammered on the detonator's trigger over and over, panicking with every uneventful click.

The vehicle that had once been Sasha's home continued its uninterruptible burn, boosting Fiona safely out of the beast.

Sasha's last thought before the detonator fired was one of smug satisfaction. *Fiona is safe, and she'll be so pissed at me.*

Minutes later, the fight was over. The Vault creature was dead, its teleportation gland detonated along with Sasha and its head cut from its shoulders by an oversized beam katana.[3]

---

3 Again. Long story.

———

Rhys found Sasha among the wreckage, his typical panic mixed with a heartbreak that almost made Fiona regret trying to keep them separated for as long as she had.

"Hey Sis," Sasha groaned through wet, broken breaths. She reached out for her gun as if it were a stuffed animal, something comforting to hold onto as she died. "The Desolator," she said, wrapping her fingers around its grip. "Not really my style, but it's a great backup weapon."

She loved the loot. The adventure. The danger. And she saw the conclusion in Fiona's eyes: Fiona blamed herself for this. Her big sister had failed somehow, as if this hadn't been Sasha's choice in the first place.

Fiona and Rhys tried to lift Sasha up. She screamed a scream that made Fiona look more heartbroken and terrified than Sasha had ever seen her.

Sasha asked for the gift Felix had left behind for her before he disappeared. A pocket watch with the words TIME HEALS ALL WOUNDS etched into its back.

Rhys sobbed so loud Sasha couldn't think. He bent over Sasha and poked at his eye as if trying to pick a stray hair out of it. "What are you doing?" Sasha asked.

"There's all those stories," he cried, "where someone's tears heal people. I really feel like that's a thing." Dumb as a rock, but he had a big heart. Had to give him that.

"This isn't one of those stories," Sasha said.

Then she died, cradling the watch in her hands.

———

The pocket watch glowed an ethereal green. The atmosphere of grief transformed into one of confusion as the watch floated into the air. It emitted a cone of green energy, bathing Sasha in soft light and pulling her from the ground. The watch hauled her limp body upward, suspending her within the flood of unnatural jade light.

"Sasha?" Fiona whispered, as much out of surprise as anything else.

Sasha's body continued to rise upward, pulled by the otherworldly power of the watch. Bright green beams of energy played up and down Sasha's lifeless form. They scoured her body, tracing every broken bone, analyzing every internal rupture.

And then Sasha came back to life.

With a gasp, her back arched and her eyes flicked open. She looked around, disoriented but serene.

"I guess Felix did…" she said, unable to finish the sentence as the beams of green light unceremoniously shut off and sent her plummeting back down to the ground.

"Ow," said the no-longer-dead Sasha.

She and her sister embraced, and laughed, and Fiona was furious at her. Sasha couldn't exactly blame Fiona; if their places had been switched, Sasha would have never forgiven Fiona for dying and coming back to life so casually.

Still, after relief blasted away their grief, the sisters put the tragedy out of their minds. There were more important things to be done.

They had riches to collect.

2
FIONA

I was standing in a Vault.

Hot damn.

Not even an hour ago, I was mourning my sister. Now, I stood within an alien cache of riches and power—typically, the kind of thing opened only by entire armies or superhuman killing machines we call "Vault Hunters" because that nickname rolls off the tongue better than "Gun-Hungry Mass Murderers Who Sometimes, Even If Only By Accident, Do Heroic Things."

But there was no army here. No Vault Hunters.[4] Just me and Rhys.

Me, the Pandoran con artist with a sharp hat and an even sharper sister.

Him, the corporate stooge who wanted to climb the corporate ladder and ended up blowing the ladder to smithereens.

And now we were standing in a Vault.

Hot damn.

Our voices echoed through the cavernous chamber of the Eridians, veins of purple energy running through cold alien rocks.

---

4 Other than me. Arguably.

We stood before a stone chest that glowed violet and hummed with otherworldly energy.

The end of our journey.

Our reward.

Sasha and the others were outside, filling their pockets with cash and weaponry. Hunting big-ass Vault monsters can be good business if you've got a good team. As teams go, we were better than most. But we hadn't gotten here without losing people. People more valuable than—

"Would you like to do the honors?" Rhys asked, cutting off my thoughts. Rhys and I hadn't always gotten along. Partially because he'd screwed me over on more than one occasion, but mostly because he was a big dumb idiot.

If there was one thing this planet-crossing, gun-shooting, sister-almost-dying adventure had taught me, though, it was this: Judge slowly.

"It's the last one," I said, thinking of the half-dozen Vault clues we'd followed and several dozen corpses we'd created to get to this very moment. "It's only right we both open it. It's the best part."

Rhys nodded, an exhausted smile threatening to appear on his lips. "Was kinda hoping you'd say that."

The alien treasure chest sat before us. Mysterious. Inscrutable.

Most stories of Vault treasure-hunting don't end particularly well. Best-case scenario, you get a handful of guns. Worst case, nobody ever sees you again.[5] But we hadn't come this far just to leave our quarry unopened.

Rhys and I put our hands on the warm lid of the chest. We pushed.

---

5 Pandora's first successful Vault Hunter, a Crimson Lance commandant named Steele, earned a sharp tentacle through her chest for her trouble. A few years later, a Hyperion engineer named Jack found a Vault on the Moon and got his face burned off in the process.

The chest slid open with an ethereal hiss, unfolding and retracting along the veins of Eridian magic etched into its surface. A bright purple light shot from the innards of the box, completely overwhelming my senses. I could hear the light. I could taste it.

Everything went white.

Ah, I thought. *So it's a bomb. An alien bomb just exploded and killed us all. If this is the afterlife, I'll be sure to apologize to Sasha at my earliest convenience.*

Then I heard a sound that convinced me I couldn't possibly be in heaven: Rhys's voice.

"Uh, the Atlas Corporation, I guess?" he said, pulling out a legalese-riddled piece of paper. "I got the rights, but they're not, uh, signed. Or legal in any way. And I'm still poor."

My vision cleared. I stood within an infinitely large, infinitely purple void. A pinprick in the distance gesticulated much like Rhys would. As the pinprick spoke, I could hear its voice as if Rhys were right next to me.

"I mean, I just want to build something of my own, you know? Blaze my own trail. Stop following false idols. Maybe restarting Atlas could help me do that? Unless… Oh god, unless that's a trick question. Like, if seeking power is bad and you're gonna, like, turn me into a big monster, like an ironic twist thing. In that case, I wish for, uhhhhhh—"

Rhys cut himself off, as if interrupted.

"Oh! No ironic twist? That's great. Super. Glad to hear it. So, uh, yeah, I guess the ownership of the Atlas Corporation and all its trademarks and—"

Pop. A chest appeared at Rhys's feet.

"Oh! So, these are the documents? That's gr—"

He disappeared.

For a horrible moment, I thought that was it. Rhys was off, free to rebuild gun corporations and hit on my sister while I languished in this royal-colored void for the rest of eternity. Stuck in one spot. Alone. For ever.

Then something worse happened.

"Hellooooooooooo, traveler," said a voice that sounded like someone had inhaled a lungful of helium and then gargled rusty nails.

I turned and, to my endless disappointment, saw a CL4P-TP robot wheeling toward me. A steward-class automaton whose designers confused "friendly" with "deeply annoying" when programming its personality.

"Be not afraid," it said. "I am not a Claptrap. This is merely a form I have chosen to make you more comfortable."

"If you want to make me comfortable, be literally anything else," I said.

The Claptrap narrowed its eye. "You're sure?"

"Yeah. Go for it."

"Fine. Then I will speak to you with the First Voice. Prepare thyself."

The Claptrap disappeared in a blink.

HOW ABOUT THIS? a voice asked from around me and inside me. HOW DOES THIS FEEL?

Every syllable punched me in the heart with a spiked iron gauntlet. My bones vibrated in fresh agony with every word. My nerve endings burned with infernal pain. My skin felt as if it would melt off my skeleton. Worse than that, I gained a true sense of my place in the universe. I was small. I was mortal. In a hundred years, no one would remember my name. My life—indeed, all lives— boiled down to a series of alternating joys and tragedies culminating in absolute oblivion. The only variable of note was whether my loved ones would die before me or I before them. Life was nothing more than the space between the parentheses of nonexistence. I was, and would forever remain, utterly meaningless.

"Yeah, this is better than the Claptrap," I said.

COOL, the voice said. SO, WHAT DO YOU WANT?

"What do I…? It's that simple?"

YES. ONE WISH.

"Oh, okay. I'd heard Vaults were a little more complicated than that."

ALL VAULTS ARE DIFFERENT. EXCEPT THE ONES THAT ARE NOT.

"Great. And who am I talking to, exactly?"

THE VOICE OF THE SERAPHIM, SPEAKING TO YOU IN A LANGUAGE AND STYLE YOU WILL UNDERSTAND.

"And you're, what? An Eridian? One of the aliens that built these Vaults?"

NO. I'M LIKE… YOU KNOW THE GUARDIANS? THOSE CONSTRUCT-ROBOT THINGS YOU FOUGHT ON THE WAY IN HERE?

"Yeah."

I'M LIKE ONE OF THOSE, BUT BETTER. ALSO, WHAT ARE WE…? WHY DO YOU CARE? YOU'VE GOT A FREE WISH AND YOU'RE DRILLING FOR LORE? FOCUS UP. GET YOUR LIFE TOGETHER.

What did I want? An hour ago, I'd wanted only one thing: for my sister to be alive again.

Then I'd gotten my wish. At that moment, everything else felt small, irrelevant. Minutes ago, my sister was dead. Now she was alive again. The relief I'd felt when she'd opened her eyes… That was, in its own way, the biggest reward I could ever receive.

I mean, sort of. I still wanted money.

I sighed. "Man, I wish Sasha were here. She'd know what to ask for."

IT IS DONE.

A gust of wind nearly blew my hat from my head as my sister popped into the empty space next to me. Her skagtooth earrings rattled in her ears, and her hairband had come loose in the teleport. Less than an hour since she'd died, and now she was being blipped from one place to another without her consent. She yelped in shock, then shrugged and pulled her hair back into a bun. I was surprised she didn't look more rattled, but that was Sasha all over— she'd learned to live with sudden, unpleasant change. Tragedies that would have reduced others to a gibbering, sobbing mess often elicited little more than a shrug from my little sister.

"Wuh," Sasha said as she appeared into existence next to me. "Where are…? What's…?"

YOUR WISH IS GRANTED. FAREWELL.

"Ah," Sasha said, snapping her fingers. "Vault. Wish-granting thing. Got it."

The purple void around Sasha and me began to fade away. Beyond it, I could see the Pandoran desert from whence we'd come.

"What? No! That wasn't my wish! Come on!"

YOU SAID, "I WISH."

"It's a figure of speech!"

YOU ARE A FIGURE OF SPEECH.

"Shut up. You haven't been waiting thousands of years just to grant a stupid technicality wish, have you?"

NO. I AM MESSING WITH YOU.

The void resolidified around us.

"Ugh. Dick."

Sasha put her hand on my shoulder. Her knees wobbled. "Fiona… the voice… it hurts."

OH, RIGHT, SORRY.

A Claptrap poofed into view in front of us.

"Helloooooooooooo, traveler! This is my alternate means of communication! I am just as capable—"

"Never mind," Sasha said, waving her hand. "Go back."

FINE. NOW, IF YOU COULD QUICKLY DECIDE ON A WISH, I WOULD APPRECIATE IT.

Sasha pulled me into an embrace. "You okay?"

"Yeah. Just need to choose a perfect wish."

Sasha blinked. "Infinite guns? Is that allowed? Can we…" She turned away from me to address the void. "Can we wish for infinite stuff?"

PROBABLY NOT.

Sasha snapped her fingers in frustration. "Ah. Well. Maybe just, like, a million guns, then? That'd give us a heck of a leg-up on the new Vault Hunter career, right?"

I shook my head. "No. Let's ask for money."

Sasha frowned. "What's going on? I thought you were beginning to like Vault hunting."

She was right, of course. Our quest to find the Vault of the Traveler had awakened something in me: a sense of purpose. A sense that, after years of conning and scrimping and scraping and hating damn near every second of it, I'd finally found it: that magic three-way intersection of something I was good at, something I enjoyed doing, and something that paid well.

Older siblings have only one job, and I had failed at it. I'd pushed it out of my head in my excitement to step into the Vault. But now that I was here, it hit me just how close I'd come to losing the one thing that mattered most. Vault Hunters were known—apart from their tremendous body counts—for overthrowing dictatorships and vanquishing villains. Exciting stuff. Dangerous stuff. On occasion, selfless, heroic stuff.

But I remembered one of the first things Felix ever taught us: To hell with everybody that isn't us.

"We're not Vault hunting," I said.

"But we're literally—"

"That's final."

Sasha narrowed her eyes. It wasn't often I pulled rank as the big sister. When I did, she knew I damn well meant it.

"If you say so," she said, trying to hide her frustration.

I raised my voice to address the Eridian intelligence. "We'd like as much money as you can give us, wired directly into our cash accounts."

I CAN'T DO THAT, it replied.

Sasha cocked her head. "Uh. Why?"

I CREATE PHYSICAL THINGS. I COULD GIVE YOU A BILLION DOLLARS IN CASH.

"Bah," Sasha said, waving her hand dismissively. "Way too heavy. You can't write us a check?"

GREAT IDEA. A CHECK. FROM A BANK ACCOUNT.

"Okay," Sasha said. "I get it—"

A BANK ACCOUNT THAT I, AN ALIEN INTELLIGENCE, POSSESS—

"—I said I *get* it."

"Give us something we can sell," I said. "Something small. And light."

Sasha clapped. "Yes! Okay, good idea. Something we can easily transport, but that doesn't scream, 'Hey, kill me and take this off my corpse.' Something like… Ah! I've got it!"

Her eyes lit up with joy. She had a look on her face I hadn't seen since we were kids.[6]

"Is it okay if I make the wish?"

I nodded. She gave me a quick hug and then turned to face the endless abyss of nothingness before us.

"I'm ready," she said.

HIT ME.

---

6 Or recently when Rhys flirted with her, but I tried not to think about that too much.

"We wish for… a mint-condition, first-edition Typhon DeLeon Vaultlander™ figurine."

WEIRD.

Silence enveloped us as the alien supercomputer considered the request.

YEAH, OKAY.

With a hiss and a pop, a small box digistructed before Sasha's feet. Its transparent front showed off a plastic sculpture of Typhon DeLeon, diminutive Vault Hunter, a shockwhip firmly grasped in its poseable hand.

NOW GET GOING, the voice rumbled. The void around us faded away as we were thrust back into the dry heat of the Pandoran desert. The dry expanse was silent save for the buzzing of biteflies that hovered around a desiccated spiderant corpse. The moon crawled over the horizon as night fell and a chill seeped into our bones.

DON'T COME BACK.

———

Before I knew it, we were back in the Badlands. No purple void. No alien supercomputer. Rhys, Vaughn, and the others who had helped us open the Vault chatted animatedly in the distance. Rhys showed off a certificate emblazoned with the Atlas Munitions logo and his name written on the bottom. He'd gotten what he'd always wanted: he was the head of a major corporation.

As for Sasha and me, our wish had been granted. And that wish had a big yellow sticker on the front reading, "push my tummy to hear my catchphrase!"

I held the box in my hand and could not stifle my sigh. "Did you just waste our wish on a toy?"

"Toy? Yes. Waste? No. Allow me to explain," Sasha said, holding the thin cardboard box in the air like a religious icon. "Though the

Vaultlander™ series of games, comic books, and action figures has yet to make a splash on Pandora, the shared Vaultlander™ Transmedia Universe[7] has taken the rest of the galaxy by storm. These toys, based on the exploits of the galaxy's most famous Vault Hunters and villains, are priceless to the right collector. Especially—" She waggled the box for emphasis. "—if said Vaultlander™ has been out of print for the last twenty years."

She pushed the action figure's tummy. "Lotta money in turds," it chirped.

"Where is all this coming from?" I asked. "You've never shown an interest in this garbage before."

"I accidentally brushed my hand against Rhys's arm and he got so nervous he wouldn't stop talking about these things for twenty minutes."

"So, you wanna sell this thing to Rhys?"

"What? No. We can do better."

"Yes! That's what I keep telling you!"

"No, not… Don't be such a mom. He's a nice guy. No, I know exactly where to find a buyer who will drop so much cash for this thing—"

"—we'll never have to work another day in our lives," I finished. "This could be our last big job."

"I dunno about that," Sasha said, cocking an eyebrow, "but still—payday. We'll be safe behind turret-gun walls, eating food with a lower than average amount of fecal matter in it. And our journey to sell it—it'll be, like, our last adventure. A last hurrah. The last big job before retirement."

She shook the doll again. Its stupid big head rattled inside its stupid cardboard box.

---

7 Otherwise known as the VTU™.

"This is stupid, right?" I said.

"Yes. And it's going to make us stupid rich."

This was what all the blood, sweat, and tears[8] had been for? A big payday from some toy-collecting nerd? I didn't know what I envisioned for my and Sasha's future, but I imagined more drama.

But drama gets people killed. So, hell with it—it was time to retire. Forget the Vault-hunting business. I was now in the Vault Hunter Collectible Whatever Toy Nerd Thing business.

"Fine. Let's say our farewells. I think I've got just enough hard cash left to buy us a couple off-planet shuttle tickets to… Where are we going, exactly?"

Sasha smiled. "I am so very glad you asked."

---

8 Rhys's.

3
FIONA

Eden-5 smelled like money. You could taste it in the air the instant our shuttle punched through the atmosphere. We'd journeyed from the old-ham-and-violence smell of Pandora to the sour, metallic recycled air of the transplanetary shuttle. We'd just come out of hyperspeed above Eden-5 and were breaking atmosphere. The planet's breathable air vented into the shuttle and I felt my muscles involuntarily relax. It smelled like the entire planet had jumped out of a warm perfumed dryer directly into a patch of freshly cut grass.

Looking around the shuttle, most of the faces looked like ours: dirty. According to Sasha, Eden-5 flew in most of its labor force from offworld. No doubt most of our fellow passengers were destined for lives of service.

"Oh shit," Sasha said, slightly too loudly. "Look."

The capital city was a shotgun blast of skyscrapers, bright lights twinkling from the buckshot wounds. A thousand towers of commerce and wealth all packed so close together you couldn't tell where one ended and another began. The city sat in the middle of an intricate web of glowing veins—power cables, all designed to siphon energy from one part of the planet and redirect it to this shrine of plastic and steel.

Near the capital city, separated by a small band of desert, sat a smaller town. Compared to the grandeur of the capital city, it looked like a pimple on the surface of the planet, just waiting for someone to pop it. Its few buildings glowed weakly with sick flickering lights.

Next to me, Sasha hugged the Vaultlander box close to her chest, as if afraid it'd leap from her arms. She kept taking it from her shoulder satchel to check that it still existed. She tapped the box. "Think they'll ever make one for us?" she asked.

I frowned. "A Vaultlander? Doubtful."

"I'll commission one for you. Once we sell this thing, I'll get you a posable Fiona made out of solid gold."

"I don't want—"

"Her hat will be made out of one big-ass diamond. And if you press the button on her back, she'll say, 'Sasha, stop it!'"

"Yeah, never mind."

"Why are you being such a bummer? You're about to be as rich as Handsome Jack, except alive and not a weird pervert."

The shuttle began its final descent to the planet below. We weaved nauseatingly between skyscrapers as we corkscrewed down to the surface.

"I just… wanted to apologize."

"For what?"

"For… what happened to you. The part where you died."

Sasha put the doll back in her satchel. Sincerity often caught her off guard. Especially when it came from me. She turned away from the aisle to face me.

"Why would you apologize for that? We had to set the bomb off. I had the detonator. It was my choice."

"You shouldn't have had to make it. It's my job to—"

"Oh, stop flattering yourself. Just because you're older doesn't make you—"

"It's my job to keep you safe," I said, too loudly.

"Hey. You're doing a pretty good job of it. How long's it been since someone shoved a gun in our faces?"

"Ah," I said. I'd intended to say, "About twenty-six hours, give or take, unless you count the autoguns at Marcus's store when we sold him the Desolator." But instead, I said, "Ah."

Because someone had just shoved a gun in my face.

"Gimme that box," rasped a voice that smelled of stale skag jerky. He stood in the aisle, a rusty Maliwan pistol clutched between his crusty fingers. He rested his gun hand on Sasha's shoulder. I couldn't tell which looked greasier and more worn out, his face or his pistol. The latter looked like it might explode if he tried to pull the trigger. He knew it. I knew it. Judging from the look on Sasha's face, she knew it too.

"In the future," he said, "you might wanna lower your voice when talking about your valuables. Give it here."

If the expression on Sasha's face could be used as a weapon, the mugger would have exploded into a thousand meaty chunks right then and there.

Sasha raised the box above her head. The idiotic face of Typhon DeLeon stared back at me as Jerkybreath tucked the doll under his arm.

"Lovely," he said. "Obviously, don't follow me."

He backed up toward the shuttle door, making sure to keep the gun trained on me even as he pushed past an alarmed shuttle attendant.

The shuttle shuddered to a stop, the harness signs clicking off as the retroboosters finished firing. The shuttle door opened and, gun still trained on us, the mugger disappeared into the procession of passengers as they filed outside.

We jumped to our feet. I flicked my wrist, sending the pistol concealed up my sleeve into my palm. It was a little thing and held only a single shot, so I'd have to make it count.

Sasha and I pushed our way through the crowd and out the shuttle. I scanned the throng of raggedy passengers all ambling their way toward the security checkpoint, but other than the human-sized floating-torso robots that guarded the spaceport exit, I couldn't see anything.

"Sasha," I called out. "Eyes on him?"

We saw it at the same time. A particularly greasy, panicked face looking back at us through the crowd as he shoved past a handful of travelers. The toy under his arm.

"There!" Sasha yelled, and dove into the crowd. Others might have had a hard time slinking their way around the mass of people, but Sasha, small as she was, was used to sliding around those who refused to move no matter how much of a hurry she appeared to be in.

I didn't bother with that if I didn't have to.

"Hi, sorry, outta my way," I yelled, elbowing people left and right.[9] After a few near-collisions, the travelers in front of me cleared a path. I saw him. I had a shot.

"Hold it!" I yelled.

He did not, in fact, hold it.

He whirled, raising his gun, which shot a bolt of elemental fire toward me that almost sizzled my ear. That's one of the better parts of your body to be almost sizzled, but still not ideal in an objective sense.

The travelers dropped to the ground around us. The thief sprinted toward the checkpoint, firing blindly over his shoulder.

I raised the gun. Took my time aiming, even as he stopped in front of the secbot at the checkpoint gate. He produced a bright

---

9 The trick is to swing from your hips—really gives you the momentum you need.

yellow work permit from his coat and started saying something I couldn't make out.

Only later would I wonder: why the hell weren't they doing anything? A crazed, greasy boy firing wildly at a crowd—surely that should count as a security issue?

As I said, though, I only thought about that later. At that moment, I thought what I always do when I'm about to fire:

Breathe in.

Hold.

Bang.

The thief's ankle exploded.

He screamed in pain as he fell to the ground mere inches from the checkpoint. A chorus of other screams around us joined his own. At first, I thought the people around us were being attacked as well. It was only after glancing around at their horrified faces and pointing figures that I understood our fellow passengers were not as used to the sight of protruding bone and spurting blood as Sasha and I were.

We ran toward his prone form at full speed—until one of the enormous secbots dropped in front of us, mammoth arms outstretched.

"NO CUTTING IN LINE."

It was even more massive up close. A floating metal torso with two bulky arms, each supporting a fist with sharpened digiclaws protruding from its knuckles. In lieu of a skull, a box atop the torso contained a single menacing light that changed color as it scanned us.

"But *he* cut in line!" Sasha shouted.

"NO TATTLING IN LINE."

Over the secbot's shoulder, I watched as the bleeding thief pulled himself toward the metal detector. He tossed his gun aside, to absolutely zero reaction from the secbots. He again raised his work permit.

"Just scan the work pass. Let me in. I'm good to go."

"SCANNING," the secbot intoned.

"He's got our property!" I protested. "He's a thief!"

The secbot before us leaned in. Its eye flashed crimson.

"IF THAT IS TRUE, YOU HAVE LITTLE TO WORRY ABOUT."

The bot nearest the thief nodded. "WORK PERMIT ACCEPTED. PROCEED."

The thief, still crawling on his belly, turned back to give us a final shit-eating grin. He hauled himself through the metal detector. It emitted a shrieking beep the moment he was halfway to the other side.

"ERROR. UNDECLARED GOODS DETECTED."

Red lights flashed over the security checkpoint. Two more bots swarmed the thief, encircling him.

"IDENTIFY," one droned, ripping the Vaultlander from his arms.

"It's a toy. For my kid."

One of the other bots pulled him up by the scruff of his neck. "YOU DID NOT DECLARE IT WHEN DEPARTING FROM YOUR ORIGINAL DESTINATION."

"*I* bought it from a friend on the shuttle ride over."

"SMUGGLING WILL NOT BE TOLERATED."

"I don't know if I'd call it smuggling," he said.

Or at least, that's what I assume he would have said. As it stood, one of the secbots decapitated him by the time he'd got out "I d—"

A single swipe of the robot's digiclaw sent the thief's greasy gourd flying toward us. A ribbon of blood twirled and spun through the air like someone writing cursive with viscera. His head landed at my feet, the wet splat of its impact speckling my boots with his blood.

A new set of screams joined the chorus from before: two younger, high-pitched voices with more agony than shock in their howling.

Beyond the checkpoint, two children ran toward the headless

form of the thief. One was the cutest child I had ever seen in my entire life. The other was fine.

I don't generally find kids very cute. They're like adults who can't talk to you about books, which is fine, but I've never seen a kid and had an emotion stronger than "I hope it doesn't wipe its hands on me."

Until I saw this first kid.

I wanted to squeeze his little rosy cheeks until his big eyes popped out of his skull. I wanted to tousle his hair until the friction turned him completely bald. I wanted to grab his little belly and throw him into a wall with all my strength. I wanted to feed him marshmallows until he popped like an overripe melon. I wanted to grab him by his little turtleneck and hurl him into the sun. Unfortunately, when he cried, he got even more pathetic and cute.

"Daddy!" he wailed. His wet, agonized face turned to the bots. "You killed my daddy!"

Oh. Well, that wasn't cute. That was sad.

"YOUR VOICE HAS REACHED AN UNACCEPTABLE VOLUME. SILENCE YOURSELF."

His older sister grabbed him by the arm. "We gotta go, Face," she said, and yanked him back beyond the checkpoint, even while her adorable brother kept reaching for the remains of his dad.

"ACCORDING TO CUSTOMS FORMS, THIS IS YOURS."

The bot's voice broke me out of my horrified reverie, and its owner shoved the Vaultlander into my arms. The cardboard felt heavy and wet in my hands, blood dripping from its edges onto the spaceport's metal floor.

"Goddammit," Sasha winced. "That's going to hurt the resale value. Oh, and you've, uh, got some... some goo. On your... everything."

How many times had I been in this exact situation? Sticky blood on my hands and my clothes. My nostrils filled with the sour-metal stench of human death. I'd grown used to those sensations over time, sure. These days, though, they reminded me of my sister's unmoving corpse.

With the greasy thief's greasy blood trickling down my arm, I realized that Sasha was right. Rich people don't get shot at. Rich people don't have to wipe bits of other people off their boots. Rich people are safe. Content.

Enough of this *getting* rich crap. It was time to *be* rich.

The secbot waved us forward.

"WELCOME TO EDEN-5."

4
FIONA

"Where you headed?"

As is the case with most spaceports, the street surrounding Eden 5's was filled with bikes and autos and copters looking to take new arrivals wherever they needed to go. Being low on cash, we opted to head for the cheapest-looking ride we could find: a rickshaw bike with an oversized passenger cart and an undersized rider. The bike had flames painted on it. The chauffeur had hair he'd shaped into flames, presumably with the aid of superglue.

The transpo-biker ran a comb through his hair, which had roughly the same effect as trying to shape a tidal wave by blowing at it. He waved us into the rickshaw with a practiced smile.

Sasha checked her ECHO journal. "Uh, the Villa Holloway, please."

"Elite District, eh? You're not dressed for cleanin'."

"We're not workers. We're… It doesn't matter." Sasha waved off the question.

The driver shrugged and kickstarted the bike. We rode past a large corrugated metal sign with "rustville" painted on it, with an arrow pointing down a filthy firelit alley.

"Little on the nose," I said.

"First time here?" the biker asked.

"No," Sasha lied.

Even over the wind rushing past us, I could hear him scoff. "Mm-hmm. Well, then you'll already know how the capital city's divvied up, then. Elites live in the east. Them what work for 'em—Rusters—live in the west, down there in Rustville. Not so named 'cause of the poor accommodations, mind you. It was founded by a missionary, name of Jonathan Rust."

"Really?"

"Nah, I'm playing. It's called that 'cause everyone's poor as shit and the buildings are all made outta rusty metal."

"Ah."

"You want me to drop you off at Dapper Delilah's on the border of the rich district? Maybe you can get some clothes that aren't so… sticky?"

I checked the small wad of cash in my pocket. It was grim. We'd spent nearly every last cent we had getting to Eden-5; the transpo-bike alone would probably tap out the last of our cash. Sasha saw the look on my face.

"Don't worry," she said. "You're always more charming when splattered with gore."

"Who are we meeting again?"

"Countess Cassandra Holloway. She blew up my ECHO practically before I'd finished making the VagueList post."[10][11]

The Vaultlander poked out of Sasha's satchel, Typhon DeLeon's

---

10 VagueList, of course, being an ECHOnet black market where buyers and sellers refuse to give concrete details about what they're purchasing for fear of attracting law enforcement. Sasha posted "Very Valuable, Voluptuous Vaultlander™," to which Countess Holloway apparently replied with an eyebrow-raise emoji.

11 If you're thinking it might have been slightly irresponsible to spend all our money to fly halfway across the galaxy over an emoji, then I wish you could have been there as backup when Sasha told me she'd already bought the tickets.

smiling face indifferent to the world around it.

"Should we take it out of the box?" I asked.

Sasha looked at me as if I'd just suggested we buy a puppy and use it as a speed bag.

"What? The box is dirty," I said. "That doesn't hurt the resale?"

"You *never* take a Vaultlander™ out of its box. Are you kidding me?"

"Then how are you supposed to play with it?"

Sasha might have jumped off the bike entirely if I hadn't grabbed her wrist. "Fiona. You're embarrassing yourself."

"What?"

"You don't *play* with these, Fiona. You set them on a shelf and stare at them for thirty seconds and pretend they're a sound financial and artistic investment. Then you never look at or think about them again until you're packing up for your next move."

"Rhys told you that?"

"He did."

"You're telling me Rhys doesn't play with these toys?"

"He told me he didn't."

"Which means he absolutely—"

"Which means he absolutely does, yeah. But somebody smarter and richer would probably be able to resist the urge. And Countess Holloway seems plenty rich."

The transpo-bike zoomed onto a boost strip. Sasha and I were pushed back into our seats by the sudden burst of acceleration. The spaceport vanished behind us as we approached the ivory spires of what our driver called the Elite District.

The entire neighborhood seemed to be made of porcelain. Shining pale buildings reflected the curvaceous luxury cars driven by tired-looking chauffeurs. The owners of these vehicles, the ones lounging in the backseats half-watching ECHOnovelas while scrolling through the newsfeeds on their personal ECHOwatches, exuded an air of immaculate health and smug beauty. I saw so many razor-sharp cheekbones, I considered buying a roll of bandages.

The thought of blood drew my attention to the secbots patrolling the streets. In every direction, I saw at least three of the floating metal torsos directing traffic, guarding storefronts, or hovering near laborers in menacing silence.

Beauty. Luxury. Killer robots. And in the middle of it all, us.

"What's to stop Holloway from just killing us and taking the doll?" I asked. "Those secbots?"

The biker laughed. "She owns the secbots, kids. Builds 'em, programs 'em, sics 'em on folks who don't stay in line."

Not spectacular news. Dealing with a billionaire would be bad enough; a billionaire with an army of robots was not the kind of trouble we were looking for.

Sasha didn't seem worried, though. She flipped the box over, revealing a blinking, eyeball-sized sphere duct-taped to the back. "Micro-nade. She tries anything, I'll detonate it. Box'll burn up along with anything in it."

"What if she takes it out of the box?"

Sasha looked at me as if I'd just wiped my ass with my bare hand.

"Right. Dumb question."

The bike slowed to a stop outside a mansion so large I couldn't gauge its full width without turning my head. A wrought-iron gate and four wall-mounted autoturrets kept it protected from the hustle and bustle of the street.

"We're here," our driver said.

The sight of the estate turned my blood cold. A fleck of goopy gray matter on my cufflink told me that, in fact, no, our gore-splattered fashion would not be looked upon kindly. We needed a change of clothes before doing this deal, or there wouldn't be a deal at all.

"Changed my mind," I said. "Take us to Dapper Delilah's."

5
FIONA

We paid the cabbie what little cash we had left[12] and stepped through the entrance of a grand building that, as I'd seen on our descent into the planet, was shaped to look from space like a giant flower. Even down here, the floral aesthetic expressed tasteful understatement; upon stepping toward the automatic doors, Sasha and I were enfolded by the scent of gardenias and jasmine.

The beauty of the shop's interior did nothing for me. In the same way that a caveman wouldn't know what to make of a distant spaceship, I regarded it with confusion rather than awe, with no real idea what I was looking at. Trying to decipher the styles on display with my limited cultural intelligence was like trying to learn a language by licking the dictionary.

Sasha didn't fare much better. "Is it me," Sasha said, "or are you also having trouble figuring out what any of this is?"

It wasn't just her. We saw mannequins engulfed by fluffy orbs, wearing bright pink belts that covered their eyes and *nothing else,* as well as one wearing a large brown blanket and floating off the ground.

---

12 Plus tip. We're criminals, not monsters.

"Help you ladies?" A sales assistant appeared before us. Her approach had been utterly silent. Her eyes were slightly too big, her smile just a bit too small to hide her disgust at our appearance.

"You know the way you're looking at us right now?" I asked. "We want something that'll get us the opposite."

She didn't flinch. "Offworlders, then?"

Sasha nodded. "Pandoran."

At that, she flinched. "I would be happy to show you some of our formalwear, as I hope you will be happy to note that I carry no cash on me."

"Shucks," Sasha said, snapping her fingers sarcastically. "I just love robbin' people so much."

I leant over. "You kind of do," I muttered.

"Eh," she said, which I couldn't argue with.

The sales assistant—her nametag said "Tammithah"—escorted us past the infinity scarves seemingly made out of puppy fur and to the back of the store. There, under dim lighting and shoved into a corner, were clothes I actually understood. Suits. Dresses.

Bowler hats.

"See anything you like?" Tammithah asked.

"I do, actually," I said, running my finger along the brim of a deep-red bowler. "Where's your fitting room?"

She laughed so hard I thought my eardrums might burst, a single enunciated "HA!" that rebounded off the near walls and leaped back into my brain a second time. "I'm afraid not," she said. "Fitting rooms are unnecessary, as these clothes auto-tailor to your proportions. Not to mention," she said, flicking an eye toward Sasha, "people use them to steal things."

"Rookies, maybe," Sasha said, holding a dark gray vest to her chest and glancing into a floor-length mirror. "Little too normie, I think. Maybe this?" She put the gray vest back onto the rack and pulled out a combination scarf and suit that clearly conveyed "I do business but I'm also just a normal dude" vibes.

I nodded, replacing the dark beaten hat on my head with the crimson one in my hand. It felt more than comfortable—it felt *confident*. I could feel the self-assuredness leaking from the hat into my scalp, down the back of my neck, and into my spine. Just by wearing it, I felt like making outlandish promises I never intended to fulfill. With this thing on my head, criticism and insult would slide off me like skin off a melting bandit. They say clothes maketh the woman. In this case, the clothes turned me into an entirely new one.

"And how will you be paying," Tammithah asked.

"Cash."

The smile dropped from her face entirely. "Unless you've parked a couple pallets of thousand-dollar bills outside, these clothes are out of your price range."

"Impossible," said a newly confident voice that happened to be mine. "Let's see here." I removed the hat and checked the price tag.

I screamed in horror.

"Whoah!" Sasha screamed. "What happened?!"

"Don't look at the price," I said, pulling the suit from her.

"It can't be that *oh my god*," she gasped, glancing at the suit's price tag and throwing up in her mouth.

"How?" I asked, my breath catching in my chest. "How can it cost so much?"

"Out!" Tammithah screamed, grabbing our shoulders and marching us toward the door with a surprising strength. "Your kind should stay in Rustville. You're lucky I don't call the secbots."

She stopped for a moment.

"Actually, never mind. Secbots!"

She shoved us out the front door and locked it behind us. Pressing a switch on her wristband, a barrier of bulletproof steel slammed down across the entrance, ensuring neither Sasha nor I would get a chance to ask about any sort of financing program.

Luckily, the Holloway estate was only an hour's walk away. Unluckily, two secbots zoomed in to flank us before we'd made even two steps.

"EXPLAIN YOUR LOWER-MIDDLE-CLASS PRESENCE," they said in unison.

I tried my best not to scoff. Which was tough. I love scoffing.

"Trying to buy new clothes," I said. "What does it look like?"

"LIKE YOU JUST MURDERED SOMEONE."

Sasha shook her head. "There was an incident at customs. You probably heard about it. There was a guy. And then you robots made it so there wasn't a guy anymore."

"IRRELEVANT. THIS NEIGHBORHOOD HAS A DRESS CODE. EVEN WERE YOU NOT COVERED IN BLOOD, YOUR ATTIRE WOULD NOT, AS IT WERE, PASS MUSTER."

"Yeah, hence us trying to buy new clothes. Whatever, Sasha, let's go. We're not taking fashion advice from a murderbot," I said.

"FINE."

"Oh. That was easy," Sasha said.

"NO. YOU ARE BEING FINED. TEN THOUSAND DOLLARS."

Now I scoffed. "That's ridiculous!"

"I SUPPOSE YOU'D KNOW, GIVEN YOUR HAT."

I had a strong suspicion that shooting a secbot in the face was grounds for an even larger fine, so I bit my tongue.

"Ten thousand dollars? Absolutely not a problem," Sasha said. "When and where should we have the money wired?"

"INTO THIS HAND," the secbot said, putting its palm out. "RIGHT NOW."

"Ah," Sasha said. "Well, we're sort of between bank balances right now. Perhaps we could work out an installation plan? One where the first installation is, say, zero dollars?"

"I SEE. APPLYING DEBT CUFF."

The secbot's chest sprang open. Inside were a series of bulky metal cuffs that looked like dog collars, all dull green and supremely rusty. The bot pulled one out and snapped it open.

"SPECIFY PREFERRED LOCATION OF DEBT CUFF, IF YOU WOULD."

I extended my arm and showed him a location of particular relevance to the situation at hand.

"PROFANE GESTURES ARE ALSO A FINABLE OFFENSE. RETRIEVING SECONDARY DEBT CUFF."

The secbot grabbed my right hand—my favorite, the one I used for flipping off robots—and clamped the dog collar around my wrist. I wasn't prepared for how damned heavy it was. I felt my shoulder being pulled from its socket and I fell to the side, clutching my arm. I pulled the collar up toward my shoulder and bent my elbow, which helped ease just a little bit of the burden on my shoulder, enough that I could get to my feet.

As I stood, the secbot clamped another cuff onto my right ankle. My entire body listed to the side and I fell again. Despite their size, each cuff weighed as much as a tenth of a human corpse.[13]

"For f— You couldn't have balanced them out?"

"I COULD HAVE," the robot said. I had the impression that if it were capable of affecting a sarcastic tone, it would have. "YOU MAY PAY YOUR FINE USING THE CONVENIENT TOUCHSCREEN BUILT INTO YOUR DEBT CUFF. PAY OFF THE FINE AND THE CUFF WILL OPEN. ANY ATTEMPT TO FORCIBLY REMOVE THE CUFF WILL BE MET WITH IMMEDIATE NEGATIVE REINFORCEMENT, IN ADDITION TO SUBSEQUENT FINES."

---

13 Or for those who don't measure weight using Pandoran units, roughly fifteen pounds.

I swung my head up to face the robot, my right arm and leg still weighted to the ground. "I'm just supposed to lug these weights around until I get enough cash to remove them? Are you kidding me?"

"WE ARE NOT."

"You don't think being weighed down by this crap might make it harder for me to earn the money to pay you back?"

"I DON'T, AS A RULE, THINK ABOUT THE IMPOVERISHED AT ALL."

"I—"

Sasha stepped in front of me. "Thank you so much for your help. We'll be sure to pay the fines as soon as we can."

The secbots stared at her. "TELLING US WHAT WE WANT TO HEAR IS ALSO A FINABLE OFFENSE."

"Oh, for—"

The bots produced another debt cuff and moved to clamp it around Sasha.

"No, give it to me," I said. "I'll take it."

"UNACCEPTABLE," the bot said, clamping the cuff around Sasha's neck. She tilted forward and would have toppled over if I hadn't put an arm out to balance her.

"Cool," Sasha said. "Great."

Without another word, the secbots floated away.

Sasha turned to me, dumbstruck. "Well. This is no big deal," she said in a voice that meant it absolutely was.

"Look," I shrugged, pointing across the street with my unburdened hand. "Most of the laborers here have cuffs like these."

On the opposite sidewalk, a wrinkled woman with cuffs around her ankles swept the entrance to a perfume store. Her terrifyingly muscular legs suggested she'd carried the debts for quite some time. In the coffee bar near her, the bartender mixed cups of brown liquid with two cuff-weighted hands. On the other block, a landscaper with a collar around his neck, just like Sasha, struggled to stand after bending over to pick up every individual piece of trash dropped by the Elites who passed by him.

"The countess will probably just assume we're some workers who stole it from a rich guy, or got it in an inheritance or something," I said. "If anything, these make us blend in more. She'll be less likely to fleece us."

"Maybe," Sasha said. She at least did me the courtesy of pretending like she believed me. Still—it's not like there was anything we could have done about it. We'd gone from having no money to having negative money, and our only way out of that hole was currently waiting to buy a gore-stained plastic doll.

I hit the Call button on the wall-mounted buzzer box.

6
FIONA

The waiting room of the Holloway estate stunned me into silence. Sasha and I had seen incredible things—Vault monsters, an exploding moonbase—but we'd never seen something so completely and utterly… tasteful.

A combination of wall sconces and chandeliers bathed the room in a comforting glow that made me feel as if I'd stepped into somebody else's dream. The warm, inoffensive ambience was interrupted by a marble statue in the middle of the room, splashed with perfectly placed spotlights that gave this austere, lithe figure—the woman of the house, I assumed—dominion over the landscape. The statue's face sported an expression of kind wisdom and merciless pity all at once.

A chair/couch thing[14] sat up against the near wall, its quiet burgundy color contrasting with the charcoal-gray bookcases set on either side of it. Most of the books were too pristine to have ever been read, but that didn't matter: They imbued the space with a

---

14 The butler called it a "shayz" and it looked so comfortable my blood pressure halved just making eye contact with it.

quiet intelligence and dignity I'd never before experienced.

It sounds stupid. A well-decorated room—big deal. But when you've spent your entire life no more than thirty feet away from human excrement at any given time, when a bumper sticker is the closest you've ever gotten to home decoration, then a comfortable space just hits you differently.

"Oh," Sasha said in the voice of someone who has not only learned that there is a God but that you're in her foyer and you're massively underdressed. She tugged at her shirt, which was still splotched with blood. "The *lamps* are better dressed than me."

The butler, a young man with two debt cuffs on his muscular left arm, rolled his sunken eyes. He gestured at the chaise. "Please take a seat."

We sat. The cushions encircled our hindquarters with a welcoming sigh, supporting us as we sank lower and lower into its pillowy mass. Though I had no memories of that time, I knew in my bones I hadn't felt this comfortable, this safe, since the womb.

"Oh no," Sasha said. "How is this so comfy?" She looked to the butler, tears forming in her eyes as the chair slowly enveloped her limbs with its softness. "What did you do? It's just a chair! How did you make it like this?"

"It is not just a chair, madam. And if you will not use it as intended, I must ask you to remove yourself."

"What's your name?" Sasha asked.

"Denboro, madam. Denboro Charlesby."

"Well, Denboro, you seem like a nice guy. I like you. But I'm going to tell you right now, the only way you're getting me off this shay-thing is if you drag my dead body out of here by its feet."

"If you continue to darken my chaise with your gore-splattered ensemble, you may just get your wish," a sharp, cold voice announced from behind the statue.

An alarmingly tall, alarmingly beautiful woman stepped into the room, the spitting image of the statue in the room's center. As she passed it, I couldn't help notice how the statue, austere as it was, didn't do her justice. The woman herself looked even more sculpted, ageless, and coldly gorgeous. The contrast was too striking to be anything but intentional. The lady's guests were meant to be gobsmacked by the statue right before her arrival smacked those same gobs a second time.

"Ah, Countess. I merely assumed that, as guests, you would wish to extend them—"

"The only thing I wish to *extend* to these 'guests' is the center digit of my right hand. Ideally out the window of a rapidly-moving automobile."

I don't mind getting insulted a bit before doing business—helps the buyer think they're in control—but if you take that kind of sass sitting down, you start to lose leverage.

I stood. "Left hand would be the smarter choice. So you could keep your dominant one firmly on the stick you've shoved up yourself."

Her eyes narrowed. The corner of her lip pulled upward ever so slightly. "Come," she said, turning on a heel. "Unless you have need to relieve yourself?"

We shook our heads.

"Good. I myself dreaded visits to the water closet so much that I received elective surgery to remove the need entirely."

"I have so many questions," I said.

"And I have so little time. You have come to do business, yes? Then business we shall do. Follow me to my office."

Apparently, we didn't respond quickly enough to her liking.

"Ah," she said. "You're confused. Apologies. An 'office' is where people do work. Now. Come."

We had to take two steps for every one of her loping strides. As we followed her through the house, she gave us a practiced walking tour of the various art pieces and rooms. I didn't understand any of it—she'd point at a painting of a crying mustachioed dog and say something like, "One of Bouffant's lesser-known explorations of interplanetary ennui"—but we found ourselves powerless to be anything but impressed. Even the way she gestured at her many art pieces was, in and of itself, a work of art: the gentle bend of the wrist, the purposeful point of a finger, the way her large (but not gaudy) jeweled bracelet dangled from her wrist. Her feet barely seemed to touch the floor. She moved like an alien. A beautiful, rude alien.

Every room we passed made the foyer seem like a well-lit dumpster. We thought we'd seen luxury, but we hadn't seen anything yet. The lounge, which sported its own robotic bartender, a half-dozen ECHOsim machines, and a massage coffin, looked like somewhere you could happily spend the rest of your life. The dining-room ceiling was so high I couldn't see where it ended, the room's dark wood furniture polished to a sheen until the hundred-candle chandelier reflected its light into every chair back and tabletop. Even though she had no use for them, the bathrooms we passed all had their own massage table, parfumerie, and turbo-bidet.

"This is a lovely home," Sasha said, doing her best to keep the saliva in her mouth.

"Yes," Holloway replied, wealthily. "I built it brick by brick, plank by plank, with my own two inheritances. Prior to this home, my family lived in a ramshackle manor barely fit for human use. It didn't even have a drawing room."

"Rough," I said. *What is a drawing room and is it a place where you sit around and doodle pictures?* I did not say.

"I couldn't have my little girl grow up in such a hovel," she continued.

A shadow passed over her face. She stopped in the center of the hall and stared at nothing. It occurred to me that we'd walked the length of the house and I hadn't seen any signs of a child living here.

"Here we are," she snapped, wrenching open a door twice her size.

The office didn't disappoint. A fireplace crackled along one wall, flanked by ceiling-high bookcases stuffed with dog-eared tomes. Unlike the ones in the foyer, these appeared to have been well read. Granted, that didn't tell me anything; she could have bought them used or, more likely, had her butlers tastefully rough the books up to simulate the wear and tear a true bibliophile would have put them through.

The other end of the room was dominated by a floor-length painting of Countess Holloway that was equal parts sullen and powerful. At the far end, a door opened on to a balcony. Orange light from the Eden-5 sunset spilled into the room.

The countess gestured at a pair of chairs near the fireplace.

I knew a trap when I saw one. She hadn't sat in her own chair as she gestured to us, which meant she had no intention of sitting. We'd sit, and she'd remain on her feet. We'd appear rude. She'd have a literal height advantage.

I scowled at her. "Really?" She had all the money. We obviously weren't from around here. She already had the upper hand a dozen times over. This small extra power play was unnecessary and more than a little insulting.

She shrugged. "Force of habit."

Holloway closed the door to the balcony, plunging the room into an intimate darkness. Only the flickering fire provided any light.

"Let's see it," she intoned in a voice like silk dipped in chocolate.

"Uh," Sasha said, removing the blood-soaked box from her shoulder satchel.

"Lotta money in turds," Typhon DeLeon chirped.

Holloway recoiled. "Is this a joke?"

"We understand the box is in less than prime condition," I said, "and are willing to offer a small discount."

"'Less than prime?' You haven't even wiped the previous owner off it! I'm assuming that's how you came into possession of it, yes? Murdered your master, thought you'd move the merchandise before the secbots caught up with you?"

"Maybe. Or maybe that's the dried blood of another potential buyer who tried to rip us off." On Pandora, it never hurts to be the right kind of scary. I hoped the same negotiation tactic applied here on Eden-5.

Holloway narrowed her eyes. "Hmm. Well. Gore notwithstanding, Typhon DeLeon is a moderately uncommon Vaultlander™. Not the first one I've seen, of course."

"That's interesting," Sasha replied. "Because I've tracked the other known copies of the DeLeon doll. One burned up in the Helios space-station crash. Several others melted into goop when somebody managed to knock the planet Hieronymus into its sun. They only made a half-dozen of this model in the first place, and nearly every single one of them has been accounted for. You know as well as I do that you might be holding the last intact, still-in-box Typhon DeLeon in existence."

Holloway raised an eyebrow. "Of course, I'll need to scan it. Verify its authenticity."

"Of course," Sasha smiled. She shot a wide-eyed glance at me. I understood the implicit question: Will a toy digistructed into existence by a Vault read as authentic, or are we about to get thrown out on our asses?

Holloway took the box to her desk. From its top drawer, she removed a circular metal plate with a digital readout on its front. She placed the toy atop it and sucked in a lungful of air, trying and failing to hide her excitement. A scanning rod unfurled from the edge of the plate and began to move around its circumference, humming with activity as it bombarded the toy with scanner rays.

"What's your asking price?" she said without looking up.

"Seeing as this piece is twenty years out of print and damn near one of a kind, we thought it'd be more appropriate for you to make the first offer," Sasha said.

A mirthless grin flashed across the countess's face. "You bring me a blood-soaked box. You're weighed down by debt cuffs. You mistake a couch for a toilet. And now you intend to negotiate? Embarrassing."

The scanner ping echoed across the room. She examined a small screen set into the desk.

"Well, how about that?"

She smirked at us. Silent. Sasha and I returned polite, neutral smiles. The kind panicked people wouldn't have.

"Despite the bits of person all over the box, it appears to be genuine."

"Of course it is," I said, stifling a sigh of relief. "Now there's just the matter of price."

"Yes."

She stared at us again. I knew this tactic. She would wait us out, force us to make the first offer. In some circumstances, it would have been a smart move. An arms dealer back on Pandora had tried something similar with me, with great success; he knew the guns I was selling were hot, and every second I couldn't get them off my hands was another second the meat-bicycle-riding bandit lord we'd stolen them from could catch up and take them off my hands. And then take my hands.

Here, though, on Eden-5, it was the wrong move, and one she'd never recover from. We stank up the place. We lowered the value of the house just by sitting in it. Our very presence clashed with the decor. Sasha and I could have happily sat in Holloway's office until the sun turned off, but she wanted—*needed*—us out of her hair.

So we waited. In silence.

"There will be no negotiation, understood? I will say a number, you will accept it, and you will leave."

Sasha and I stood. I put on my best expression of righteous indignation. "That's hardly in the spirit of—"

"Ten billion. Take it or leave it."

The number struck me in the face like a sniper round.

"One moment," I said.

I turned my back to Holloway and faced Sasha, whose eyes were now the size of dinner plates.

"Hnnnngh," I whispered.

"Mmmmmf," she whispered back, biting her lip.

"Be cool," I said.

"I'm cool. I'm cool as hell. You be cool."

"I'm cool, too. Just give me a second."

Ten. Billion. With that kind of money, we could buy a house, then buy a smaller house and store it inside the first one for emergencies. We'd never have to work another day in our lives. Never again have to wash chunks of random people out of our hair.

I straightened up. Took a deep breath. Turned around.

"Countess Holloway, I think we have a deal."

That's when the room exploded.

7
GAIGE

The lights of Eden-5's Elite District burned bright through the evening, a beacon of civilization in an ocean of darkness, bordering the island of weak, flickering flames that pockmarked Rustville.

A young woman moved past those flames, past downcast and hopeless faces and shivering, whining collections of bones and loose skin that used to be cats and dogs. Her eyes focused on the twinkling lights in the distance.

Behind her floated a dismembered metal torso covered in rust. It remained exactly five paces behind her at all times, its monocular head sweeping back and forth as if scanning for threats. These threats seemed unlikely to present themselves, as the mere approach of the robot was enough to send most pedestrians running back into their hovels.

The woman tapped a button on her wrist, clearing her throat.

"Greetings, o loyal ECHOcast subscribers," she said, pigtails bouncing with every step. "And as always, greetings to the pigs trying in vain to track my signal through this quintuple-encrypted stream. Get dunked on.

"For those of you new to the channel, lemme catch you up. A

few years back, there was an accident—not my fault—"

She scrunched up her face in thought.

"—well, sort of my fault—and a rich kid died. Since then, her mother has spent a whooole buncha time and money trying to track me down. Which was fun! For a while."

Her gait slowed to a stop. A shadow crossed her face.

"Till it wasn't. But I don't wanna talk about that part."

With a shake of her head and another clearing of her throat, she resumed her march toward the city of lights. The starving flames of Rustville faded into pinpricks behind her as the asphalt turned to dust and dirt under her feet. In the liminal desert between Rustville and the Elite District, the darkness enveloped her.

"But tonight, it comes to an end. That's right, cops and narcs, I'm back on Eden-5 again. Back home. And it's way, way too late for you to do anything about it. Deathtrap, we're here."

The towers of the Elite District were close now, albeit safely behind the walls that separated the city from the desert. Walls covered in spikes, electric razor-wire, and the remains of those confident or stupid enough to try to scale them.

Behind her, the robot's head ignited. A bright, tight beam of light revealed an ECHO tower, its peak disappearing into the clouds, sheets of corrugated metal patching the wear and tear around its base. Midway up the tower, higher even than the border wall surrounding the Elite District, a single rope dangled from an exposed strut. Down on the ground, the woman grabbed on and climbed.

"Just like gym class," she said, reaching and pulling up her body up as best she could, grunting with every inch. "And just like gym class," she continued, panting, "my upper-body strength is… the worst. Deathtrap, can I get a boost?"

The robot zoomed underneath her. She placed her feet on its armored shoulders and sighed with relief. "Thanks, babe," she said.

The bot's hoverthruster glowed brighter and, inch by inch, the girl and the bot ascended the ECHO tower.

"Did a lot of reading on the way over," she said between gasps for breath. "Well, I listened to audio transcripts of books, which, same thing. Don't be jerks. And there are just not many revenge stories that really work for me, you know? Most of the time it's, 'Muhh, revenge is bad and you should just, like, turn the other cheek,' or whatever.

"But I, dear listener, do not subscribe to that philosophy. I believe in grabbing your cheek, shoving razor blades into it, then hitting their cheek with your cheek over and over until their face is slashed to ribbons, and yeah, maybe that means your own cheek is torn to shreds too, but that's a small price to pay for ruining the face of the woman who murdered your FATHER!"

The word echoed through the otherwise silent desert. The Vault Hunter tried to regain her composure and reduce the volume of her angry, heaving breaths that sounded as if they might turn into sobs if not stifled.

She shook the thought from her head as she and the bot rose higher.

"Never mind. Not worth talking about. Here we are! The jumping-off point."

The girl hoisted herself onto the strut overlooking the border wall. If she'd been a bird, she could have easily flapped her wings and sailed over the walls and into the city.

However, she was not a bird.

However however, she had a floating robot—just as good.

A giant metal hand encircled the girl's forearm (also made of metal). The bot's hoverthruster glowed brighter and louder than before as it floated toward the barrier, the young woman dangling from its arm still streaming video to her followers.

"Once we're over the wall, things get even simpler," she said.

"She won't be hard to find, and I won't miss."

Her ECHO device emitted a chime, the sharp tone traveling far and wide in the expanse of the desert.

"Ah. SpicyFrogRulez asks what I'm gonna do after I've killed her, once I'm being swarmed by secbots. Great news, SpicyFrogRulez— it doesn't matter! They can laser me into tiny cubes of cute-girl meat, but so long as she's dead, I'll have done my job."

The robot made a sound like metal scraping against a tougher, angrier metal.

"Don't whine, DT," she said. "I'm *probably* not gonna die. I mean, it's me. We'll be fine." She patted the robot's arm.

Still floating toward the city, the girl's ECHO device chimed again.

"JinothyKimothy asks, 'Isn't this a step down for a Vault Hunter? It wasn't long ago you were taking down a fascist army and saving the world.' Yes, Jinothy, I did. And I liked it a whole lot and it made me smile and everything was good. But since somebody had to go kill my dad, I haven't really liked anything and I've forced every smile and life feels like it has no meaning so long as my fingers aren't dripping with the blood of my father's killer.

"Thanks for subscribing, by the way," she chirped, displaying another forced smile.

The Vault Hunter and the robot passed over the upper lip of the wall, the girl hugging her knees to her chest so as not to clip the top with her feet.

"Hard part's over," she said, which is just about when the secbots folded out of the parapet walls and started firing at her. Without another word, her own robot released its grip and she tumbled to the ground, rolling with momentum and coming to a stop with a gun already digistructing into her hands.

The girl's robot charged the security forces, its digistruct claws rending the polished steel with every swipe. The girl fired her shotgun with reckless abandon, but somehow the pellets managed to ricochet and find a home in the artificially intelligent brains of the robotic guards. After a few moments of deafening laser fire and shotgun blasts, the shiny corner of the shiny city fell silent, its spotless streets now strewn with robot guts.

"Thing about these crime-buster bots, or whatever the security forces here call their army of robothugs," she said into her ECHO device. "Are they cheap, pathetic ripoffs of my boy Deathtrap? Yes. But—credit where credit is due—they're deadly in most circumstances.

"Most. See, they're programmed to defend from all sorta threats—petty criminals, offworld soldiers, voracious wildlife— but there's no programming in the world that can prepare you for a vengeful Vault Hunter.

"Deathtrap and I are coming for you, Countess Holloway," she growled. "And right before a bullet splits your head in two, you'll know it was me."

8
SASHA

"Gaige!" Holloway spat through the smoke and fire, that one syllable containing enough hatred to daze Sasha just as much as the explosion that preceded it.

Moments earlier, a thunderous boom had engulfed the room. The balcony door exploded inward, sending a thousand splinters of wood toward Sasha and Fiona. They dropped to the ground and covered their faces. Countess Holloway didn't react as quickly. She screamed as a dozen shards of wood embedded themselves in the arm she'd thrown up to protect her perfectly proportioned face.

Sasha yanked an incendiary Maliwan SMG from her satchel and flicked off the safety.

"You got one for me?" Fiona asked.

"There wasn't room."

"You could have brought a smaller gun."

Sasha scoffed.

Two figures appeared in the blasted-out balcony doorway. One of the intruders was all too familiar, if only in shape: it seemed to be a more ramshackle version of the secbots they'd been dogged by since landing on Eden-5. Someone had painted skulls onto its arms and back, which, to Sasha's eye, made it less intimidating. The rocket launcher in one of its fists, though, did a lot to balance out its fear factor. A wild-eyed girl dangled from its other hand, her eyes laser-focused on the countess.

Sasha couldn't explain why, but the woman struck her as the more dangerous of the pair.

The girl wore spiked shoulder pads over a ragged vest. Her hair was pulled into two pointy pigtails. She held a Torgue pistol in her cybernetic left arm, the barrel of which never wavered from Countess Holloway.

She glanced at Sasha and Fiona for a heartbeat before returning her gaze to Holloway. "Keep an eye on those two, DT," she said. In response, the ramshackle secbot leveled the rocket launcher at them.

Sasha aimed her submachine gun at the bot. If the robot hadn't been made of metal, and if it hadn't held a device that could blast both her and her sister to chunks with a single trigger-pull, and if the bulky debt cuff around Sasha's neck weren't throwing off her aim, this might have been a proper standoff. As it was, the bot and the girl had Sasha at their mercy.

Holloway glared at the intruder. Sasha had already felt that Holloway despised them, but once she saw the scowl on Holloway's face, she understood *true* hatred. Even a perfectly plascrete-surgeried face such as Holloway's could not contain her spite.

"You," she spat.

"Me," the girl replied, smiling. She sat on the edge of Holloway's desk, inches from the Vaultlander.

Holloway reached for her watch. Sasha assumed she had some sort of way to trigger the alarm remotely.

"Ah-ah-ah," the girl said. "Wouldn't make a difference anyway. Security already heard the boom. And you're gonna be dead long before they get here."

Sasha cleared her throat. Holloway would be considerably less inclined to pay them for the doll if she were dead.

"Ah," Sasha said. "That's actually not going to work for us? We were about to make a sale. So…"

Without looking, the girl with the gun asked, "If you knew the things this woman had done, you wouldn't be willing to tolerate another second of her. Do you know what she did to my father?"

"Killed him?" Fiona said.

The girl frowned. "Yeah. Good guess."

Fiona shrugged. "Context clues."

"Oh," Holloway laughed. "The murderess wants to get judgey, does she? After what you and that *thing* did to my Marcie?"

"It was an accident," the girl said, pulling back the hammer of her pistol. "Unlike this."

"Wait!" Fiona shouted. She flicked her arm forward to unholster her wrist gun, but the weight of the debt cuff threw her off and she fell forward, the cuff all but pinning her to the ground. Sasha didn't consider the moment very dignified and, given that the barrel of Fiona's popgun was now pointed directly at a very expensive rug, it also wasn't getting anyone closer to a proper standoff.

Then Fiona saw the micro-nade on the back of the Vaultlander.

"You pull that trigger, you die next," Sasha said, working some bass into her voice in the hope of offsetting the fact that Fiona was high-fiving the hardwood floor.

"That's right," she said, pointing at the Vaultlander. "That box next to you? You make a move we don't like, it pops. And you along with it."

The girl glanced down at the box and the explosive charge attached to it. "A micro-nade? Next time you want to bluff, maybe don't try it with someone who knows their explosives," she said.

Half of bluffing, Sasha knew, was about reading your mark.

You can come up with the most believable lie in the world and it won't matter if you spend it on the wrong person. In this case, the person appeared to be a punk-rock youth between the ages of sixteen and twenty with robotics skills, weapons experience, and a pronounced hatred of authority. The kind of person, in other words, who probably didn't spend a lot of time researching the street value of collectible action figures.

"The micro-nade isn't what you need to worry about," Sasha said. "It's the molded bomb inside the box. One pound of plastic explosive, formed in the shape of a rotund Vault Hunter. If the micro-nade pops, the Vaultlander, and then all of us, go with it."

"What?" Gaige asked, annoyance twisting her face.

"Vaultlanders," Sasha said. "A collectible—"

"I know what Vaultlanders are. They screwed up the proportions on mine. I look like a kindergartener."

Ah, Sasha thought, *she's a Vault Hunter. That explains the… well, everything.*

Gaige stole a glance at Typhon DeLeon's oblivious, grinning face and failed to hide the brief flicker of panic across her own. Sasha could see it in her eyes. Sasha was probably bluffing, sure, but why else would a couple of out-of-towners be selling a stupid-looking toy to Countess Holloway? The box was in garbage condition—if it was *just* a valuable doll, nobody would buy it with the packaging covered in blood. What if these two Pandorans had made the box themselves *and* built the bomb inside? It was far-fetched. Probably a bluff. But she couldn't know for sure.

That's what Sasha hoped was going through Gaige's mind, anyway. She could just as easily be thinking about how fun it'd be to stain a bullymong-fur rug with their brain matter.

"Shoot her," Holloway spat. "Kill her and the bot or you're not getting a cent out of me."

"I see so much as a finger twitch and you won't live to spend your lunch money," the girl said.

Finally, a proper standoff.

Time slowed down. Fiona always said that when you're overwhelmed, you gotta take your problems one at a time.

First, the robot's Hyperion-brand rocket launcher, with a custom homing module mounted to the barrel and heat-seeking rockets—bad. Good: it had a max mag size of two. And one rocket had already been spent on blasting the door in.

Second, the gun pointed at Holloway. Torgue brand. Explosive shot. Even if the Vault Hunter somehow missed at point-blank range, the splash damage alone would still blow Holloway inside out.

Third, the robot itself. Even after solving problems one and two, it could still unsheathe its digistruct claws and cut Sasha and Fiona to ribbons before they could bring it down.

So. Three unsolvable problems. Now how about some solutions? Sasha scanned the room.

Her submachine gun. Its flaming bullets could turn the Vault into a lump of smoldering goop but wouldn't do anything against the non-flammable bot.

Fiona's wrist gun. Currently weighted to the floor. Even if she hoisted her arm up, the shot wouldn't cause much more than a flesh wound.

Fireplace. Warm. Crackling.

Decorative sword on the wall. Sheathed. Might be glued to its mount. Even if Sasha had time to pull it down, it—

Wait.

Fireplace.

Heat-seeking rockets.

Sasha's SMG.

Sasha hurled her only gun into the fire.

"Uh," Fiona said.

The robot didn't wait to see what happened next. With a thunderous boom, it fired a rocket straight at them.

An eternity passed between heartbeats. Sasha thought about the things she'd accomplished in her life. The list didn't take as long as she'd hoped.

The gun in the fireplace sparked. Somewhere in its sleek metal innards, an elemental charge—the power cell that allowed the gun to digistruct fiery bullets out of raw matter—sizzled. Flames licked at its plasmetal casing until—

WHOOM.

The gun exploded. A plume of flame blossomed out from the fireplace. The ball of fire that burst forward was barely an explosion compared to some Sasha had seen before—it was far too small to hurt anyone, and not sustained enough to give them cover for a retreat. It was, however, hot enough to confuse the mid-air rocket's heat-seeking sensor.

The moment before the explosion, it had locked onto Sasha and Fiona as the hottest things in its target range. The moment the gun exploded, it suddenly detected a greater threat and heat source—the fireball—and veered toward it.

It didn't have time to change direction as much as Sasha would have liked.

The rocket impacted against the far corner of the fireplace and the ensuing explosion and shockwave knocked everyone who wasn't a hovering robot to the ground.

The Vault Hunter's explosive pistol pointed at the ground. Fiona had maybe a second before she raised it back up at Holloway and pulled the trigger.

Fiona wrenched her wrist pistol out of her anchored right hand. She wasn't a leftie, but this would have to do. She raised the popgun and took aim at the girl's pistol. All she had to do was knock it out of her hand, give Holloway time to find cover.

She pulled the trigger. And shot the Vault Hunter in the chest.

The girl yelped in pain as a puff of crimson appeared just under her right shoulder. To her credit, she maintained her grip on the gun and tried to raise it at Fiona. Holloway took the opportunity to spring to her feet and grab the girl's cybernetic arm holding the gun.

The girl's robot charged toward Holloway, digiclaws at the ready.

It became obvious to Sasha that this was normally the part where she and Fiona would run. They didn't know any of these people, and it's not usually a great idea to stick around after you've nonlethally shot someone who owns a murderous robot.

But the Vaultlander sat on the edge of the desk, perilously close to the fighting women. They may not be able to sell it to this soon-to-be-murdered billionaire, but if they left without it they'd be screwed ten times over.

Sasha and Fiona sprinted to the desk, the latter limping with every weighted step.

The bot pulled its arm back to strike.

Holloway slammed the girl's arm onto the desk, knocking the gun loose from her grip.

The girl growled with anger. Grabbed the Vaultlander.

And smashed it over Holloway's skull.

The micro-nade exploded with a dull pop. Holloway shrieked in pain, smoke rising from her burned face. She scrambled blindly for the pistol and wrapped her fingers around the grip.

At that moment, the doors behind Sasha and Fiona exploded inward. A half-dozen secbots, shinier duplicates of the one that'd just shot at them, entered the room and fired their lasers at the girl.

Barely dodging the storm of energy beams, the girl smirked at Sasha. "Good bluff," she said and snapped her fingers. "We're outta here, Deathtrap."

The robot re-sheathed its digiclaws and slung an arm around the girl's stomach. Its hoverengine spat blue flame as the two would-be assassins boosted their way back through the broken balcony doorway, the secbots' lasers impacting against the assassin robot's back.

Sasha and Fiona were too slow to stop them. Too slow to do anything. All they could do was watch. Gaige looked back into the office, staring at Holloway with hatred as the secbot-that-wasn't-a-secbot flew them over the balcony railing and out of sight.

As they disappeared from view, Countess Holloway's raspy screech echoed through the room: "I'll find you, Gaige! I'll find you and I'll reprogram your little friend to peel your skin off while I watch!"

The smoke cleared as Sasha searched amidst the wreckage.

"Oh no," she said. "Oh no, no, no."

She held up the Vaultlander. What was left of it, anyway.

The box was blown wide open. No longer a box, even, but a singed blossom of paper and transparent plastic. The micro-nade had reduced the Vaultlander itself to an unrecognizable mess of melted putty and burnt doll clothing. A glob of what used to be Typhon DeLeon slid to the floor with a wet plop.

"Moneyyyyyyyyturrrrrrdssssss," it said.

"Darn," Fiona said. "She took it out of the box."

9
FIONA

As Holloway's live-in plascrete surgeons painstakingly reformed the size, shape, and number of her nostrils to what they'd been before she'd headbutted a grenade, I asked for some compensation for saving her life. The lights of her own surgery room were warm and soothing. Combined with the relaxing sound of waterfalls and birds chirping, the surgeons probably could have cut my face too and I wouldn't have noticed.

She patted my shoulder, a gesture that exerted the skin on her neck just a bit too much and caused a split. The nearest surgeon quickly sprayed it down with liquiskin before the blood could seep through. "First rule of business, you poor little thing: if you're working without a contract, you're working for free."

I grimaced. "Next time there's a gun to your head, I'll be sure to negotiate price before I do anything heroic."

She removed her hand from my shoulder and wiped it down with a silk handkerchief before throwing the handkerchief away. "Now you're getting it. If you happen to run into a *second* one-of-a-kind Typhon figurine, you know where to find me."

"Who's the girl?" Sasha asked.

Holloway grunted in irritation. "A fugitive. None of your concern."

"Considering she just janked us out of a fortune, I'd call her pretty concerning. There a reward on her head?" Sasha said.

Holloway furrowed her brow, pulling her forehead skin so taut you could see the blood vessels beneath it. "If you're in a suicidal mood, certainly. Years ago, I put a bounty on her so big it would, and did, attract bounty hunters from across the galaxy. None of them succeeded. As tends to happen when you hunt someone who chases Vaults for a living."

"Well," Sasha said, putting a foot on the operating table's footrest and an elbow on her knee, "we're not most bounty hunters. And we've opened a Vault or two in our time."

I shoved Sasha's knee off the footrest and put an arm around her shoulder. "What she means is, we'll be going." I turned to go, forcing Sasha in front of me.

"Sixteen billion if you bring her in alive," Holloway said, stopping us both in our tracks. "Dead, half that." It was a lie, of course; nobody would pay that much for a single bounty. Not to mention that Sasha and I were gutter trash as far as Holloway was concerned; she could just as easily send us packing as pay us, and there'd be nobody for us to complain to.

Apparently Sasha didn't seem to see it that way, as she eagerly said, "It's a d—"

"We'll think about it," I interrupted.

Holloway dismissed us with a wave of her hand. "Makes no difference to me if you get killed chasing her. Just get out of my home."

———

On our way out, a pair of secbots corralled us in a security room. A wall of monitors showed camera feeds covering every inch of the grounds, and a secbot worked a console full of hundreds of blinking buttons and switches to keep it all moving smoothly. Holloway's personal secbots were suspicious we might have had something to do with the intruder, but after a half-hour of questioning that went nowhere, they tossed us out onto the street.

Outside, we sat down on the sidewalk and sulked.

"You know, we could always call Rhys for backup," Sasha said. "Three Vault Hunters against a girl and a bot—"

"We're not Vault Hunters, so stop thinking about it." I put enough force in my voice to make her shoulders slump. I'd made my decision, and there was no way she could capture Gaige without me.

"So," she said. "It's over."

"Seems so," I said.

She closed her eyes. "I attached explosives to a priceless action figure. I'm such an idiot."

"You couldn't have known somebody'd use it as a bludgeon."

She buried her face in her hands. "We were so close! We were almost out of... all this. Now we got less than we did before. Don't even have the cash to get back to Pandora. Shit, was this all for nothing? Hunting the Vault, meeting Rhys, killing the big monster? Hell, if I'd known it would have led to this, I wouldn't have wasted so much effort dying."

"Not funny," I said. "But we can get back to Pandora easy enough. We could always call Rhys. Maybe Janey and Athena. They could spot us enough money for a ride home."

"Yeah, and then what? Back to hustling for scraps? That doesn't bother you?"

Of course it did. It's one thing to live knee-deep in shit when the stink is all you've known. It's another thing to step out, clean your boots, and then get shoved back in face first. Even getting thrown onto the pavement hurt worse since our butts had known the feel of expensive cushions.

"Of course not," I said. "Long as we're together, that's all that matters."

Sasha nodded. If she didn't believe me, she was polite enough not to say anything about it.

My arm ached. My ankle felt heavy. The debt cuffs were beginning to really weigh on me. The thought that I'd be stuck with these things for longer than a couple of days made me want to grab a hacksaw and a tourniquet. I wanted to lie face down and sleep for a year straight. I wanted to go back to the Vault and ask for a do-over. I wanted a lot of things I wasn't going to get. Most immediately, a place to sit.

A secbot across the street saw us harmlessly resting on the curb and decided that couldn't be tolerated. It zoomed over to us, its face light flashing red. "NO LOITERING. MOVE OR YOU WILL BE FINED."

"Yeah." I said, beginning the long process of pushing myself up to my feet. "No problem. Where should we go?"

"NOT HERE," it said.

"While you've got us here, I have a question," Sasha asked. "Does the name 'Deathtrap' mean anything to you?"

The bot leaned over, putting its monoeye so close to Sasha and me that we could see ourselves reflected in it. "CONSORTING WITH KNOWN FUGITIVES IS A FINABLE OFFENSE."

"Good thing we didn't do any consorting then, just… I just heard the name."

"CONSIDER UNHEARING IT."

———

We walked all the way back to the shuttle docks. I couldn't decide which was more irritating, the secbots giving us the digital stinkeye with every step or the rich folks who went out of their way to ignore and avoid us. It was a hell of a walk even without my entire right side anchored down.

When we finally arrived, we found an ECHO terminal in the shuttle bay, but didn't have the cash to call anybody—I'd forgotten I'd spent the last of our cash on the cab ride to Holloway's. The lady at Dapper Delilah's was right to kick us out—I couldn't have paid even if the clothes were in the same price galaxy as me.

"Great," I said. "So we're stuck."

"We just need enough for an ECHO call, right?" Sasha replied. "A few hours of panhandling could get us there. Or are your fingers feeling sticky?"

I shook my head. "Neither. I'm sick of being embarrassed, and there's not enough cash around here to be worth lifting. 'Scuse me," I said, waving at one of the dockworkers. "You-all got a bounty board around here?"

"There's a few in Rustville," he said. "Mostly just odd jobs for the Elites. I wouldn't get your hopes up."

I adjusted my hat. "That won't be a problem."

———

You know the image that comes to mind when you think of a place called Rustville? You know the smells and sounds your brain comes up with?

Rustville was exactly like that.

Flaming barrels provided warmth to shivering, huddled forms. Piles of human feces dotted the street like landmines, which first makes you think, *agh, how disgusting*, until you realize there are no outhouses or indoor bathrooms, so then you think, *agh, how inevitable*. But you still breathe through your mouth.

"Bounty board?" I asked a girl on the street. She looked up from her "toys"—two shell casings she clinked together while making fight noises with her mouth—and nodded down a side street. I couldn't help but notice a big fat debt cuff looped around her stomach. I tried to put it out of my mind as we headed for the jobs board.

If you want something done and don't particularly care how or by whom, you post it on a bounty board. It's a bulletin board connected to the ECHOnet that displays every manner of odd job you can think of.[15]

We heard the bounty board's presence before we saw it. A dozen shouting denizens elbowed each other to get first pick of the day's new jobs (elbows that were granted much more momentum by the debt cuffs every single laborer wore). Glancing over their shoulders, I could see jobs like MANSION ROTATION, VISCERA ACCUMULATION, and FOOTREST.

"Let's give them a second," I told Sasha. If we waited long enough, there might be some jobs more dangerous and interesting than menial labor still remaining. The locals looked like they needed the jobs worse than we did, and if there were any gigs left that were considered too dangerous for the average worker, Sasha and I could probably handle them without breaking a sweat.

After a few minutes, the crowd dispersed. Each laborer left with that mixture of glee and dread that often accompanies a new job—glad to be paid, irritated to have to deal with a brand new buffet of bullshit.

The remaining job postings ranged from the imaginatively demeaning to the physically impossible.

"Oh, good," Sasha said without reading the copy of the top job request. "This one asks for sisters. Oh, wait. Never mind." She scowled like she'd smelled something foul. "It doesn't even pay that well."

She took a deep breath. "Can I try something?"

"What?"

"I just want to see about that Gaige girl. Just out of curiosity."

Sasha tapped Gaige's name into the bounty board's search engine. The screen spat a thousand different offenses at us,

---

15 Though often these jobs reduce down to collecting something, killing something, or standing in a particular area for a particular amount of time.

mostly of the murder or assisted murder varieties.

"What do you think you're gonna find?" I asked. "It's just a rap sheet. It's not going to list a super-secret way to take her out or something."

"Just gimme a second. Let's see the bounty itself."

An image of the girl who had shot at us flashed onto the screen. She looked slightly younger and considerably happier. The legend below it read: *Wanted: Gaige DiMartino. Crimes: Illegal experimentation, murder. Reward: $16,000,000,000.* Even having heard the number from Holloway, it still gave us chills to see that many zeroes.

"Well," I said, "I guess Holloway wasn't lying."

"There are some video files attached," Sasha said. "Let's see…"

One button-press later, the bounty board filled with grainy surveillance footage of what looked to be a high-school gymnasium. A dozen students littered the gym, awkwardly standing next to dioramas and test tubes and large pieces of posterboard with questions like "Is sand edible?" scrawled on them in permanent marker.

"Science fair," Sasha said. "And look." She pointed at one of the students. She looked younger, but there was no doubt: it was the girl who destroyed our Vaultlander. The Vault Hunter. She stood next to what appeared to be her secbot friend who'd launched a rocket at us. The display board she'd set up next to it read, "mechanized anti-bully deterrent, a.k.a. project dt."

"When's this from?" I asked.

"A little over seven years ago."

The girl—Gaige—held a trophy in her hand. Third place. She looked irritated. The irritation only increased when another girl entered the frame, with her own secbot in tow and a first-place trophy. The bot looked like a shinier version of Gaige's. Nearly identical to the secbots on every street corner of Eden-5.

Gaige shouted. Pointed at the other girl's bot. "Marcie!" she yelled, and then something about "rip-off cop-ass police-state-ass robot," and then, "narc."

"Marcie," Sasha murmured. "Holloway mentioned a Marcie, didn't she?"

Gaige thrust her fists into the air. "Anarchy forever!" she cheered. Other kids and parents turned toward the commotion.

Marcie pointed and laughed at Gaige. Pinched her cheeks.

Gaige pushed Marcie away.

Marcie shoved Gaige back. Hard.

Gaige went down and hit her skull on her display table. Blood trickled down her forehead.

And DT obliterated Marcie.

It was quick. It was bad. In one moment, DT floated placidly next to its creator. The next, its claws were out, it slashed once, and Marcie the bully was just… goo.

Screams. Panic. Running. Gaige grabbed her pigtails. "Ohhhhh nonononono," she shouted to the fleeing crowd. "I didn't mean to! It was an accident! It—"

The security footage ended.

"Yikes," Sasha said. "No wonder Holloway hates her so much."

"Yeah. Any other files?"

Sasha scrolled through the feed. "Some rumors. Lotta folks saying she fled to Pandora, hunted Vaults for a while. Lotta gibberish." Sasha dragged her finger across the screen. "Official death certificate for her dad. Pretty recent. Says he died in debtors' prison a week ago. Looks like Holloway forced him to serve out Gaige's sentence." Sasha turned back from the bounty board. "Not like him dying is gonna make Holloway go any easier on her, though."

I nodded. "So, she leaves, Holloway takes her dad, and spends seven years pumping him for information. Then he dies, and his little girl comes back looking for revenge. In the process, she skunks our deal and our one shot at a happy life." I chewed my bottom lip. "In theory."

Sasha narrowed her eyes. "Is that interest I detect?"

"It's just... I dunno. I assumed this girl was just some revolutionary, a terrorist or something. But if she killed Holloway's daughter... then Holloway would actually pay up. She'd have to—the crime's too public for her to get away with screwing us, and too personal for her to even mind the hit to her bank account."

"Yeah," Sasha said. "But like you said. Sixteen-billion-dollar reward and no takers. You think there might be a reason for that?" This was a favorite argument tactic of Sasha's, to restate my position back to me and force me to argue against it.

"None other than the fact that she's a Vault Hunter with a floating deathbot. She can't have too many connections out here. Anyone who knew where she was would sell her out the second they could. So, wherever she is, she's alone. Other than the deathbot."

"Right," Sasha said. "But... I'd also like to point out that, between the two of us, we have a whopping one gun." She tapped my wrist. "If we can even call it that."

"Rude," I said, patting my faithful wrist pistol. "But didn't you hear me? We don't need to worry about getting guns. She's a Vault Hunter."

Sasha squinted in confusion before she realized what I was suggesting.

"Wow. Okay. You want to sneak into a Vault Hunter's stash and kidnap her by stealing her own guns? That's an incredibly reckless idea."

"And with any luck, it'll be our last one."

"What?"

"Because it'll work and we'll get rich," I clarified. "Not because we'll die."

"Great. Wonderfully worded."

I sat on the ground. "Look, I know it's a long shot, but we spent the better part of a year hunting a Vault, hoping that when we got there it'd somehow… I don't know, change *everything*. That we'd be different people. A year of build-up. A year of hoping that this time, *this* would be the job that fixes everything. And then when we got there, what happened? You died. Right in front of me."

Sasha flinched. "Yeah, but—"

"But nothing," I said, my voice cracking with the effort. Bewilderment crossed Sasha's face, then concern. I could see, plain as day, that she'd been so focused on her own feelings about death, she'd not stopped to see how hard it had hit me, too. Not that I blamed her; I'd made a concerted effort not to show her.

"I saw you dead on the ground, Sasha, and I don't… I *can't* see that happen again. So we've got a choice. We can do some lousy odd jobs to pay our way back to Pandora and then keep doing lousy odd jobs until one day one of us takes a bullet we don't come back from. Or, we can get a big payday right here, right now, and retire in safety."

Sasha raised an eyebrow. "You're worried about me getting hurt, and your solution is… to fight a Vault Hunter."

"Look, I didn't say it was an amazing plan, but we either take a million small gambles or a single big one. We're putting ourselves at risk no matter what. And besides, we've fought Vault Hunters before."

Sasha ran a hand through her hair and closed her eyes. It's what she always did when she was about to agree with me. "So, to get guns, you wanna do, what? 'Stalker in the—'"

"'Stalker in the Skag Den,' yeah."

"And her robot pet? How do we handle that?"

"I have a plan," I said, as I furiously tried to come up with a plan.

"Shit." Sasha shook her head and extended an arm to help me up. "Let's go Vault Hunter hunting, then."

10
FIONA

"Is this going to kill me?" I asked.

"Definitely not. Probably not. That's why I'm starting with the one on your ankle."

Sasha sat next to my leg, a handful of multicolored wires running from the ECHO device on her wrist to my debt cuff.

I focused on the wires, trying and failing to make heads or tails of how Sasha intended to remove the cuff. "What makes you so sure this'll work?"

Sasha waved her hand in the universal don't-worry-about-it gesture. "Rhys taught me a ton of stuff about hacking. If these things are designed to just snap open once you've fed enough cash into them, it shouldn't be hard to flip some ones to zeroes and trick them into thinking they've been paid off."

"You lost me at 'Rhys.'"

Sasha threw her hands up, nearly yanking the wires out of the cuff. "You want me to leave these on? I can leave them on. You can try to fight a Vault Hunter with an extra hundred pounds weighing down your right side."

I got to my feet. This was stupid. "Maybe you should. The

secbots said something bad would happen if you tried to take them off."

Sasha grabbed my ankle and held firm. Whatever she was doing, she was nearly done. "Everybody says stuff."

"Wow," I said. "You should put that on a T-shirt."

We probably would have kept sniping at each other like that if the cuff hadn't started beeping. The beeps quickly grew louder and more high-pitched, and the cuff began to vibrate around my ankle.

"Um," I said.

"It's fine," Sasha said.

"DETONATING IN FOUR SECONDS," the cuff said.

"Sasha!"

"I know! Just lemme—"

"THREE—"

Sasha typed faster. The cuff vibrated harder and harder, like something inside it was about to burst.

"TWO—"

"If I don't survive, you call Athena and—"

"Shut up! I've nearly got it!"

"ONE—"

The cuff sprang open. Sasha grabbed it and flung it down the alley. *Move!* she yelled, pushing me behind a dumpster. I didn't understand her panic—the collar was no bigger than an ordinary grenade. Its explosive force couldn't possibly—

The entire world went white with sound and fire.

My ribcage rattled as the shockwave hit us, my heart damn near liquefying in my chest. I couldn't hear anything but a high-pitched ringing, and my entire body felt as if I'd stepped directly into an oven. Debris rained from the sky for what felt like minutes. When the chaos finally came to an end and the whine in my ears was replaced by the angry shouts of distant bystanders, I looked at Sasha with horror.

"That was awful," I said. "Let's never do that again."

"Agreed. After I get this one off my neck," she said, reaching for her collar.

I grabbed her hand. "No, you are absolutely not."

"I figured it out! Easy hack. I won't cut it so close next time."

"How sure are you? Zero to one hundred."

"About… n—"

"You weren't about to say one hundred."

Sasha shot me the face all younger sisters whip out for those moments when they think their older sister just said something really stupid. "Uh, it's my neck, Fi."

"And I'm your older sister, which makes that neck my responsibility."

"I'm not twelve anymore," she said, rolling her eyes.

"Yeah, thanks to me for keeping you alive all these years." I kept talking through her scoff, not wanting to give her the opportunity to shut me down. "Enough messing with the collars. We need to find Gaige."

"And how do you propose we do that?"

———

The receptionist of the Eden-5 debtors' prison was more pleasant than I expected. She gave me a quick glance and asked, "You wantin' to stay with us?"

"Oh, no. I've just got the two cuffs. I'll have them off in no time."

"Aw, bless yer heart," she said, patting my hand. She was a balding woman with a scar on her face and a debt cuff around each wrist. She'd painted them floral colors and drawn little cat faces on them. It was cute, in a sad kind of way.

"If you change your mind, we got room. At least in here we

can give you three square meals a day. You just can't leave until you're cuff-free."

"No, we don't need to go in," I said. "I was just curious about an ex-prisoner here. Name of DiMartino?"

"Oh, we're not allowed to give out any information on inmates."

This? This is where I thrive. Using my wits to get people to part with things they don't want to part with. Things like money. Like information.

If I could find out where Gaige's father's body had been sent, I suspected I could find Gaige herself. After all, she'd come all the way back to her home planet, so there was a good chance she wanted to see or bury her father while she was here. Follow the corpse, find the girl.

But there were a variety of different paths I could take with—I glanced down at her nametag—Laurel the prison guard. A complex tree of possibilities, one choice amplifying a single branch while pruning all the rest.

As I often did in moments like this, I let the little voice in my head decide which path to take. The voice wasn't terribly consistent, but it seldom steered me wrong.

Turn on the charm—turn to page 82

Bribe her—turn to page 83

Relate to her financial situation—turn to page 84

…—turn to page 86

TURN ON THE CHARM

"Laurel. Can I call you Laurel?"

"Aw," Laurel said. "I'd love it if you did."

"Laurel, I don't want to bog you down with the details, but a very dangerous person is on the loose. And if I can find where

Mr. DiMartino's body went, I can take them off the streets and make things a lot safer. I'm a Vault Hunter, you see. That's what I do: I protect people."

"I thought Vault Hunters just sorta killed everything that looked at 'em sideways."

I put my hand on hers. "Some do. But not me. I'm a nice one."

"*We're* nice," Sasha confirmed. "We only kill the bad people."

"That sounds subjective."

"I—it—yes," Sasha stuttered. "But in this instance, the person we're hunting killed a teenage girl."

"Aw. That's sad."

I leaned forward. "It is. Now, I'm asking you, Laurel, will you help me? Will you give me this teeny-tiny bit of information that'll help me bring a murderer to justice?'

Laurel's face softened. She took a deep breath. "Well, when you put it that way…"

Turn to page 86

BRIBE HER

"*Of* course," I said, "I'd never expect you to part with privileged information for free."

"Of course," Sasha agreed.

"I'd be happy to make the exchange worth your while."

"All right." Laurel shrugged. "I'm open to bribes. What do you got?"

I stared at her. Oh god, what did I have? Apart from a spare handful of bullets for my wrist gun, my pockets were completely empty. Still, I'd never let that stop me before.

"What don't I have, Laurel? I can get you the autograph of—or, if you're lucky, a picture with—the two Vault Hunters who found the Vault of the Traveler."

She nodded, smiling. "I don't know what that is!"

Sasha's eyes widened in exaggerated shock. "You don't know what…? Wow. Laurel. Wow. A very dangerous Vault. There was a big, big monster—"

Laurel pointed at me. "I like your hat."

I grabbed Laurel's pointer finger and gently pushed it away. "Hat's not for trade. Anything else appeal to—"

"Fi, she likes your hat," Sasha said.

"So do I. That's why I'm wearing it."

"You wanted to trade, she just told you what she wants in trade."

"I don't want the hat anymore," Laurel said, waving her hands. "Too much drama."

"She wants the hat, Fiona," Sasha said.

"I don't want the hat," Laurel said. "I want money."

I nodded at Laurel. "You drive a hard bargain, ma'am. So I'll give it to you straight. The person we're hunting? She's named Gaige, and the reward on her head is sixteen billion dollars."

"Oooh," Laurel said. "Neat."

"If your tip helps us catch her, you'd be entitled to some of the reward. Say… one percent."

"Hmm," Laurel said. "Well, when you put it that way…"

Turn to page 86

RELATE TO HER FINANCIAL SITUATION

"Like I said, I'm not allowed to give out any information on inmates past or present."

I leaned on the front desk and put on my best we're-all-in-this-together smile. "Sure. You know that, and I know that, but the people upstairs? The ones who put these debt things on us? They don't know what we're going through."

"I don't follow," she said, still smiling.

"Laurel," I said, because people like hearing their own names repeated back to them. "How long have you worn those cuffs, Laurel?"

"Since school, so... 'bout twelve years?"

"Twelve years. I've only had these ones for a few hours. I can't imagine how much they'd chafe after twelve years."

"Considerably!"

Sasha leaned in. "But, I mean, the bank that put the cuff on you. They send you lotions, right? Bandages. Stuff to help with all that. Right?"

Laurel, confused, shook her head.

"They *don't?*" Sasha asked in her best fake outrage. "That's... Laurel, that's preposterous."

"It is?"

Sasha nodded. "It *is.*"

"It is," I agreed. "And we're all wearing these cuffs for the same reason."

"You've got student loans too?"

"No, Laurel. We're wearing these cuffs because we played their game. We played by the rules. Rules they don't have to live by."

"They sure don't," Sasha said.

"Those rules—to the rich folks, they're just words. But to us? They're as solid as the very bars of this prison, Laurel, squished squarely under the big guys' thumbs."

"Are they prison bars or are they thumbs? Bit of a mixed metaphor."

"They're... It doesn't matter. The point is, Laurel, people like us have to stick together against people like them. Sometimes that means big rebellions. Sometimes that means little ones, like giving out information they don't want you to give out. What do you say, Laurel?"

"Well, when you put it that way..."

Turn to page 86

...

I stared at Laurel in silence.

She smiled placidly back at me.

I continued to stare. This was the most arcane and risky of persuasive arts: the silent treatment. By continuing to stare daggers at her without a word of elaboration, Laurel would be tempted to fill the negative space with something—anything— to ward off the awkwardness.

Sasha froze in place. The smallest movement, the smallest noise, could break the impeccably crafted atmosphere of uncomfortable silence I had plunged Laurel into.

"Oh," Laurel said. "This is kinda nice. Just enjoyin' silence. So often, you know, conversations are about back and forth, everyone tryin' to get their points in. Almost like a competition. But this? This is nice. I could sit like this for a while."

And she did.

For forty-five minutes.

She just… smiled calmly at us. Taking deep, intentional breaths. Enjoying the silence.

It was awful.

Sasha broke first.

"Oh my god, can you please just tell us where you sent DiMartino's body?"

"Aw. I thought we were havin' a moment."

"We were," I said. "And it was lovely. But we would really, truly love to find out what became of poor Mr. DiMartino."

"Well, when you put it that way…"

Turn to page 86

"Nah," Laurel said.

"But," Sasha said. "But the whole… We had a moment. We had, like, one of four moments."

Laurel pursed her lips in what seemed to be genuine sympathy. "I know. But this job's all I got, ma'am. If it comes back that I helped you, these cuffs are gonna get a whole lot heavier."

Well. That was that. I can talk my way out of a lot of things, but apparently I can't talk someone into not being afraid of their boss.

"I see. Thank you for your time, Laurel."

Sasha made for the door.

"We could always just ask random folks in Rustville. Somebody must have seen a redhead with a killer secbot boyfriend."

"Oh! You're looking for her?" Laurel interjected.

Sasha and I spun on our heels.

"She came by a couple days ago askin' pretty much the same thing 'bout Mr. DiMartino. Pigtail girl and her rusty pal."

"And you—" I winced. "—didn't think it was worth telling us that?"

Laurel shrugged, her debt cuffs clinking against the desk.

"Laurel," Sasha said. "Would you happen to know anything at all about where this girl and her robot went?"

"Oh, for sure. She asked me where her dad's body was and I told her I couldn't tell her, so her robot got kinda scary on me, and she stopped the robot from hurtin' me and told me if I ever had a change of heart and decided I want to help her bury-slash-avenge her dad, I just needed to go out to the Tetanus Wilds to find her. Then she told me not to tell anybody that."

"So… why are you telling us that?"

"Oh, that's easy."

IF YOU TURNED ON THE CHARM:

"You won me over with your charm!"

IF YOU BRIBED HER:

"One percent of sixteen billion bucks sounds pretty good to me."

IF YOU RELATED TO HER FINANCIAL SITUATION:

"Class solidarity. You convinced me. A girl with no cuffs tells me not to help a girl *with* cuffs? Nah. You also said my name a bunch and I liked that."

IF YOU REMAINED SILENT:

"I had such a good time enjoyin' that silence with you. I feel like we're connected, you know? Spiritually."

I nodded and held out my hand. "Laurel, I'm glad we met."

"Aw, shucks," she said. "Samesies."

"Hey," Sasha said, pointing at the ECHO device on her wrist. "I got the Tetanus Wilds here."

The digital screen showed aerial surveillance pictures, likely taken by secbots, depicting a wasteland of rusted metal and shattered concrete that used to be a neighborhood until a higher power decided it'd be better off as a graveyard. It was connected to the far side of Rustville like a pimple on top of a boil.

"ECHOnet says this place used to be for the Upwards," Sasha said.

"Upwards?"

"Halfway between the Rustville folks and the rich ones. Poor folks who were starting to make a lot of money."

"Why'd they tear it down?" I asked.

"Dunno. Maybe the Elites didn't want the Upwards getting any ideas. Stay in your lane and all that."

I took a deep breath. This was going to be fine. I wasn't in over my head. I'd fought Vault Hunters before. I'd taken down a score of alien Guardians. I was a badass. I could do this.

And I could do it alone.

"Yeah," I said. "Wait here. I gotta make sure Laurel doesn't tell anyone we're here. Check the photos for anywhere that might make a good hideout—someplace Gaige might be lying low."

"Already on it." She nodded and continued to pore over the images with the focus and intelligence I'd admired ever since we were kids. She was always smarter than me where it counted. That's the great secret of all older siblings: We know we don't really deserve what little authority we're given. I've run a lot of great cons in my life, but the greatest one—the one I was still running—was convincing Sasha I knew what the hell I was doing. That I knew best. That I'd keep her safe. All the while, I'd continued to rope her into grand schemes and back-alley brawls and high-speed chases until one day she'd run into a blast zone with a detonator in her hand.

This time would be different. This time I would keep her safe.

"Laurel," I whispered. "I actually do want to take you up on your offer."

"Oh? What's that?"

"My sister here. I think debtors' prison might just be the safest place for her."

"You sure? She's just got the one cuff round her neck. Usually folks don't come in until they're so weighed down they can't work no more."

"I'm sure, Laurel. So, however we start that process, I'd like to do that now."

"Works for me," said Laurel with a shrug. "Lemme call in the escorts."

She pressed a blue button on the desk. The iron barred door behind her slammed open and two secbots zoomed in, arms outstretched.

Sasha looked up from her ECHO. "What? What's going—"

My poker face must have failed me. When she looked into my eyes, her expression darkened. She knew exactly what I'd done.

"No," she said as the secbots lifted her up by her shoulders. "You dumbass, you're going to get yourself killed!"

"Then we'll be even," I said.

"You dumb motherf—"

The secbots took her through the iron door, which slammed shut behind them. And for the first time in a long while, I felt something like relief. Sasha was safe. All I had to do was bring in Gaige and pay off Sasha's debt with the reward money.

Couldn't be simpler.

11
FIONA

It wasn't that hard to track down Gaige's hideout in the Tetanus Wilds. Most of the wilds were a minefield of architectural shrapnel, with very few walls still standing. Only two buildings stood defiantly against the ruins surrounding them: a holo-theater and, on the opposite side of the wasteland, what appeared to be the remnants of a hip juice bar. On the upside, that meant there were only two possible places she could be hiding; on the downside, that meant I'd have to cross a lot of treacherous terrain to get anywhere.

The sun hung low, turning the sky a burnt orange. Rather than making the place appear more beautiful, it bathed the jagged ruins in a sickly red that turned the Wilds into one big open wound, a gash on the face of Eden-5, cut into its crust with such violence and speed that it'd never fully close.

I took my first step into the Wilds and nearly impaled my foot on a spike of rebar. Beyond that lay a field of broken glass and tangled metal wire. Animal bones marked the ground every few paces. The Wilds were an ocean of pain and metal and exposed sharp edges, save for a few islands of flat, collapsed concrete that looked less like places to rest and more like almost-comfy places to bleed to death from your journey through the rusted metal sea.

Whatever guilt I'd felt about tossing Sasha in prison[16] evaporated as I looked out across the wasteland of suffering. She wouldn't have enjoyed crawling through this jungle of rebar any more than I would.

I realized then just how great a hiding spot this was for a girl with a hovering robot that could carry her above the detritus.

The holo-theater was closer. Three of the walls were still standing, and the roof had collapsed at just the right angle to still provide a decent amount of shelter to anyone huddling beneath it. I decided to check it out first.

———

I posted up behind a collapsed, broken neon sign and watched the old theater. For ten minutes, nothing came in or out. If I had a robot buddy, I'd probably have them at least patrolling the perimeter, so either this wasn't the hideout or Gaige didn't want her toy visible from the outside. Or, of course, Laurel's info was crap and they'd left the Wilds days ago.

Manhunting was already more difficult than I'd expected. Vault hunting was simple by comparison. You find a clue. You follow the clue. You try not to die along the way. Not a lot of ambiguity. But this? Stalking a single person across a wasteland of filth on the say-so of a complete stranger?

I couldn't know for certain if Gaige was in the theater and planning to head out, if she was out somewhere and coming back soon, if she was at the juice bar on the other end of the Wilds, or if she was just sleeping.

I hoped she was sleeping.

I crawled along on my belly, slow and methodical. Broken glass scratched the sleeves of my coat. The weight around my wrist

———

16 Not much.

made every movement twice as hard, but the collapsed theater got closer and closer with every inch I crawled.

What would Athena have thought? She was possibly the greatest—or at least deadliest—Vault Hunter in history. You hear stories about Vault Hunters walking into a town and either blasting or picking up everything that moves, but Athena wasn't really like that. She once told me about her time as an assassin for the Crimson Lance. "It was ninety-five percent waiting," she said, "and five percent fighting." Athena was smart. She knew when to be sneaky. Knew how to turn a crappy situation to her advantage.

I'm not the praying type, but in that moment, as I shuffled my way over rusty nails and toxic clouds of drywall toward a possible enemy hideout, I considered praying to Athena. Granted, I have no doubt, had she actually been there, she would have said something like "Separating from Sasha was a tactical error," or "Your crawling posture is wrong," or "Thanks for helping me repair my relationship with my girlfriend. I super-appreciate it and you look very nice today, Fiona. This compliment means a lot coming from me, a Vault Hunter."

One can dream.

I reached the theater and leaped to my feet in a shadowed alcove. The easy part was over. Now I had to go looking for the hard part.

Beams of drywall-scattered light shot through the holes and cracks of the decaying walls, the only illumination afforded to the place. The shadows were so dark I could slink from one to another without fear of exposing myself, but anyone could be hiding in the dark and I wouldn't know until I bumped straight into them. My heart beat out a stuttering refrain as I moved further into the building.

The main theater auditorium was almost intact. The far wall, where the screen would have been, had completely fallen away. As it was, the auditorium now functioned as a grand hall for the

display of the Tetanus Wilds themselves: two hundred chairs, all
pointed toward an open wall and a view that made you want to
take a bath.

It'd take a long damn time to search each row of chairs for Gaige, so
I figured I'd explore this room last. A sign on the west wall advertised
a snack bar just beyond a set of collapsed double doors. I tiptoed
toward them, stupidly hoping that maybe there were still some
preserved candy bars among the wreckage. Or a wanted murderer.

I ended up finding both.

Imagine a normal snack bar. Transparent plastic cases filled to
the brim with all manner of sugary treats. Overflowing tubs of air-
popped steakbites slathered in grease. Spurting fountains of juices
that turn your pee festive colors.

Now replace everything edible with a gun.

Someone had hastily converted the snack bar into an armory.
Where I'd expected to see Sour Slices, there was a double-barreled
shotgun. Where there should have been Sugar Rockets, there were
actual rockets. There were enough armaments to conquer a small
planet. Gaige had put the "attack" in "snack attack."

I'd stumbled onto the linchpin of any good "Stalker in the Skag
Den" maneuver: getting to your mark's armory and holding them
up with their own stash. I hadn't heard a single noise since stepping
into the theater. Good chance Gaige and the bot were out. How
many guns could they possibly have on them? Three? Four?

Meanwhile, I had a proper arsenal at my fingertips: a rocket
launcher, two shotguns, a sniper rifle, four pistols, an assault rifle,
and a bandolier of grenades.

It was time for an ambush.

I closed my eyes. *Think it through. See the different possibilities that
might unfold, just like Athena taught you.*

If Gaige and her bot were out and about, there was a good

chance they were out on some sort of recon job: Gaige would want another shot at Countess Holloway, who'd have tightened security since the girl's last attack. That meant there was a good chance Gaige and her bot would be coming back low on ammunition. Which meant their first step, upon returning to the hideout, would be to come here and stock up on ammo.

I'd give 'em ammo.

So: entry points. I couldn't take for granted that they'd come here the same way I did, so I checked the rest of the room and found an additional doorway that led to what would have been the street. Two ways in and out. I had to choose one to watch.

The doorway to the street was half-collapsed, which meant she'd make noise climbing through it. I could aim at the other door, then—the one leading to the auditorium—and swing to the street door if I heard anything.

I hid the bandolier of grenades near the street door, under some rubble. A single rocket might not take out the robot… but a rocket and a half-dozen grenades, all going off at once? That might seal the deal.

I grabbed the rocket launcher and lifted.

"Hnnnngh," I said, because holy shit are those things heavy. "Haaaahhh," I said next, because the weight around my wrist made it even harder to lift. "Hell yeah," I concluded, finally managing to balance the damned thing on my shoulder.

So, Plan A: If the bot comes through the door first, blast it to pieces. Then drop the rocket launcher, grab the assault rifle, and start spraying.

Plan B: If Gaige comes through the door first, wait and see if the bot follows her in. If it does, see Plan A. If it doesn't, wait until she's far enough into the room and calmly give her an ultimatum: toss her weapons to me and call in the robot, or die.

Plan B-2: If she refuses, blast her. I wasn't too excited at the prospect of killing somebody, but—if only for Sasha's sake—lethal force had to be on the table. And though it's never the preferred method of delivery, a big sack of body parts can still be DNA-matched for the purpose of collecting a bounty.

I looked through the sight of the rocket launcher, the world turning red and white. A universe of ambiguity shrank down to fit into the gunsight. There were only a few possible ways this could go.

My heart pounded in my chest. My stomach hurt. My finger tickled the firing button on the rocket launcher.

I was ready.

12
GAIGE

Gaige spoke into a microphone, transmitting her words to her fanbase. "Deathtrap has heat vision. I saw her, like, twenty minutes ago."

13
FIONA

That's when Gaige's robot punched through the wall behind me and put me in a chokehold.

Weaponry exploded out from the snack bar, scattering across the floor. The rocket launcher instantly fell from my shoulder. I felt myself lift off the ground, the pressure around my neck immediately unbearable.

"Nfffffr," I said. I meant to say, "No fair," but a metal arm against your windpipe has a way of squeezing out your vowels.

Gaige strolled in from the auditorium. She leaned up against the doorframe, a makeshift bandage wrapped around the hole I'd put in her shoulder. Two seconds ago, she would have been right in my sights and I wouldn't have been gasping for air.

"Good job finding us. If it weren't for DT, you might have gotten the drop on me. Go ahead and kill her, babe."

Somehow, he squeezed harder. Darkness crept in from the edges of my vision. My face tingled, like someone was prodding me with a hundred tiny needles.

I flicked my right arm forward. My wrist gun slid forward into my hand for what I hoped would not be the last time. Summoning every ounce of strength I had left in my body, I lifted my arm, even as gravity and loss of consciousness and a heavy hunk of metal debt tried to pull it down. I raised the gun higher… higher…

…And Deathtrap batted my arm down like the irritation it was. My entire right side slumped in defeat. I'd spent everything I had and it hadn't been enough.

Everything went dark. I was going to die and I hadn't managed to fire a single shot.

I thought of Sasha. Would she be stuck in that debtors' prison forever? All I'd wanted to do was keep her safe, and now I'd guaranteed a life of imprisonment and servitude. She trusted me. She loved me.

…But thankfully, she'd never once listened to me.

An earsplitting explosion brought me back to consciousness. Suddenly, I could breathe again; suddenly, I was falling.

I hit the ground face first. Couldn't hear a damned thing over the ringing in my ears, and as light began to creep back into my vision, I saw a pile of rubble where Gaige had been standing. The robot clawed at the detritus, sending chunks of mortar and drywall flying in every direction.

I turned and saw a Sasha-shaped silhouette drop a rocket launcher to the ground. She shoved a shotgun into my hands.

"Get up," she said. "And don't you dare die until I've had a chance to yell at you."

She pulled me to my feet just as Deathtrap pulled Gaige from the wreckage by her cybernetic arm. The pigtailed Vault Hunter leaned against her robot friend and narrowed her eyes at us. I saw recognition dawn on her face: We'd been the ones at Holloway's. She smiled—then pulled her pistol and fired at the same time we did.

Deathtrap swooped in front of her, its arms out and its body juddering from the hail of bullets. Gaige's single pistol was no match for our weaponry. Even though the floor was littered with guns, she'd have to expose her and her bot to far more gunfire to grab anything worthwhile. We were completely overwhelming the two of them with gunfire, and they knew it. They had no choice but to back up into the auditorium and try to draw us out.

You can imagine my surprise when they started moving forward.

Gaige blindfired over Deathtrap's shoulder, most of her shots landing nowhere near us. But that didn't matter: The Vault Hunter and her bot crept toward an assault rifle in the center of the room. She'd have to step out from cover to grab it, but—

My thought process was interrupted by, in order: a stray bullet hitting a beam far above and behind me; my brain taking a quick second to think, It'd be crazy if that bullet bounced off that beam and hit me; and then that exact thing happening as the bullet slammed into my left shoulder blade.

I was so surprised I forgot to cry out from the pain.

"How the hell did she do that?" Sasha shouted over the gunfire. "She ricocheted the bullet into you!"

The thought of dying entered my head. Then the thought of Sasha's magic fob watch bringing me back to life entered my head. Then came the thought that Gaige would probably, upon killing us, take the fob watch and not ever think to open it and bring us back to life. In the back of my head, I'd been thinking of the watch and its weird green life-giving energy as our ace in the hole, but an ace wouldn't be any good if Sasha and I were too dead to play it.

"Stop being impressed and reload that launcher!" I hissed.

I'd been favoring most of the shotgun's weight in my left arm. With my shoulder bleeding, it couldn't take that load anymore. My one good arm was useless. Great.

With Sasha rushing to reload the launcher and me finding a way to balance the end of the shotgun on the snack case, Gaige had all the time she needed to duck out of cover and grab the machine gun.

A tidal wave of bullets crashed onto the snack bar. Sasha and I dropped to the floor as shards of glass and concrete peppered us from above. Eyes squeezed shut, Sasha slammed a spare rocket into the end of the launcher.

The gunfire somehow got even louder. That could mean only one thing: Gaige and Deathtrap were covering her approach. With a hail of bullets clearing the path, she could stroll up to the snack bar without a second thought. She'd be at point-blank range, and we'd be trapped with nowhere to go.

"When she reloads," I shouted, dropping the shotgun and grabbing a Hyperion pistol in my weighted right arm, "I'm gonna split their focus. No matter what, you take the shot."

"She'll kill you!" Sasha shouted.

"Not when she sees you with the launcher. She'll hesitate. She won't know which one of us to aim at."

Sasha hesitated. I could tell she hated the plan. Even more, she hated the fact that it was the best shot we had. She nodded, clutching the rocket launcher to her chest.

We waited for what felt like an eternity. Finally, the bullet storm ceased. We had seconds at most. I intended to make them count.

I dove over the right side of the snack bar, completely exposing myself. In the air, time seemed to slow down. Gaige slammed another ammo belt into her machine gun. Sasha stood in Deathtrap's path, launcher hoisted on her shoulder. Deathtrap wound up a swing, its digistruct claws already sizzling in the air.

I hit the ground, my finger pressed to the trigger. The bullets went wide thanks to the goddamned debt cuffs, but it was enough to get Gaige's attention. She turned her gun toward me, and then...

She hesitated.

Her eyes flicked over to Sasha, and she suddenly realized the danger her bot was in. Too slowly, she swung the machine gun back in the other direction.

Sasha braced her foot against the snack case and pushed back as hard as she could, putting a few extra feet between her and Deathtrap.

Those few extra feet probably saved her life.

She launched the rocket directly into Deathtrap's chest at nearly point-blank range. A fireball exploded out from the robot as a thunderous boom shook the building. The explosive plume threatened to engulf Sasha, but the extra space she'd given herself saved her, and the shockwave from the detonation sent her hurtling back through the open wall Deathtrap had destroyed.

The squeal of metal mixed with Gaige's shriek. The explosion launched the robot directly into her, the heap of flying metal knocking her to the ground and slamming into the opposite wall. It crumpled to the ground, unmoving.

"DT!" Gaige screamed, scrambling to her feet as I did the same. She took a second too long worrying about her robot. By the time she'd turned around, fire and tears in her eyes, I'd already limped to within arm's reach.

I threw the hardest punch of my entire life, the force of the blow significantly increased by the extra weight on it. My fist collided with her chin with a loud popping noise and an explosion of pain; I'd punched her so hard I'd broken my own fingers.

Fine. Once I'd brought her in, I could buy myself new fingers made out of diamonds.

She reeled back from the blow, giving her the space to unholster her pistol and level it at my stomach.

Grabbing her wrist with my unbroken hand, I winced as the bullet wound in my shoulder reminded me it was there.

She struggled to point the gun back at me, and the strength was draining out of my body.

"You shouldn't have come here," she spat through heaving breaths.

"You shouldn't have been worth so much money," I tried to say, but my exhaustion deleted half the consonants. The result was a slurred "Youshoubeeworthmoney" that completely failed to intimidate her.

I didn't love the idea of those being my last words, so I did the only thing I could think of: I drove my forehead into her nose as hard as I could.

You ever read about people throwing headbutts and think there must be something about the hardness of your forehead that makes it hurt less, right? Surely that's why everyone uses headbutts—because they don't hurt you that much. Right?

Wrong. It hurt a lot.

I nearly knocked myself unconscious as my skull collided with Gaige's. I felt something soft in her face snap, and then something warm and wet trickled down my face. But she hadn't dropped the gun.

That was the moment I learned that there is something that hurts even worse than a headbutt, and that's punching someone in the face with a broken hand. My five-fingered sack of bone shards and meat hit Gaige square in the jaw, and the weight around my wrist made damned sure the punch followed through. I put every ounce of remaining strength into that punch, and the pain of impact almost made me black out again.

Gaige's eyes rolled back into her head. Blood trickled from her nose. Her legs finally buckled. She hit the ground and lay still.

I collapsed to my knees. Sasha appeared in the blasted-out wall near the snack bar, taking in deep, pained breaths. She glanced at Gaige and the robot's unmoving forms. Nodding, she gave me a half-hearted thumbs-up.

I spread my arms toward Sasha. "What did I say? Couldn't be simpler."

I passed out.

14
FIONA

When I woke up, we were flying. Wind stung my face, but I forced my eyes open. An Eden-5 secbot had an arm around my waist as it zoomed through the sky. Sasha struggled against the bot's other arm, shouting something I couldn't quite make out over the wind but sounded like *hospital*.

Another secbot just ahead of us carried the prize: Gaige's unconscious body dangling from one hand, and Deathtrap's wrecked chassis in the other.

It was too loud and cold and I had some blood loss to be getting back to, so I passed out again.

The next time I awoke, I was tied up and getting cursed at, two of my least favorite things to wake up to. The room I was in was small, windowless, and very clean—the kind of clean that implied this room was designed to be cleaned thoroughly and often, because the sorts of things that happened in it necessitated thorough cleanup.

Sasha, Gaige, and I were tied to chairs, all facing one another. I struggled against the rope, which only tightened. Plasteel cabling. More or less unbreakable in my current situation.

"Heya, sleepyhead," Gaige said in a voice whose brightness I was unprepared for. "Just so you know, I'm going to escape. And then I'm going to kill ya."

"Okay," I said. I've learned it's best to meet threats with indifference. It starves them. I turned to Sasha. "Where are we?"

"Holloway's estate," she said.

"And we're tied up because…"

"PRECAUTIONS," the secbot said.

Sasha leaned toward me. "Right after you passed out, I called them to the Tetanus Wilds and gave them the whole story. I dunno, maybe they're worried we might be secretly working with her or something."

"Do you even know who you're working for?" Gaige interjected.

Sasha raised an eyebrow. "Uh, a super-rich lady whose daughter you murdered?"

"I didn't… 'Murder' is so mean. Like I meant to do it or something. It was an accident, okay? Accidents happen. That's no excuse for torturing my dad to get to me."

"Certainly isn't. But—" I attempted to shrug. "—here we are."

"You know she's a bad guy, right? You're literally working for the bad guy."

Sasha and I exchanged glances.

"I mean, we got that vibe, yeah," Sasha said, nodding.

"Yeah, that's definitely the odor she gives off," I agreed.

Gaige's irritation turned to understanding. "Oh, I see. So you're just a couple of assholes. Bandits."

I don't love being called an asshole, but I especially don't love being called a bandit. I'd heard enough of that garbage growing up.

"Vault Hunters," I corrected her.

Gaige cackled. "Vault Hunters! Big-time heroes, huh? Yeah, I remember when Roland and Brick went on The Adventure Of Kidnapping A Puppy Because Some Rich Dickhead Asked Them To."

"Oh, you know Brick, huh?" I asked.

"Uh, yeah, I know Brick."

"Me too. Athena and I fought him together."

Gaige rolled her eyes. "Doubt it. Your bones are all still inside your body."

"Hey," Sasha said, "if it makes you feel better that the two women who beat your ass *aren't* Vault-hunting badasses, believe whatever you want to believe."

Gaige rolled her eyes. "So what's your plan, huh? Take the money, fund your own bandit clan? Try to make yourselves queens of some podunk moon out in the space-boonies?"

"I was thinking that," Sasha said, "but then I sat in this really comfortable chair, so I'm kinda thinking we stay here a while and see what a life of luxury is like."

"Oh, good," Gaige smiled. "This place really needs another rich jackass with their boot on its neck."

Sasha shook her head. "Are you even aware of how much money you're worth? That kinda money can change things for people. For the better. And not just us."

Gaige laughed so hard she turned red. She literally stamped her feet.

"Yeah, I'm sure adding another billionaire to Eden-5 will fix everything right up. I'm super-psyched for you two."

The door hissed open. Countess Holloway entered, followed closely by two secbots. She locked eyes with Gaige upon entering the room and never wavered, even as she addressed Sasha and me.

"My people have investigated the Wilds and your story checks out." She gestured at us. The secbots unsheathed their digiclaws. I strongly suspected Holloway was about to kill us rather than pay up.

"Well, hold on, surely we can make a…" I began, only to stop myself when the bots expertly sliced through our bonds.

"Right," I said.

"And the reward?" Sasha asked.

The countess grimaced, as if Sasha had told her there was a plug of steak between her front two teeth. She beckoned Sasha with a snap and a come-hither gesture. Sasha came thither.

The countess tapped her ECHO device on her wrist, then tapped hers to Sasha's like she was swatting a fly.

"There," she said. "Eight billion."

"The bounty said sixteen," Sasha protested.

"And I did half the work by luring her from Pandora. You'd be wise not to nickel-and-dime me right now, bounty hunter."

I cleared my throat and put on my best peace-making voice. "You lured her here, yes, but we did what your army of security robots couldn't. I'm sure that's worth an extra nickel. Or *two*."

She narrowed her eyes, weighing the extra cost against her desire never to see our faces again. Which was a shame because I think I have a very welcoming face.

"Ten," she spat. "A reasonable price to pay for ensuring Gaige spends the rest of her short life staring at the walls of the Eden-5 Maximum Security Penitentiary. But I will not remain reasonable much longer."

"Ten is fantastic, thanks," I said, grabbing Sasha by the arm. "Now, if you'll excuse us, we're going to go on a spending spree. At the nearest hospital."

———

I sat on the hospital bed, staring at the ECHO in disbelief.

Ten billion.

Ten. Billion.

A ten, then a comma, then three zeroes, then a comma, then three zeroes, then another comma, then another three zeroes. When I was a kid, I'd thought about how much money it'd take

to keep Sasha and me fed and sheltered for the rest of our lives. A
million dollars, I figured. Which meant we now had enough cash
to retire ten thousand times over. Minus the two hundred thousand
for our debt cuffs and the medical expenses, but still: nine billion,
nine hundred ninety-nine million, eight hundred thousand dollars.

I didn't know how to feel about it.

"I've died and gone to heaven," Sasha said. Apparently, she did
know how to feel about it.

"This can't be real. We did it. We're rich." My eyes couldn't
focus. My mouth felt dry. It didn't make sense. Good things didn't
just *happen* to us.

Sasha kept nodding in disbelief. "Apparently so."

"You want to buy a house?"

"I guess so?"

Sasha tapped her ECHO. "Done."

The speed of the house purchase snapped me out of my daze.
"Oh. I meant, like, at some point. Are you sure you wanna live
here? We could always build a… house… back home never mind
that's a stupid idea—"

"Who would build a home on Pandora? That's a stupid—"

"I know. The second it left my mouth I knew it sounded dumb."

"Why not build a house in a toilet lined with razor blades?"

I scratched under my hat. "So what's our… What's the house like?"

"I dunno. It cost a billion dollars, so… big, probably?"

I tried to sit up and could feel the stitches in my back straining.

"You spent a *billion dollars* on a house we haven't even seen?!"

"Yeah. You know how much money we have left?"

Sasha leaned in so close our noses touched.

"*Nine billion dollars!* I don't even know how we're going to
spend the rest, unless we just start eating thousand-dollar bills for
breakfast."

She squinted. I could see her doing the math in her head.

"At that rate, we'd eat it all in… twenty-seven hundred years."

"You're drunk," I said.

"I'm rich. Can you imagine how insufferable I'll be once I've got some thousand-dollar champagne in me?"

"I'd really rather not," I said, laughing. As manic as she was, this was the first time I could remember that Sasha seemed relaxed—not worried about getting to a big pile of money before the other guy, not losing sleep trying to think through the intricacies of our next big con. I mean, she was bouncing off the walls, sure, but she was calm. She was content. I never thought I'd live to see her like that.

"Oh, and by the way," she said, and punched me in my bad shoulder, hard.

"Ow! What the—?"

"That's for throwing me in prison. Do you have any idea how hard it was to get out?"

"No?"

"Well. Not very hard, actually. Laurel folded after I asked her nicely a few times. But there was a good half-hour when I was ready to kill you."

"I'm sorry. Really. I thought I was protecting you."

"And yet you're the one in the hospital bed."

"Speaking of which, I'm bored."

I sat up on the edge of the bed. I could feel myself smiling.

"Let's go see what our new house looks like."

15
FIONA

I'll say this: a billion dollars can buy you a pretty nice house.

Our three-story estate came with an ostentatiously large foyer complete with a dual staircase leading to the second floor. The kind of staircase that you wanted to descend in an evening dress while a horde of gobsmacked guests watches you in awe. Banisters you want to slide down while dual-wielding pistols.

The first floor, with its lounge, dining hall, and ice-cream room was for entertaining guests. We lived on the second floor, with its five-poster beds and dopamine misters. The third floor was dedicated to hedonistic delights such as a zero-gravity swimming pool and a fully interactive ECHOsim room.

All in all, the home came with all the amenities. A hovertennis court. A butler who solves murders. Audioshowers. A bank vault guarded by a guy who always tells the truth and his brother who tells only lies. A big painting of Sasha and me that I don't know who painted or how they got our likenesses down so well. Seven bathrooms.

And most importantly, a 24/7 security system consisting of surveillance cameras, wall-mounted Sabre autoturrets, and a nuclear-bomb-proof panic room with enough food and water to last a decade.

We'd done it.

I waited for the floor to fall out from under us. For the twist. For things to get bad. Or for me to learn that I didn't *actually* enjoy being rich—that *actually*, the big house and incredible catered meals and buying whatever we felt like buying without worrying about our bank accounts was nice, but that after a few weeks it all started to feel hollow and empty.

But it didn't.

Being rich was awesome.

We'd fled from poverty all our lives, and we'd finally outrun it. This was the life we'd always dreamed of, and the dream had finally come true.

See, money isn't money. It's not currency, it's not barter, it's not a construct. It is two things: freedom and safety. Freedom to do whatever you want, and safety from the consequences.

Not to say all my problems were solved. Even if I rationally understood that we'd escaped the black hole that is poverty, I still felt its gravitational pull threatening to yank me back into oblivion.

Suddenly, we had something to lose. Suddenly, we had a home to protect—or at least, a home without wheels.

I spent the first two weeks waiting for every wine merchant to sneak poison into my Chablis or our gardener to attack me with shears. So much of our lives had been concerned with treating every single stroke of good fortune as a potential threat. Now that things were actually good, I didn't know what to do with myself.

Sasha, by contrast, had a much easier time relaxing. Once she'd realized we could order sheets that were both soft as silk *and* tasted like greenberries, she seldom wanted to leave the house. She ECHOchatted with Rhys almost every day, trying her best not to rub his face in the fact that we were doing fantastic while the Atlas Corporation was hemorrhaging money.

The first week, we threw a housewarming party and invited every billionaire in the neighborhood. Though their discomfort at our presence was obvious—as many acidic perfume showers as we took, the stink of Pandora apparently never goes away—their housewarming gifts alone justified everything that had brought us to this point. It turns out the answer to "What do you get the woman who has everything?" is "Gift cards worth at least two million dollars each." We'd sunk a billion into buying the house, but we damn near got it all back in the form of gift cards to ECHOnet megamarts that sold everything you could possibly need. Evidently, the only thing better than having a lot of money? Getting even *more* money. Not because of greed,[17] but because every little bit we accrued, whether in hard cash or gift cards, made me feel that much safer. That much more certain that the blood and death were far in our rearview.

Still, I didn't let my guard down completely. I tossed handfuls of money around the ECHOnet to get all the information I could about Gaige and the whereabouts of her disassembled robot. One day she might get out and come looking for revenge, and I needed leverage.

I needed to feel safe.

Even when an old-money Eridium magnate did get poisoned at one of our brunches, our butler, Fitzwiggins, identified the culprit almost instantly. ("It appears," he said, "that this titan of industry was brought down by another sort of tightening: his side squeeze.")

Was I anxious? Yeah. Turns out that's my default state. Was I happy? Surprisingly, also yeah. I'd passed some bribes around and learned where Deathtrap's wrecked chassis was being held. From what I heard, it was being stripped down and analyzed by some freelance roboticists in the tech district. In other words, it wasn't

---

17 Well, not just because of greed.

going to be in much of a position to seek vengeance on us anytime soon. We had, for the first time, nothing to worry about.

Our first month in that house was buck wild. Cleaning crews worked full-day shifts to ensure we never had to pick up after ourselves. The best chef in the district crafted us three artisanal meals a day.

And Sasha had even more fun once she realized money could buy you the most delicious meal of all: revenge.

16
SASHA

"Big mistake," Sasha said. "Huge."

"That's what you're gonna say to her?" Rhys asked, his holographic form cocking a skeptical eyebrow.

"Yeah. I read up on it—the salespeople at Dapper Delilah's make most of their money off commission. So if I did buy a suit from her, she'd make a fortune. But I won't, because I don't buy suits from dicks."

"And you're gonna head back and tell her that."

"Yeah. Is that too petty?"

"Nah. Petty would be naming your first line of guns after yourself to remind all your ex co-workers who used to bully you that you're more successful."

"Right," Sasha said. "And how is the Rhys's Pieces weapons line selling?"

"Oh, real bad," Rhys said. "But money isn't everything."

"Exactly! Hence the 'big mistake'-ing. But, uh, on another note, you know how I said we should maybe be on pause until I had things figured out?"

"I do remember that."

"I kind of… have things figured out now. So, I dunno. Maybe you might wanna come by and visit or something? We've got a guest house with a smaller guest house inside. It's like a guest-house turducken."

Rhys winced. "God, I wish you'd told me that a month ago. I'd love to, but—"

"It's fine, don't worry about it."

"No, honestly. This isn't an excuse. The company is on fire."

"I get it."

"Literally. Somebody lit a cigarette in one of my munitions warehouses and it's still burning."

"Oh," Sasha said, raising her eyebrows. "Okay, that actually makes sense. Maybe later, then?"

"Yeah. I do, uh, honestly miss you. So… uh." Rhys often talked like a malfunctioning robot once it was time to be honest about his feelings, and this occasion was no different.

"Hey, me too," Sasha said in a voice that, through years of con artistry, perfectly split the uprights between "romantic" and "platonically friendly." Even if Sasha wanted to shut it off, she couldn't; the muscle memory was too strong. Men tended to be more amenable to everything if they weren't quite sure where they stood with you.

Frankly, Sasha wasn't quite sure where she stood, either. He was a kind, handsome himbo with ambition, but she had no interest in corporate mergers or office politics or any of the things that seemed to give Rhys a reason to wake up in the morning. This long-distance thing they had was a trial run for both of them: Were they, in fact, better off in their own separate worlds? Would one of them sacrifice their life's direction to spend more time with the other? Hell, they hadn't even been on a proper date yet. How do you move forward in a relationship when technically the relationship hasn't even started yet?

Danger had brought Rhys and Sasha together. Was it the danger she was attracted to, more than the man himself?

It was at this point that she realized he'd been talking for the last ten seconds.

"…a lot to me, and I know this is a weird situation, but I'm grateful you're giving it a shot, and…" He was blushing with confused, amorous exertion.

Nah, Sasha thought. She liked the danger *and* she liked the guy.

"You're good," Sasha said. "We're good. But you sound busy. Maybe you get back to work, and I'll ruin the day of a very mean store lady."

———

"But you didn't have the money," Tammithah said. "What was I supposed to do?"

"Oh, I dunno," Sasha said, her upper half hidden behind the stack of clothes in her arms. She'd walked right into Dapper Delilah's, grabbed the first salesperson she saw who wasn't Tammithah, and filled her arms until the salesperson ("Quynn," she'd said, "pronounced just like it's spelled") could put their family through college off the commission. "How about not call the fuzz on me?"

"It's store policy," Tammithah said. "I didn't… I'm sorry!"

"Yes," Sasha said. "I think you are."

Sasha swiped her wrist-mounted ECHO device through the payment scanner. The funds hit Quynn's account instantly, causing the salesperson to faint with delight.

"Here you go," Sasha said, tossing the clump of clothing at a startled Tammithah. "Donate these to charity. They're not my color."

Sasha sashayed out of the store. If she could have made the world crawl to slow motion just to give Tammithah another glimpse at her smug strut, she absolutely would have.

Was it mean? Yeah. Was it petty? Absolutely. But did it scratch an itch that had gone un-scratched ever since the sisters had come into their wealth? One hundred percent. The rush of adrenaline, the joy of defeating an enemy… Granted, dressing down an hourly employee didn't have the same kick as outrunning a horde of bandits, but it was the closest she'd gotten in a while. An itch that hadn't been scratched in a long time.

Maybe it was time to scratch harder.

17
FIONA

At the risk of belaboring the point, things were really good. Safe, warm, soft, and delicious.

During our first five weeks in the house, the closest thing we had to a tangible problem was when Sasha bought an expensive rug and then slid down the grand staircase into a bunch of Pandoran Girl dolls I'd bought before I caught her and explained that Pandoran Girl dolls aren't bowling pins, they're meant to be treated with dignity and respect, and Sasha said, "Wait, you didn't understand Vaultlanders but you understand Pandoran Girl dolls? How does that work?" and I picked up the Pandoran Girl dolls and grumbled something like, "Pandoran Girl dolls are about the courageous spirit of girls everywhere and keeping them boxed would be like keeping that spirit boxed," but then I took a bath in a strawberry sundae and everything was basically fine. But I'll spare you the details of everything we bought. Nobody wants to hear about the things rich people waste money on.

Initially, I found it odd that, of all the rich people we'd seen on Eden-5, of all the Countess Holloways of the world, none of them seemed to smile much. I didn't understand why they weren't in the constant rapturous joy that consumed Sasha and me during every hour of that first month.

Okay, sorry, one more thing: We bought this bubble-bath solution that was full of tiny parasites that massaged every micromuscle in your body and then, because they're bred to love giving massages, they die of happiness, and when they die it makes the bath smell like lavender and it cost two million dollars a bottle.

But back to the story.

After a couple of months, though, our hedonistic lifestyle had made quite a mess. The house began to stink of dried sugar and boredom. I thought I'd never get tired of the good life, but there are only so many sundaes you can eat before they all blend into one vague, lactose-fueled blur. The new-money smell wears off and you're left with the same problems you had before. For myself, they revolved around a nebulous anxiety that, despite all evidence to the contrary, Sasha and I were still not safe, that we were one mistake away from being kicked out onto the street.

As for Sasha, her problems manifested as a desire to get herself stone-cold killed.

One night, as I was drifting around the hoverpool, listening to true-crime ECHOcasts, Sasha tossed a shrimp tail at me. I removed my headphones and leaned over the edge of my velvet hoverchaise to look at her. She was smiling, which was a pleasant surprise. The last few dinners we'd shared together had elicited little from her beyond a sort of lost, sullen silence and a palpable air of discomfort.

"Pack your stuff," Sasha said. "We're going on a trip."

"Okay," I said, deactivating the hoverpool. "Where to?"

"It's a surprise. Don't worry about it. The tickets are already bought, and I've handled everything."

The hoverfield gently lowered me to the ground. "I could use a hint," I said.

Her smile grew wider. "One hint. Once this trip is done, we're not gonna be Vault Hunters."

I cocked my head.

"We're gonna be," Sasha said, "*Vaults* Hunters."

Sasha correctly read my open-mouthed squint as confusion.

"Okay, screw hints. I've been studying satellite data and I think there's a Vault on Gantis. Well, one of its moons. And nobody knows it's there but me, probably, 'cause it's totally out of the way and basically just one big planet of pain and angry stuff nobody in their right mind would wanna go to, so we can go and open the Vault!" She hugged me around the neck. "Surprise!"

My stomach dropped. My ribcage tightened around my heart. I grabbed her by the shoulders and tried to break the hug as gently as I could.

"You want to hunt another Vault?" I asked, hoping against anything that I'd misheard her or that this was some bizarre practical joke. I wanted her to say, "No, of course I don't. This was some sort of weird test and you passed."

Instead, she raised an eyebrow and said, "Uh, yeah. Obviously."

I grabbed two fistfuls of my hair and leaned against an articulated gold statue of myself for support.

"What?" she asked. "What's the problem?"

"The problem," I said, too loudly, "is that we're not going to hunt another Vault. We wanted to get rich, we got rich, and now we spend the rest of our lives enjoying the relaxing sounds of people not trying to strangle us with our own intestines."

"Oh, come on." Sasha rolled her eyes. "I know you're bored too. Don't pretend you're not."

"Boredom has nothing to do with it. We're as safe as we've ever been, and we need to stay that way."

Sasha shook her head in disbelief. "So, I don't get a say?"

I stood. "We're finally safe. And now our job is to stay safe. So no, Sasha, you do not get a say. I get to pull big-sister rank on this."

Sasha's jaw set as her disbelief switched to anger. "You tried this already. You tried to lock me up, and if I hadn't escaped in time, you'd be dead."

"And you *did* die," I shot back, moving to within an inch of her. "Back on Pandora. Do you have any idea how that felt—"

"Do *you?*" Sasha yelled back, her voice echoing through the cavernous halls of our mansion. "You're gonna, what? Tell me I can't do this because *you* felt bad when I died? You don't know what I went through. You didn't so much as ask!"

"You seemed fine," I said. "You were making jokes about it."

She rolled her eyes so hard I thought they might get stuck. "For the love of… Come on, Fiona. You're smarter than that."

I opened my mouth to argue, but nothing came out. She was right. Even after we'd left Pandora, even after we'd made our billions and had nothing but time on our hands, I hadn't asked what had happened. How it had felt. If she needed anything.

I always saw Sasha as unflappable, someone who could handle anything. It never even occurred to me to ask her if she was all right.

Or maybe I just didn't want to spend more time thinking about how my decisions had gotten her killed.

"You know what I saw when I died?" she asked. "I was looking at you, and Rhys, and the others, and then… there was nothing. When you used that… shard thing to bring me back, it was like no time had passed. Like I'd just been knocked out or something. At first I thought, 'Oh, that's good, then. Death doesn't hurt. It's just… nothing. Not being there.' But the more I thought about it, the more scared I got. If we're nothing before we're born, and we're nothing after we die, then this," she said, gesturing at everything around us, "is just a tiny vacation from all that nothing."

She wasn't crying. She wasn't shouting. I could tell she was still angry, but otherwise she just looked tired. In all our years together, I'd never seen her like this.

"I'm sorry," I said. "I know that's probably scary—"

"You *don't* know. That's my point."

"But that's even more reason to be careful!" I shot back. "After what you experienced, I don't understand why you're in such a big hurry to throw yourself in front of gunfire again."

She spoke just above a whisper. "Because *this is it*, Fiona. It's just *this*. I'm not going to spend what little time I have sitting around, amusing myself with stupid junk like *that*," she said, pointing at my statue.

"That statue was your idea," I said.

She nodded. "Yeah, 'cause I thought it'd be cool. But it turns out it's boring. Just like everything else in here. Just like *you*. But when we were on Pandora, when we were hunting that Vault… I dunno. I'd found something that mattered." She shook her head at me like I was some sort of wounded dog. "I thought you had, too."

Blood rushed to my face. I could handle anger. I could handle feeling like a bad sister. I couldn't handle being pitied.

"Yeah," I said. "I did love hunting Vaults. And then my kid sister died and I thought maybe I should grow the hell up."

I held her furious stare and waited for a retort that never came. She pushed past me on her way to the front door.

"Where are you going?" I called out.

She squeezed past the butler and grabbed the doorknob as he reached for it.

"Somewhere that doesn't smell like goddamned strawberries," she snarled, slamming the door behind her.

18
SASHA

Sasha walked through the streets of the Elite District, her sister's words still echoing in her head. Had Fiona been right? Was she just being childish? She'd gone from the height of excitement in Vault hunting to the height of luxury in retirement. What was wrong with her? Was she really just bored?

No. That wasn't it. She loved their home just as much as Fiona did. The edible picture frames, the singing shower heads, the crime-solving butler—all of it was delightful to the senses. Wonderfully distracting.

Maybe that was the problem: it was all just a distraction.

But from what?

Her feet carried her across polished cobblestones, past closed jewelry stores and clothing boutiques that smelled like cinnamon and roses even this late at night. She came upon a crossroads—a literal one. To her left, a path through Eden Park, with its burnt-orange trees and birds trained to land on extended fingers. To her right, the road to Rustville.

She went right.

The cobblestone road gradually gave way to a dirt footpath. The trees got smaller and sparser as she got further from the Elite

District. Eventually, there was nothing to mark her progress across the seemingly endless expanse of dirt and rock. Nothing but the dim lights of Rustville itself, gradually growing brighter as she walked, and the floating superhighway far above her.

It was dark. She was alone and unarmed. This wasn't the best idea. But still she walked, eager to put the empty comforts of her home behind her, eager to find… something. She wasn't sure what. The desert wind tousled her hair and kicked up dirt on her path.

When she was about an hour away from Rustville, there was a loud click and she was suddenly bathed in light. A spotlight, perched atop a circular building to her right, held her frozen in surprise. The circular building's dark, muted color palette made it all but invisible in the shadows. With the spotlight off, Sasha could have walked within arms' reach of its wrought-iron gates and never known. Barbed wire coiled around fenceposts topped with autoguns. Armored vans loomed in the parking bay.

This was a prison. Not a debtors' prison like the one in Rustville, but a proper maximum-security lockup for hardened criminals, sitting almost exactly between Rustville and the nicer districts. It made a sort of sense; the wealthy would never allow a prison anywhere near them, but they also wouldn't trust the unwashed masses of Rustville to keep the convicts behind bars.

She felt her feet moving toward it, dragging the beam of light with her. There was a Vault Hunter inside she wanted to talk to.

———

"Life is crap—clean it up! Life is crap—clean it up!" the janitor sang to himself, eyes down, his ankle cuffs clanking against each other as he danced his mop across the linoleum floor. Security cameras turned back and forth across the entrance hall. Large metal doors dotted the circumference of the room, each leading to a different wing of the prison. Each was protected by a human guard wielding a small armory's worth of firepower.

Sasha tapped the janitor on the shoulder.

"Gah!" he yelled, sparing a quick glance around the room to catch the guards' reactions. He seemed nonplussed by their shrug-and-look-the-other-way strategy. "How'd you get in? And why aren't the guards doing anything?"

Sasha winked. "A super-secret stealth tactic I just came up with."

"Oh yeah?"

"I paid the guards several million dollars to let me in."

"Oh," the janitor said, brow furrowed. "Guess that serves the owners right for cheapin' out. Not splurgin' on secbots."

"Guess it does," Sasha said, nodding. And then, "Would *you* like several million dollars?"

The janitor straightened his back. "Indeed I would."

"Then I need just two things. I need someone to erase what's on those," she said, hooking a thumb at a security camera. "And I need you to take me to the redhead."

———

Sasha tried her best not to gasp when she pulled the cloth bag from Gaige's head. The Vault Hunter's face was more bruise than skin. Her nose looked like it had been broken, fixed, and broken again three times over. She looked as if she hadn't eaten anything in days.

"Oh, hey!" Gaige said, her chipper voice belying the pain she must have been in. She waved at Sasha as best she could with her arms chained to the wall behind her. "It's you! Hey, could you lemme kill you real quick for blowing up my robot? Just gimme your neck. I'll be real quick. My chompers are strong as hell."

"I'm sorry," Sasha said.

"That's cool. Just gimme that sweet, sweet carotid artery and we'll be even stevens."

"Are the guards hurting you?"

Gaige shook her head. "Oh, you mean my new *au naturel* look? Nah. Holloway applied this particular makeup. She's part owner of the prison, so she just comes in whenever and beats the hell out of me to relax. It's okay, though—I've got an escape plan."

"Which is?"

"A secret. The kind I don't typically share with people who kill my best friend."

Sasha knelt to Gaige's level, just out of carotid-chomping distance. "Well, I don't know how good your escape plan is, but I know I've got a much better one. And all we need to do is work together."

Gaige looked her over through swollen eyes. "Pardon?"

"I will get you out of here. Safely. Quietly. And in return... I want to hunt Vaults with you."

"*Ha!* Fun joke. So, about that neck of yours..."

"I'm not joking."

"Neither am I!" Gaige hissed. "You think I'd spend another second around you if I had half a choice? You and your ugly-ass-hat-wearing sister helped Holloway, the woman who killed my dad."

Sasha pulled a bronze fob watch from her pocket, the words TIME HEALS ALL WOUNDS etched into its backplate. "What if I knew a way to bring him back?"

"Blegh," Gaige groaned. She rolled her eyes, then winced from the pain of it. "I've had the immortality pitch before from people more convincing than you. I know a scam when I smell one."

"I'm from Pandora," Sasha said, screwing the backplate off the watch, "and I'm not here to talk about urban legends." The plate came off into her hands, revealing a shard of glowing green crystal. "I'm talking about this."

"Fun glowy rock! I don't care."

"I died. A little while ago." Sasha swallowed against the lump in her throat. "My dad, Felix, he gave me this in case of emergencies.

This green thing? This brought me back."

Gaige stared at her. "Can… Is my eyebrow raising? I'm trying to raise an eyebrow but it hurts. Can you see it?"

"No."

"Well, you can imagine what it looks like. It's a reaction I have to people trying to shove BS down my throat."

Sasha bit her lip in concentration. "Yeah, fair enough," she said, standing to her feet and pulling a revolver from her coat.

Gaige clenched her jaw and giggled. A stream of blood dripped from her mouth and down her chin. "Go ahead! Try it. I dare you."

Sasha raised the gun. Pulled back the hammer.

And put it into Gaige's hand.

"Uh," Gaige said. "What?"

Sasha pried the crystal from the watch. "This'll probably work," she said, more for her own benefit than Gaige's, and popped it into her mouth.

"What is this?" Gaige asked, rotating the gun in her hand. "This a trick gun? It gonna backfire and kill me? What's your game?"

Sasha placed the barrel of the gun against her heart. Her cheek bulged and glowed green, the crystal secure in her mouth. "No gane. Kull ge krigger."

"How stupid do you think I am?" Gaige whispered, but there was no force behind it. Confusion painted her features as she examined Sasha's resolute face.

Sasha set her jaw. "Stupid enough to let your robot friend d—"

The gunshot was deafening in the close quarters of the prison cell. Gaige gasped in shock. Sasha stumbled backward, a patch of dark red growing bigger and bigger over her heart.

The human brain can maintain consciousness for roughly fifteen seconds once the heart has been ruptured. Sasha spent her fifteen seconds:

saying, "Ow"

sitting down on the ground

winking at Gaige

saying, "See you in a bit"

making finger guns at Gaige.

———

And then her fifteen seconds were up. She slumped to one side, finger guns still finger-pointing at the woman who'd killed her, her blank eyes staring at the floor, a smirk frozen on her face.

"Uh," Gaige said. "I don't... Hey. I don't like this, man. That was weird. Was that a squib?"

The blood soaked through Sasha's shirt and dripped onto the floor.

"Yeah, okay. No, that's... that's too much blood for a squib. You just... you just died. Cool. Fun. Real weird. Kiss my ass, I guess, for killing Deathtrap and stuff, but. Weird."

Sasha's corpse did not respond. Gaige was once again alone in her cell. She was happy to have the hood off but, to her surprise, less happy that the only thing she could look at was the corpse of the woman who had helped to put her here.

Two minutes later, Sasha stopped being dead.

"*Gah!*"

She sat up with a start, pulling great heaving gulps of air into her lungs.

Gaige's jaw dropped. "What? No. What? No."

Sasha tugged at her shirt, which was sticky with blood. "You killed me," she said, showing Gaige the hole in the fabric. She spat the crystal into her hands. It was glowing brighter than when she'd taken it from the watch, almost blinding. "And this brought me back."

"Oooookay," Gaige said. "That's weird."

"Yeah," Sasha said as she pushed herself to her feet. "No idea how it works, but I'm not complaining. So. How about it? I break you out. We bring your dad back. We hunt a Vault."

Gaige cocked her head. "You seem messed up. I'm into that."

19
SASHA

Sasha punched the prison guard in his bank account as hard as she could. Her wrist ECHO slammed into the one embedded in his upper arm. With that single punch, Sasha turned the man into a millionaire.

There are a lot of ways to win fights—violence, bribery. In this case, a combination of the two.

Gaige and Sasha made it about twenty feet out of Gaige's cell before the guards caught them on security cameras. The women found themselves surrounded by far, far too many men to beat in a gunfight.

An idea occurred to Sasha.

Well, two ideas.

Well, one and a half ideas.

Idea one: Holloway wanted to torture Gaige for years and years. This meant she would not allow Gaige to die.

Idea one point five: people like money.

One of the guards reached toward the gun in Sasha's hand. "You're gonna want to give that to me," he said.

"Oh, I wanna give you something, all right," said Sasha, handing him her gun with one hand right before slamming her ECHO device against his with her other arm.

Thirty guns racked, their owners both unsure what the hell Sasha had done and frightened at the possibility of hitting Gaige at such close quarters.

"Uh," the guard said, thumbing on his radio. "I quit?"

"*What?!*" barked the officer on the other end of the conversation.

"I'm a millionaire now, so. Byyyyye? I guess?"

The newly affluent guard dropped his gun to the floor and, as politely as possible, shoved his way through the sea of perplexed former co-workers.

Sasha raised her ECHO device. Its illuminated screen displayed her considerable bank balance.

The guards stared slack-jawed for a moment before charging the women all at the same time.

It took everything in Sasha not to fall back on her instincts and start blasting people, and she could only imagine how much harder it was for Gaige. She swung her ECHO device back and forth, knocking it against heads and shoulders and, occasionally, the ECHO devices of the other guards.

The cacophony of the crowd soon gave way to jubilant shouting as, one by one, the guards tossed their guns down and raced from the prison.

Soon, there was no one left to stop the two women—that is, until there came the tromp of heavy steel boots approaching.

Not interested in seeing who the boots belonged to, Sasha grabbed Gaige's hand and ran for the door. Unfortunately for the two of them, they weren't fast enough.

A large, bald, mustachioed man with a patch on his shirt reading WARDEN blocked the door. His mass was such that, just by him standing in front of the open double doors, the moonlight itself couldn't breach the threshold of the prison.

He vibrated, red with anger. His fingers tightened around a

nightstick the size of Sasha's leg. When he spoke, his lips barely moved.

"You two are not going anywhere. I can't be bribed."

Sasha showed him a number, and then added two commas to it.

"I have changed my mind," he said, and stepped aside. Sasha booped his ECHO device with hers and made the man so rich he burst into tears.

The two women walked into the night, toward the flickering lights of Rustville.

20
SASHA

Sasha crouched next to Gaige in the shadows, watching the secbots patrol around Gaige's father's grave. Gaige had barely said a word since they'd escaped the prison. This job—mission?—already felt different than any she'd been on with Fiona. More dangerous. More volatile. Though maybe that was just Gaige herself.

"Damn," Gaige said, nodding at the secbots. "Dead for more than a month and they're still guarding him."

Holloway had buried Gaige's father in the smack-dab center of Rustville's town square. Bullet holes and scorch marks dotted the street, evidence of the fight Gaige had survived when she'd first come to Eden-5 to pay her respects to the dead.

"Maybe they're scared of folks paying tribute, turning him into a martyr," Sasha said. She shoved a magazine into the handle of a Hyperion submachine gun and handed it to Gaige.

"Or they just forgot to give these rip-off rustbuckets new orders," Gaige muttered. "Ugh. Just look at these things. All the function of DT, none of the beauty."

She smiled with her mouth but not her eyes, and it struck Sasha that she was both sad and angry, in a way that suggested she shouldn't bother trying to delve too deep.

"Right," Sasha said. "I mean, they look sorta identical. Except these don't have skulls on them."

"Exactly," Gaige said as the submachine gun vibrated in her hand. "None of the beauty. You sure you don't know where they're keeping him, by the way?"

Sasha shook her head. "Sorry."

Another mouth-only smile. Gaige waved her hand. "Ah, it's fine. They'll wanna take it slow, analyzing DT for all the improvements I made, and that'll take ages. More than enough time to open a Vault, come back, find out where he is, and kill every single person who wants to stand between me and finding my robot."

Gaige's smile, Sasha noticed, *did* spread to her eyes when she talked about killing the people who stole her robot. It occurred to her, not for the first time, that she was alone with a Vault Hunter she barely knew.

It would probably be fine, though. Surely.

"First time I was here, they had five secbots waiting for me," Gaige said. "You believe that? I helped kill Handsome Jack. And they thought *five* bots would do the job. Friggin' trifling." She shook her head.

"Right," Sasha replied. "But there's five bots patrolling the square right now. And you don't have Deathtrap. And, uh, what's going on with your…" She gestured at Gaige's arm, which hummed and rattled with vibration.

"Oh, this? This is anarchy," Gaige replied, nodding as if that explained everything.

Against her better judgment, Sasha asked a follow-up. "Anarchy. Right. Is it, uh, dangerous?"

"Extremely!" Gaige grinned. "I installed servos into my bionic arm that spin really, really fast and vibrate at *juuuuust* the right frequency to make my bullets hurt way, way more. Granted, it messes up my aim real bad, but whatever. These five won't be a problem. *Anarchy forever!*" she yelled abruptly, running out into the street with her gun belching bullets in every direction but the one in which she pointed it. Hot metal shot from the gun's barrel like water squirting from a hose.

"So... so follow you? Or..." Sasha yelled over the gunfire, but Gaige was too busy cackling with mad glee to answer. Every single one of her bullets missed its target, but that didn't seem to bother her very much.

There wasn't time to think. Sasha had to either follow Gaige's utterly unhinged lead or stay back and run the risk of letting her be cut to ribbons. She was surprised to find herself sprinting out of cover toward the gunfire, a Maliwan revolver in her hand and serious doubts about Gaige's emotional state in her head. *Maybe,* Sasha thought as Gaige continued to spray lead at anything and everything that wasn't a secbot, *this was not my best idea ever.*

Five sizzling beams of energy lashed out at Gaige. She rolled to the left, finger still squeezing the trigger. One of the secbots lunged for her—

—and then, with an explosion of metal and electricity, it did not exist anymore. In one heartbeat, it was an intelligent, highly deadly weapon of the ruling class. The next heartbeat, it was spare parts.

"Smash the system!" Gaige yelled in triumph, charging toward another secbot. Two of the others peeled away and aimed their eye lasers at her exposed back.

Ah, hell, Sasha thought. *Now I have to save her.* She was used to this—Fiona often needed to be saved just as often as she did the saving—but Fiona was nowhere near as reckless as this redheaded mercenary. Gaige was likely used to running headlong into danger and trusting Deathtrap to watch her back. Tonight, she had no Deathtrap, and her back was about to be cut into sizzling pieces by a pair of red-hot laser beams.

Sasha aimed her corrosive revolver at the nearest secbot and pulled the trigger until the battery had depleted itself. The bot shuddered from multiple bullet impacts, the acidic rounds eating through its armor and spreading their corrosion throughout its chassis. It clawed helplessly at itself as its hoverengine failed and it collapsed to the ground.

That left one secbot aiming at Gaige's exposed back, and Sasha's gun empty in her hand. If she didn't do something quickly, the bots would kill Gaige, and then they'd kill Sasha, and then the crystal would bring Sasha back to life, and then the bots would wonder why she'd revived, and Sasha would try to run, and they'd capture her and take her to Holloway, and Holloway would learn about the green shard and do evil-rich-lady experiments on it, and then everyone in Eden-5's highest tax bracket would be immortal and would probably try to rule the universe as god-emperors or something.

These thoughts led Sasha to do the only thing she could think of: punch the secbot as hard as she could. Which, it turned out, was not very hard. Certainly not hard enough to damage its metal shell, anyway. It was, however, an aggressive enough action to gain the bot's attention. It swiveled its torso away from Gaige's exposed back and toward Sasha, who tried to slam a fresh battery into her gun with newly throbbing fingers.

Sasha dodged a punch from the robot by falling straight onto her back. The battery clicked home with a satisfying hum. She raised the gun and fired once, twice, three times into the bot's expressionless eye. It crumpled to the ground, the acid still eating away at its neck hole.

Gaige still had two bots to deal with. Sasha raised her pistol, but there was no need. At that same moment, the laws of probability finally decided to work in Gaige's favor and two bullets, like the iambic-pentameter output of infinite typewriters helmed by infinite jabbers, zoomed straight into the chests of the two remaining secbots and detonated them like overripe melons.

"ANARCHYYYYY!" Gaige yelled.

"It's the middle of the night," Sasha said.

"*Anarchyyyyy!*" Gaige whispered.

The two got to their feet and grabbed a couple of secbot arms to use as makeshift shovels. As they dug, Sasha asked, "So, what made you wanna be a Vault Hunter in the first place?"

"I didn't choose. I was on the lam. I had no options."

"Right. Well, it's lucky you enjoy it so much."

"'Lucky' is an interesting choice of words considering we're digging up my murdered dad, but I love the optimism!"

After another hour of digging, Sasha's shovel thumped against something hard. The color drained from Gaige's face.

"I, uh." She swallowed. "I didn't get to see him," she whispered. "The first time I was here. It's been months. I don't know if I'd... how he'd look. If I'd even..." She trailed off, still staring at the hole in the ground.

"You don't have to look," Sasha said. "I can just do the crystal thing myself."

"Yeah. I think that, uh..." Gaige blinked away tears. "I think that'd probably be a good idea."

"Go have a seat. I'll handle the rest of this part."

Gaige nodded. She walked across the town square and sat on the ground, her back to the grave.

Sasha cleared away the remaining dirt and pried off the coffin lid as respectfully as she could. The moment the odor hit her nose, she felt glad Gaige wasn't around to see the coffin's contents. The decomposition had reached the point where nobody, not even his daughter, would recognize her father as the man he was in life.

She placed the crystal against his chest.

It glowed.

21
GAIGE

Gaige stared at the ground, her breath caught in her chest. Sasha's eyes darted from her to the corpse and back, waiting for some sign of change from either of them.

They stayed like this for some time, the Vault Hunter and the billionaire.

Minutes passed.

The billionaire asked, "What was Handsome Jack like?"

"Killable," the Vault Hunter responded. "What's it like having a sister?"

The billionaire scratched her arm. "Painful." Her gaze drifted to the cobblestone road. "Some days, anyway."

An hour passed.

"It should have worked by now," Gaige said, still facing away from the grave, still staring at the cold Rustville dirt.

Sasha wrung her hands, as if unsure how to respond. Gaige accepted the silence for what it was. She pushed the heel of her metal hand into her forehead and winced in irritation.

"Yeah," Sasha said. "I'm sorry."

Gaige waved her hand through the air as if batting away a fly.

"Pah," she said, forcing a smile onto her face. "What's to be sorry for? He was dead before, he's just as dead now. So," she said, the words spilling out of her mouth so quickly that Sasha couldn't interrupt her, "you said you wanna hunt a Vault? Let's go hunt a Vault."

The pigtailed orphan strode away from her father's body at something less than a run. Sasha broke into a jog to catch up.

"But it didn't work," Sasha said, her eyes narrowing with worry as the Vault Hunter speedwalked away from her unburied father.

"Nope," Gaige said. "So I don't owe you squat. But I'm a real friendly gal—you'll learn that soon enough. Besides," she said, looking at Sasha to avoid catching a glimpse of her father's body, "I'm sick of this planet."

Sasha opened her mouth to speak, but Gaige's cheeks were wet and her smile indistinguishable from a grimace. Perhaps noticing Sasha might speak, Gaige turned back around and increased her pace, alone with her anger.

The Vault Hunter did not speak again until they'd reached her ship, hidden under a filth-covered tarp deep in the desert between Rustville and the Elite District. A Derringer-class light transport, the ship was covered in hardened grime and spacedust and emitted a metallic wheeze when Gaige slapped its hull.

"Lotta folks name their ships," she said as the entrance ramp hissed and lowered to the dusty earth. "Not me. I don't give a skag's ass about this thing, honestly. Stole it from a bandit—well, I guess you can't *steal* from the dead, technically—and I only keep it in good enough shape to fly. Don't wanna pay too much attention and get Deathtrap jealous."

Her eyes glazed over. "Deathtrap…"

"I'm sorry," Sasha said once again.

"Nah," Gaige smiled. "It's no big. I told you, he's still kicking somewhere. I'd know if he wasn't. So, once I'm through being extra nice and showing you how to Vault Hunt even though you couldn't save my dad, I'll go get Deathtrap back."

Sasha furrowed her brow. "Are you sure?"

"*Of* course I'm sure," Gaige said, her eyes growing slightly too wide.

"Okay. Because you don't sound sure."

"Look, Sash," Gaige said, ignoring the way Sasha winced at the abbreviation. "If Deathtrap were dead, that would mean I'd lost everything. And obviously I haven't lost everything, because if I lost everything, I would have killed every single aristocrat on this planet. And I haven't done that yet, so Deathtrap isn't dead!" The last sentence exploded across the desert sands like a shockwave.

"Okay," Sasha murmured as Gaige traipsed up the gangway and into the bowels of the transport. "Where are we going?" she called after her. "I heard some rumors there was a Vault on Gantis."

In the cockpit, Gaige sat in the pilot's seat, next to a console of multicolored lights and dials. She flipped a bright yellow switch and the engines kicked into life, vibrating the entire ship with a pleasant hum. "Gantis is a trap," she yelled over her shoulder. "Bandit ambush site. They're more common than you think."

"Oh," Sasha said, slightly crestfallen.

"Good thing you're with me, kid," Gaige said, though she and Sasha were almost certainly of a similar age. "No, we're headed to a little unnamed moon about a parsec away. Got it on good authority there's a Vault hidden there. Planned to go after it with Dad once I…" She shook the thought from her head. "Woo! Let's hunt a Vault!"

The ship juddered as Sasha tentatively stepped inside. "What do you mean by good authority?"

"The bandit who owned this ship? Deathtrap got that map off him." Gaige hooked a thumb over her shoulder at a stretched square of leather bolted to the bulkhead. It depicted a star map of a nearby sector. A miniscule moon dead center, a Vault symbol scrawled next to it in the reddish brown of dried blood.

"Ugh," Sasha said, recoiling from the map, her hand covering her nose and mouth. "Why does it smell?"

"I told you," Gaige replied. "Deathtrap got it off him."

Sasha squinted at the map. In the corner of the map, just below the compass rose, Sasha could make out a pink circle with a round bump in its center.

A nipple.

"Ah." Sasha nodded. "Ah," she said again, to no one in particular.

"Strap yourself in," Gaige said, "and get some rest. Couple days from now, we'll be facing down a big-ass alien made of anger and purple glowy bits."

"Just like that? We don't have to find a key or anything?"

"Already did," Gaige said, tapping her temple. "Stop worrying."

"But—"

"Ababab. Stop freaking out. We'll kill a space god, get paid, and you'll be back before your sister even knows it. Trust me—this is my job."

The ship's engines engaged and the Derringer-class transport juddered into the air.

"Yours too now, I guess," Gaige said. "Welcome to the life of a Vault Hunter."

22
SASHA

They were about four hours into their journey when Sasha realized Gaige wasn't going to talk about her father or Deathtrap.

Not that Sasha was particularly keen to hear about her companion's grief—there was always the chance Gaige would conflate it with her anger at Fiona and Sasha for putting her in prison, which wouldn't help matters—but she didn't much fancy the prospect of facing down a distracted Vault Hunter alongside a killer alien monster.

Back on Pandora, focus was everything. Focusing on the task at hand, the variables at play. Feelings never entered into it. You had to know what you wanted and what you were willing to do to get it.

What *did* Sasha want?

Here she was, flying away from Eden-5—from her sister—at full burn, on her way to hunt a capital-V Vault. The sort of capital-H Heroic thing that capital-I Important people did.

But she didn't feel heroic or important. Not right now, anyway. At this moment, all she felt was anger. Anger at Fiona for keeping her on a leash. Above all, anger at herself for being so damned bored.

Why wasn't it enough? She and Fiona had spent years together fighting tooth and nail for every cent, barely staying one step ahead of the poorhouse or the gallows. Now, those days were over. She should have been able to relax, slow down, enjoy her retirement. Instead, she was on her way to open a Vault with a homicidal tech whiz. If Fiona knew, she'd be pissed.

Sasha told herself that was why she'd wanted to send Fiona a message before leaving Eden-5—to gloat, to make her worry: *Hey, sis. About to go get into a gunfight. Wish you were here. XOXO.* But the sinking feeling in her stomach told her that was a lie. It had been less than a day since she'd left her sister, and things already felt wrong somehow. In fact, this was the first time the two of them had been separated for any real stretch of time since their childhood.

After a few years of apprenticing under Felix, the two girls had got into an argument about whether to stay on Pandora, as Sasha had wanted, or to head for one of the less cannibalistic planets on the inner rim. They'd spent the better part of a week trying to work as solo thieves and con artists before Felix all but kidnapped them and forced them to acknowledge that they were helpless without each other.

But whatever. That was years ago. Separating from her sister might have been stupid back when they had nothing to their name beyond a handful of bucks and a few spent shell casings, but now they had enough money to survive no matter what happened.

That was it, Sasha realized. It was necessity that kept her and Fiona together. And now they didn't need each other anymore.

She closed her eyes. She wasn't sure how to feel about that.

Focus.

Her eyes snapped open as she felt herself rise a few inches from her seat. The ship was descending at a moderate speed, the rush of wind past the hull implying an atmosphere. The anti-grav was off, and the brief whisper of weightlessness as the ship fell to the moon below conjured a sense-memory of her and Fiona taking a speedbump too quickly in their caravan after fleecing a pelt seller.

No. Enough about Fiona. It was time to do Vault Hunter stuff.

Gaige unbuckled herself from the flight harness in the cockpit and banged a panel on the wall with the heel of her hand. It spun around, revealing a half-dozen weapons of varying size and lethality.

"Pick your poison," she said.

Sasha stepped to the rack and wrapped her fingers around the grip of a Hyperion submachine gun. No matter how much she and Fiona had practiced, her aim had never been great or even consistent, a fault that Hyperion's auto-accuracy drive helped mitigate.

"Oh, good," Gaige said. "That's my least favorite one." She hauled a bandit shotgun off the rack, its ammo drum fit to bursting with shells that looked as if they'd been haphazardly shoved inside by someone with only a rudimentary knowledge of how guns worked.

The Hyperion SMG's clip—or magazine; Sasha could never remember which was which—was full. She flipped the sight up and raised it to her eye. Gaige handed her a surprisingly heavy grenade, which she clipped to her belt. "So," Sasha asked, "what's the plan?"

"Ha!" Gaige slapped the weapons rack with her metal hand, sending a deafening *clang* through the confines of the ship. "Plan. That's cute. You're, that's fun." She chuckled as she kicked a release lever near the door. The entry ramp slowly descended and Sasha got her first taste of the dusty, barren moon air. She panicked briefly before realizing that neither she nor her Vault-hunting companion were suffocating.

"Got an atmosphere, so no need for an Oz Kit," Gaige said. "But be careful you don't jump too high. Gravity might not have the stank to pull you back down again. Ready?" She nodded at movement in the far distance: a dozen or so humanoid figures walking back and forth beyond the waist-high moon rocks dotting the landscape.

Gaige was out the door and blasting before Sasha could respond. The distant figures stopped and dove in alarm toward the nearest available moon rock for cover. Bullets and laser beams pinged off the ship's hull as the distant figures, whoever the hell they were, started shooting back. When a sniper round punched a fist-sized hole through the ship's metal exterior, Sasha decided she might be safer outside it than within.

Scrambling down the entrance ramp, she spotted Gaige sitting behind a particularly nondescript moon rock, her back up against cover and her shotgun slung lazily over the lip of the stone. She was blindfiring with reckless abandon, not bothering to aim or time her shots, and giggling to herself.

Sasha dove behind a neighboring boulder. *"What the hell are you doing?!"* she screamed.

"Softening 'em up," Gaige said, shooting Sasha a thumbs-up. "Only a few ricochets will actually hit anybody, but it'll scare 'em so they don't charge us all at once."

A quick glance from cover confirmed this. Gaige's storm of buckshot mostly went wide, but miraculously a few pellets bounced off the landscape at the correct angles and found homes in the heads of their enemies. Sasha squinted and could now make out the figures of who was shooting at them. About half were shirtless, their dirty white masks smeared with a brown substance that Sasha hoped was mud. The other half, clad in every ramshackle piece of ballistic armor they could seemingly find, fired hot lead and coarse language with equal vigor.

"Moon bandits?" Sasha exclaimed. "You didn't say there'd be moon bandits!"

"Cult of the Vault," Gaige said with a shrug. "They're popping up everywhere. You should be psyched! Means we're in the right place."

An incendiary grenade landed at Gaige's feet. Without bothering to look, she slid her foot underneath it, kicked it into the air, grabbed it, and hurled it back at the bandits. The distant boom of an explosion, followed by the all-too-familiar sound of men burning to death, told Sasha the grenade had hit its mark.

Her chest tightened. Her brain burned inside her skull. This felt wrong. Why did this feel wrong? Because Fiona wasn't here?

No. That was dumb.

It was the bandits. The last time Sasha had attacked a Vault, she'd only had to fight off the mechanized alien Guardians protecting it. Yes, that was it—she'd been preparing herself to deal with the tactics of the highly mobile Guardians rather than the bandits, who either stuck behind cover and took potshots or ran screaming at you, buzz axe in hand.

Yeah, that had to be it. Which was good! So what if she wasn't expecting bandits? She'd lived her entire life rolling with the punches, and this was no different than any other. So Sasha did what she always did when a job changed on the fly: she took a deep breath, put on her best fake smile, and rolled with it.

Then she stood up and a buzz axe hit her in the chest.

"Ow," she said. Blood spurted from the wound, the axe still embedded in her sternum. She wrapped a hand around its hilt and yanked it out, releasing another thick jet of crimson from the gash in her chest.

"Whoah," Gaige said, more impressed than anything. "You okay?"

Sasha nodded and pulled the green crystal from her pocket. "I've died twice already. That was nothing."

It was a lie, of course, though Sasha was hardly about to tell the truth to someone she barely knew. Knowing what awaited her after death—or to be more precise, what did *not* await her—made every wound, every brush with death, immeasurably worse. It was one thing to cheat death when the thought of a shiny, benevolent afterlife awaited her. It was quite another to do so once you knew nothing awaited you beyond the chilly indifference of nonexistence.

The axe wound sealed itself as the crystal tingled in her hand.

Gaige scoffed. "Where's the fun in that? Covering fire!" She leaped to her feet, and Sasha hurriedly leveled her machine gun and blasted pockmarks into the lunar landscape. The bandits, not hugely impressed at Sasha's stream of bullets, hesitated for only a moment. Gaige used this brief pause in the bandits' bullet storm to step forward, pumping and firing the shotgun with every step. The weapon bucked fearsomely in her hands, but her aim and her mood remained steady even as a few courageous bandits peeked out of cover to fire back at her. Sasha couldn't decide whether to be impressed or frightened, settling on impressed for now.

Sasha leaped out of cover and opened up with her submachine gun, spraying wildly at the bandits until the Hyperion actuators took hold and choked her bullet spread into a fine point.

"Little girlies!" one of the bandits screeched. "I'm gonna carve you into [sound of bullet entering through mouth and exiting through back of skull]!"

Sasha nodded. There it was. That's what she was looking for, right? The thrill of being shot at; the joy of not being hit. The satisfaction of blowing away somebody who wanted you dead.

And best of all, it was all to a greater purpose. Not just survival. Not just outrunning the next catastrophe. Every bullet she fired was another step toward something that truly mattered: a Vault.

Nobody knew what the hell the Vaults were, why they'd been built, or why there were so many of them, but one thing was clear: they were tied to something bigger. A grand, horrible design by distant, hateful gods? An arms race for alien power? Just a bunch of big doors filled with tentacles and bullets? There was no way to be certain, and besides, it didn't matter—not to Sasha, at least. What mattered was that they were important. They were dangerous. And now, she was going to open one too. She and Fiona would be even. Equals.

Yeah, this was good. Definitely.

The moon bandits ultimately presented a poor challenge. After a few well-placed bullets in a few poorly placed explosive barrels— "They use the fuel inside to power their generators," Gaige said, cutting off Sasha as the latter opened her mouth to ask why the hell they kept explosive barrels around in the first place—the lunar brigands offered little resistance. After only a few minutes of gunfighting, the bandits had fled into the gray desert and the path to the Vault was clear.

A path littered with the corpses of Guardians. Their white and purple bodies lay sprawled in unnatural poses, their limbs broken and bent backward as if they'd been airborne when they were cut down. "Cult of the Vault must have wiped them out," Gaige said. "Lucky for us! One less thing to worry about."

Sasha couldn't help but feel a little disappointed. "I'm pretty good at fighting Guardians, actually."

"I never liked fighting them, honestly," Gaige said, stepping over the corpse of an alien robot as if she'd done it a thousand times before, which she had. "They're just kinda… less satisfying to kill? Than bandits? 'Cause they're robots. Mostly robot, anyway. Robotish. Does that make sense, or does that sound insane?"

"It sounds a little insane," Sasha said.

"It's a little insane," Gaige acknowledged, nodding. "But in the words of a great philosopher, life be like that sometimes."

The path of corpses led them through a tunnel deep underground, past glowing purple crystals and emissive runes that the galaxy's archaeologists had yet to decipher. With every step that brought them closer to the Vault, Sasha felt her chest grow tighter, her stomach more pained, with the anticipation of spectacle mixed with the fear of imminent violence. Even with her magical, tension-destroying green crystal, things could go very bad very quickly. If both she and Gaige died, and if Sasha lost her hold on the crystal, that'd be it. Nobody would come looking for them. Nobody knew they were here.

Not even Fiona.

Sasha caught herself. *Focus.* A large, imposing door loomed at the end of the tunnel, beckoning the Vault Hunters closer. As they approached, the image of the Vault symbol glowed brighter and brighter, the symbol's apex lining up with the seam in the door's middle.

"Here we go," Gaige said, thumbing another shell into the breech. "This is where it gets rowdy. Well, rowdier."

Sasha's footfalls grew softer and slower as they approached the Vault, as if in reverence. Gaige's were as loud and fast as ever, the footsteps of somebody who had places to be and aliens to kill.

"Now, when this thing comes out, it's gonna be armored to hell and back. We just gotta find the spot where the armor's weakest and plug away at it until it stops moving."

Sasha raised a hand, then felt stupid for raising her hand and brought it back down. "What if it doesn't have a weak spot?"

Gaige smiled and shrugged. "Then we die, I guess. I dunno. It'll be fun! Stop thinking so much." Gaige shot Sasha a thumbs-up. "The Scuttler," she said.

"What? Are you trying to give me a nickname or something?"

The chamber rumbled beneath their feet. Ancient rock crumbled above, sending fist-sized lumps of stone clattering to the ground. Light spilled from the seam of the Vault as its doors parted open.

"No," Gaige said.

"Then what was that?" Sasha asked, the submachine gun held firm in her grasp. "What'd you say?"

"The password," Gaige shouted, shotgun resting lazily against her midsection. "These Vaults, they all got different keys. This one's was the name of the thingy inside."

"What thingy?" Sasha said, and then, "Oh, okay," because she saw the thingy.

The thingy in question crawled through the crack in the Vault, its six legs punching holes into the door. Despite its magnificent size, it effortlessly gripped the door like a spider, scuttling—*Ah, Sasha thought, I see*—onto the wall and around the chamber with a speed and agility that almost instantly made Sasha nauseous. Each one of its hairy, armored legs ended in a purple spike that, with each step, punctured the wall with the ease of a dagger slipping between the bones of a human ribcage.

There was also a large humanoid eye on its back—an eye that never tore its gaze from Sasha and Gaige.

Sasha fired an entire magazine of ammo at the Scuttler's eye, each bullet piercing the gelatinous membrane and floating around the swirling liquid inside. A viscous, milky substance leaked from every bullet hole, dripping down the Scuttler's carapace and onto the chamber floor below.

"Ohohohoho," Gaige cackled. "Gross. That's nasty. I love it."

Sasha agreed with the first two sentences.

The Scuttler leaped from the wall, the dagger-sharp tips of its legs ready to perforate Sasha. She barely managed to dive away as the creature landed and, with a terrible lack of hesitation, immediately leaped into the air again. It turned its body upside down and attached itself to the roof, where it proceeded to shoot a hot sticky gob of purple matter from its pupil. The putrid hunk splashed inches away from Sasha's foot, sending flecks of purple guk onto Sasha's shin.

The substance ate through her pant leg almost instantly. When it reached the skin, it burned with a white-hot intensity like nothing Sasha had never felt in her life and hoped like hell she'd never feel again.

She hit the mag-release on her submachine gun and slammed a new clip home, all the while grunting aggressive profanity to distract from the pain in her leg. "Dodge the spit!" she shouted to Gaige.

"Well, yeah," Gaige replied, moving underneath the creature and firing more shells into the now-closed eye of the Scuttler. The pellets bounced harmlessly off the chitinous eyelid.

Suddenly, all six of the creature's legs detached from the roof and it fell to the ground eye first, stomping Gaige into the cold rock floor of the chamber.

"Hngh!" Gaige grunted through broken ribs. "Get it off!"

Sasha shoulder-checked the Scuttler as hard as she could, which had the net effect of giving her a sore shoulder and nothing else.

With a wet cracking noise, the Scuttler's legs inverted position while its body stayed in the same place. Its needly feet dug into the ground. What Sasha had thought of its underside was now on top, and its unarmored eye was on its bottom, facing Gaige's prone form. Gaige raised her shotgun and fired as fast as she could.

As Sasha and Gaige's bullets bounced harmlessly off its carapace, the Scuttler once again leaped into the air. It opened its eye, focusing on Gaige, and brought all of its legs together, evidently aiming to plunge them directly into her chest.

"Oh boy," Gaige wheezed, and blasted upwards with the shotgun. Though the buckshot tore a sizable chunk from the creature's eye, the Scuttler seemed no worse off for it.

Sasha had an idea.

She pulled the grenade from her belt and yanked the steel pin from its housing. "Catch!" she shouted, tossing the grenade underhand to Gaige, who snatched it from the air.

"What are you—?" Gaige began, but just then the Scuttler fell, legs first, toward her. She rolled to the side at the last moment, but it wasn't enough. The six hardened clawfeet punched straight through her steel arm, sending gouts of viscous oil and hydraulic fluid spurting from the wound. The Scuttler raised several of its legs again, presumably unsatisfied at not hitting flesh, and stabbed downwards again. This time, Gaige rolled toward her messed-up arm and thrust her remaining arm, grenade in hand, toward the Scuttler's open eye.

The Scuttler looked at Gaige with its big, leaking, gelatinous iris, narrowing its eyelids ever so slightly, as if unsure what was about to happen.

Gaige shoved the grenade into its pupil. Her fist easily pushed through the membrane protecting the eye. She released her grip on the explosive and yanked her arm out just in time for the Scuttler to, presumably realizing its predicament, screech in pain.

There was a muffled pop and the Scuttler's eye exploded, gouts of some obscene white fluid spewing out directly onto Gaige, mixing with the black oil from her leaking arm to coat her in a dull, vaguely upsetting-looking gray ooze.

White ichor still spewing from the hole in its eye, the Scuttler's corpse fell to the side, its armored limbs clacking off one another as it collapsed into a heap.

Gaige turned to Sasha, putrescent and viscous fluids dripping from her face and body. "Hehe," she said, her off-white smile visible through the muck.

Sasha turned from the two and looked into the open Vault. The light within was too bright to gaze at for more than a moment. "So, what do we do now?" she asked. "Do we go in?"

"Yeah, maybe," Gaige said, trying in vain to wipe her face clean with her functional arm. "Some of 'em, you go in and get the treasure. Some of 'em, you stay where you are and they spit stuff out."

A high-pitched whine emanated from the open Vault door. The room, once again, began to shake.

"Ooh," Gaige said. "Looks like we got a spitter."

With a sound like that of an angel singing and belching at the same time, Sasha imagined, an explosion erupted from the bowels of the Vault. The rumbling steadily grew louder, as if a hurricane were about to issue forth from the Vault's mouth.

"Here it comes," Gaige said. "The best part." She stood, arms stretched open to welcome what was about to come. She closed her eyes. "The lootsplosion."

A torrent of weaponry erupted from the Vault fissure, along with stacks of cash, packs of ammo, and crystals of Eridium. The gear hit Gaige with considerable velocity, but she did not flinch. As a shiny ultra-rare sniper rifle collided with her chest, she could only laugh in ecstasy. "Come here!" she called over to Sasha. "You're missing it!"

Sasha joined Gaige within the shower of armaments. This was it, the climax to her quest. The Vault was hunted. Now for the prize.

A golden pistol nailed her in the kneecap. A stack of hundred-credit bills hit her in the throat. As she coughed, an Eridium crystal flew into her mouth. Sasha ducked out of the lootsplosion as quickly as she'd entered it, pulling the alien mineral from the back of her throat.

The loot tsunami slowed to a trickle, and then stopped altogether. With a grinding of stone on stone, the Vault doors swung closed. Moments later, the doors crumbled away entirely, as if the eons they'd stood there had finally caught up with them. Where there once had been a portal to some Eridian-engineered mystery dimension, there was now only a patch of blank wall.

Gaige lowered her arms. It was done. "Well? Whaddya think?"

"Uh," Sasha said, rubbing her neck. "It, uh, it felt…"

What? Exciting? Scary? Fun? Kind of all of those, but also, like nothing. It's not that Vault hunting was boring, per se. It was just that… she'd spent so long thinking about opening a Vault on her own—ever since Rhys and Fiona got to enter the Vault of the Traveler—that she'd expected to feel… more. More joy. More exhilaration. Most importantly, more purpose. This was supposed to fix everything, bringing together all the disparate, floating parts of her personality into a cohesive whole. Vault hunting was supposed to make a better Sasha.

But it hadn't. She was the same old Sasha, just with better loot.

"It was fine," Sasha said. "It just wasn't what I was looking for. I guess."

Gaige awkwardly grabbed another assault rifle and slid it under the growing pile she held in her arms, then nodded at Sasha. "Yeah, that's what I figured. Seemed like you came out here to cure a symptom without understanding the disease."

Sasha flinched in surprise. "Uh, yeah. Maybe. That's astute of you."

"Uh, yeah," Gaige mimicked, no longer visible behind the tower of guns she'd balanced in her arms. "I'm emotionally intelligent as hell."

"Do you wanna talk about your dad, then?"

The tower toppled over, leaving Gaige empty-handed. "Hey-hey! Guess who just earned themselves a completely silent trip back to Eden-5!" she replied.

23
FIONA

I kicked the cell door open.

"What the *hell* did you say to her?" I shouted at Gaige. She trembled in her restraints, her breath quickening under the dark bag covering her head. Her cell was a spartan affair, her body chained to one wall and only a single lightbulb dangling from the ceiling. A few feet from Gaige's restrained form, there was a large brown stain on the concrete—dried blood. Too far away to be Gaige's, unless they'd laid into her before chaining her up.

Whatever. Didn't matter. I needed to find my sister.

"My ECHO device pings. Somebody in my account is spending an awful lot of money from this location. Imagine my surprise when I learn it's a max-security prison. Good thing the guards are so bribable."

I waited for a response until it became obvious I wasn't getting one. "Look," I said. "I know she asked you about Vault hunting."

Gaige cocked her head. Maybe I'd caught her attention.

"She and I opened a Vault back on Pandora. It was a good time." I paused. It hadn't been just a good time. It had been exhilarating. It had been important. It had felt like our entire lives had led to the moment we'd fought the Traveler and opened the Vault. But none of that mattered anymore. All that mattered was getting Sasha back safe. I knelt beside Gaige.

"Just tell me where she is. I know she hasn't left the planet, so just—" I ripped the hood from her face.

A middle-aged man smiled back at me.

"You're not Gaige," I said.

"Nah. But you're Fiona, I assume?"

I nodded and headed for the door.

"Life is crap," he sang. "Clean it up!"

At that moment, I agreed. But I would have used a stronger word than "crap."

———

I spent the better part of that day skimming the ECHOnet for any sign of Sasha or Gaige. My emotions bounced between sisterly anxiety and a spiteful, smug, not-really-earnest hope that something *would* happen to Sasha just so she'd understand how right I was.

After a sleepless night and still no word from her, the spite cooled into ice-cold worry, extinguishing the fires of my anger. I lay on my two-million-thread-count sheets, staring at the canopy of my four-post lux-bed and feeling—no, *knowing*—that if something happened to Sasha, it would be my fault and nobody else's. She'd wanted to leave, and I'd told her not to. What the hell had I thought would happen?

I should have gone with her. I should have indulged her. Even if I'd thought it was stupid to go off looking for people to shoot at us—and I did *think* it was stupid—she would have been better off with me there than without me. Just like I couldn't have caught Gaige without Sasha's help, or found the Vault of the Traveler, or survived Bossanova's circle of slaughter, or a thousand other near-death experiences that Sasha had prevented from being actual-death experiences.

I cursed. Not loudly, but it didn't matter; the emptiness of the mansion meant I could hear my F-bomb echo throughout the vacant rooms of my home. My crime-solving butler had gone home for the day. For the first time in quite a long time, I was alone with my thoughts.

I don't recommend it.

That was the nice thing about a life on the run: we moved too fast for our brains to catch up. When every day was a mad sprint to the next sunrise, we didn't have the time to second guess ourselves. But the night after Sasha disappeared, time was all I had.

It's moments like that when I remember my favorite sound: Sasha's snoring. It's truly abysmal and sounds like a buzz axe cutting through sheet metal. Just when you think you've acclimated to it, it changes pitch and you get woken up all over again.

But if she's snoring, it means she's unconscious. And when you're unconscious, you can't be hungry, or scared, or upset. You're at peace.

You're safe.

I turned my ECHO receiver up and tried to remember the sound of Sasha's snore.

———

She came back two days later.

Our ostentatious front door swung open with little more than a whisper. The rest of the house was dead silent, so the slide of the well-oiled door hinges rang out with the intensity of a gunshot.

I sprinted from my bedroom and took the stairs three at a time on my way down to the foyer. The anger and the fear were gone, replaced with a pure elation that she was finally back.

That's when Gaige poked her head in through the door.

"Nice digs," she said over my cursing.

A flick of my wrist saw my pistol slide directly into my palm. I leveled it at the Vault Hunter. "Where is she?"

Gaige scowled at me like I'd merely been impolite instead of threatening to shoot her. "Literally two steps behind me. Stop being a nerd." She shoved the door open further, revealing my sister.

Sasha looked like a recently kicked dog.

"You look like a recently kicked dog," I said, then immediately wished I hadn't. Sasha, her eyes on the floor, nodded at me and moved past Gaige. I would have happily taken an angry outburst or a sullen scoff. Whatever this was, this quiet acceptance of her circumstances, I didn't know what to do with it.

"What's going on?" I called at her back as she ascended the stairs. Failing to elicit a reaction, I turned to Gaige. "What happened?"

"We opened a Vault," Gaige said. "Went great. She's just been bummed out. Also, is it cool if I crash here? I'm wanted, and I think I'm gonna rescue Deathtrap and give killing Holloway another shot, so..."

"Bummed out? What do you m— No, you can't stay here! You're lucky I don't call the secbots for taking Sasha out of here in the first—"

"Boooo! Narc." She snapped her fingers. "I'm outta here." She turned on her heel.

"I know where Deathtrap is," I said. She continued turning on her heel without stopping and once again faced me.

"Aaaaand what is that information worth to you?"

"Leave my sister alone. For good."

"Sure," she said. "I'll pretend I wasn't going to do that anyway. You got a deal."

"Deathtrap's in the Tech Triangle," I said, referencing the wealthy neighborhood full of programmers, innovators, and people with enough money that they could pretend to be both while being neither. My ECHOnet bribes had borne fruit almost immediately; I'd known Deathtrap's whereabouts before Sasha had even broken Gaige out of prison. "Stead Robotics. Top floor."

Gaige gave me a cocky two-finger salute. "Aye aye," she said.

"Pleasure doing business with you, except for, you know, every single interaction we've ever had."

With that, she disappeared into the darkness with a speed and stealth that I wouldn't have expected from someone so loud.

I considered chasing after her. Once Holloway learned Gaige was missing, it wouldn't take her much time to figure out Sasha had been the one to help her escape. Only by shoving Gaige back into her cell could I ensure Sasha's safety.

But it seemed like Sasha and I had bigger problems at the moment.

She was lying atop the covers on her bed, trying hard to fall asleep and trying harder to pretend I hadn't just entered the room. I sat at the foot of the bed and tried to think of something smart and sisterly and empathetic to say.

"I wiped the footage," she said, her eyes still closed.

"From the prison?"

She nodded. "I ran the guard bribes through a shell company, so we should be good there."

"That's good. That's smart."

She didn't respond. We stewed in the silence for a moment. Ultimately, I was the one to break it.

"I'm sorry," I said.

Sasha opened her eyes. "For…?"

"Treating you like a kid."

She sat up, resting her back against the carved spacewhalebone headboard. "Yeah. You did."

"We're partners," I said. "I'm not in charge. So if you wanna go hunt Vaults, then let's give it a try togeth—"

"I don't," she murmured. I tried to catch her gaze, but she was doing what she often did when deep in thought: closing her eyes and cocking her head, as if trying to block out everything else and focus on what was going on inside her head. "This house made me feel like an asshole, and I thought doing something important would fix that. But I still feel like an asshole."

Hadn't expected that. I'd assumed she was just bored. Sasha's not an asshole. She's one of the least assholish people I know. As far as con artists go, anyway.

"We're not bad people just because we finally hit it big," I said.

"We're bad people because we're not doing anything with the money." She looked at me, conviction burning in her eyes. "Nothing that matters. Nothing *good.*"

"What, you want to donate most of it to charity? We can do that. We'd still be unbearably rich."

"I don't know," she said, shaking her head. "I mean, yes, we should definitely do that. But it still doesn't feel like enough. I think… we should help Gaige."

I cocked my head skeptically. "You wanna help her kill Holloway?"

"Yeah. Maybe."

"So, your cure for feeling like an asshole is to… murder someone?"

"'Murder' is a strong word."

"I don't think so."

She threw her hands into the air. "You *just* said you're not deciding what we do or don't do!"

"I—" I closed my eyes. She was right, as much as I hated to admit it. I'd nearly lost Sasha once by telling her what to do, so maybe it wouldn't hurt to hear her out. At the very least, having a proper conversation about the whole thing would make it easier to convince her to give up on the idea.

"You're right," I said. Sasha raised her eyebrows in surprise. I didn't let her say what we were both thinking—that I hadn't said those two words to her in quite a long time. "But why? Because Gaige says so? She *did* kill Holloway's daughter."

"By accident, yeah," Sasha said. "And then Holloway killed her dad. Tortured him to death." She looked at her feet. "I saw the body. He didn't go out well. And the only time I ever experienced silence on that entire trip was when I asked Gaige about her father. To piss off a Vault Hunter so bad they single-handedly declare war on an entire planet? Holloway's gotta be a special brand of cruel."

"And she's an asshole," I ventured.

"And she's an asshole."

"If we're gonna do this—and I'm not saying we are—we'd have to be smart about it. Make sure it never comes back to us."

Sasha leaned back and stared at the ceiling. "It'd just be about giving Gaige an opportunity to take her out. Maybe we invite her to, I dunno, tea time. In a secluded field with a tree big enough to hide a redhead and her robot." She ran a hand through her hair. "Maybe not. Maybe this is a stupid idea. Maybe I'm… Maybe I should think about this harder."

I shrugged, trying my best to conceal my joy at Sasha's newfound rationality. "Maybe we sleep on it. Talk about the whole murder thing over breakfast tomorrow. Deal?"

"Deal," she said.

We never got the chance to have that breakfast, though, because the next morning Sasha tried to kill the countess anyway.

24 FIONA

Dawn had just begun to break through my autocurtains. I lay atop the warm, gelatinous cushion of my god-emperor-sized bed, fighting the battle so many of us fight every day: namely, to conquer the parts of yourself that want to stay under the blankets for the rest of your day/week/lifespan.

"The Countess Cassandra Holloway seeks audience," our butler intoned through the home speaker system. "Shall I escort her in?"

I shot up in bed, my blood running cold. *She knows. She knows Sasha helped Gaige escape. Holloway knows we're (maybe) plotting to kill her.* I thought we'd at least have a day or so to prepare. Apparently not.

"Sasha," I whispered over the intercom, "stay in your room and do not come out." She responded with what basically boiled down to agreement.[18]

Holloway would expect to meet me in the lounge.[19] I needed

---

18 Technically, she said "No" and "I'm getting dressed" and "I'll meet you downstairs," but the subtext was that she agreed with me.
19 One of the many tips I learned from reading The Stupid Moron's Guide to Coming Into a Lot of Money Very Suddenly, whose chapters were titled things like "If You Have a Choice Between People Finding Out You're New Money Or Drinking Poison, Start Chugging" and "Owning Human Beings: More Ethically Complex Than You'd Think?"

to be there, waiting for her, wearing my best look of bored resentment. If she caught me cozy in bed wearing only my jim-jams, any chance I had of dominating the conversation would evaporate like teardrops in the Arid Wastelands.

The front door was directly next to the lounge. I was on the top floor, two stories above it.

I grabbed my most condescending evening gown and sprinted downstairs, past the half-dozen cleaners from Rustville who scrubbed and disinfected our home every other week.

The doorbell clanged over and over as I formed battle plans in my head. Was it possible she wanted to meet for any reason other than to confront us about Gaige's jailbreak? Did she, perhaps, randomly decide at six a.m. that she desperately needed to hang out with a couple of dirty offworld bounty hunters?

The doorbell continued to blare through the house as she pressed the button over and over again. A formality more than anything else; she likely had a cadre of security robots with her that could have sliced the door from its hinges in a half-second.

I nearly lost my footing on the second-floor landing. Our crime-solving butler, Fitzwiggins,[20] stood stiff-backed near the door. "Wait eight more seconds and let her in," I whispered, grabbing his shoulder for leverage as I made a hard ninety-degree pivot toward the open lounge door.

I slid into the room, kicked my shoes off while still in motion, and performed a diving leap onto the high-backed velvet chair facing the fireplace. My lounge wasn't terribly dissimilar from Holloway's: fireplace, bookshelves, tasteful paintings of sad-looking women. Through the doorway in my periphery, I saw the butler escort her

---

20 "Madam," he'd said earlier in the week, gingerly gesturing at a curly golden hair attached to the bloody dagger that protruded from a census taker's spine, "I believe our culprit may be of the… *canine variety.*"

inside, pausing only briefly to note a penny-sized drop of blood on the doorframe that would eventually result in the entire defensive line of the Eden Earthshakers being hanged for murder.

I put on my game face—slightly raised eyebrows and pursed, confused lips, like I'd just bitten into a lemon that tasted of steak— and kicked the nearest bookcase. A worn hardcover copy of *Wuthering Fights* leaped from the shelf into my hand.

"Ahem," said a wealthy voice behind me.

I turned around in the chair, already feigning delight and surprise. "Countess Holloway," I purred. "What a delightful surprise!"

She was alone. No security detail. That was either very good news or very, very bad news. She took a gift-wrapped box from under her arm and handed it to me.

"A gift? Countess, you shouldn't have," I said, tearing the wrapping paper off as elegantly as I could.

"And yet I did," she said.

It was a Vaultlander™. Specifically, a new-in-box Claptrap unit. It included three hundred unique voice lines, a battery that lasted two years without needing a recharge, and a volume control that could be turned up but never down.

I had never felt more insulted in my entire life.

"Thank you so much," I said through gritted teeth. "Please, have a seat." I gestured at the chair beside me. Her eyes never wavered from mine as she lowered herself into it. I placed the "gift" on the drinks table between us and looked her in the eye.

Now came the boring part of every social conflict: waiting to see who speaks first. Whoever breaks the silence reveals they've got more to lose. They lose the high ground. They—

"Spending the morning in?" Holloway asked. Her perfectly proportioned features didn't change. Her voice didn't waver. To anyone else, it would have been a perfectly innocent question, but I knew and she knew (but she didn't know that I knew) that she was desperate.

Desperate. No secbot backup. She was fishing. She had every reason to suspect Sasha and me of helping Gaige escape, but she wasn't sure. I had no idea why the prison guards hadn't sold us out, but I wasn't one to look a gift horse in the mouth.

Holloway had come here to see if I would break, and she'd managed to undercut herself before I could so much as offer her a drink. All I had to do was play it cool for the next half-hour and she'd head home the same frustrated, confused ball of passive income that walked through my front door.

Things were looking up.

Then I saw Sasha standing in the doorway, pointing a silenced assault rifle at Holloway's high-backed chair.

I leaped to my feet and, as hard as I could, kicked the top of Holloway's chair, which tipped backwards, taking Holloway with it. I felt a gust of wind blow past my face as Sasha fired a silenced round at where Holloway had been.

Holloway yelped in surprise and anger. "What is the meaning of this?!"

"There was a bug," I said. "A big one. I'm so sorry. I haven't even offered you a drink."

"This is ludicrous! I'm not thirsty!" she protested, her feet flailing in the air as she attempted to right herself.

"Nonsense," I said. "You'll catch your death of dehydration from that fireplace. Just look at it! And keep looking at it until I come back." I strode toward the door making I'm-going-to-kill-you eyes at Sasha, who waved at me to move out of the way. Instead, I grabbed the barrel of the gun with one hand and her shoulder with the other, taking both of us out of the lounge and toward the staircase.

"I thought we were gonna talk this over," I whispered.

"We're talking now," Sasha replied. Fair point. "No harm in getting a bead on her while we do."

"Look, morally I'm totally fine with it. She just gave me a Claptrap Vaultlander."

"Oh my god. Decision made. Step aside, Fi. She's about to get got."

"*Butbutbutbut*," I said. "This isn't Pandora. You kill somebody rich and powerful, they put you in chains."

"Not if you're also rich and powerful," she replied.

"I…" I furrowed my brow. I couldn't disagree with that. Holloway had plenty of friends and business partners, sure, but none who would mourn her death. They'd be more than happy to divvy up the spoils of her empire among themselves. As much as I wasn't a fan of cold-blooded murder, Holloway *was* a pretty lousy person. And maybe Sasha wouldn't be as depressed if she could just kill a lousy person every once in a while.

She put a hand on my shoulder. "Look, I remember what Felix said: 'To hell with everyone who isn't us.' I know it'd be easier to just sit on our hands and let Holloway and the rest of these rich jerkbags do whatever they want to whoever they want. But, like, screw this chick. I don't wanna spend the next thirty years with Holloway as a neighbor."

Did I know, logically, that this was a stupid idea? Of course I did. But was I equally terrified at the prospect of spending the rest of our lives suffering drop-ins from the countess?

Yeah. Hell with it.

I guess it's true. You can take the girls out of Pandora, but you can't take Pandora outta the girls.

"Okay, screw it. Go nuts," I said. I moved to one side of the doorway, providing Sasha with a clean shot at Holloway's back. I knew the consequences. I knew what we were doing. I think I was just, more than anything, bored. I saw the shape of the rest of our lives—eating great food, sleeping in comfy beds—and the sheer predictability of it all filled me with existential dread. If I couldn't live a life where murderous jerks get shot every once in a while, what was the point?

Sasha's finger moved to the trigger guard.

To my surprise, however, Holloway was not only facing us but grinning from ear to ear. She got to her feet and leaned against the doorframe with an effortless, casual grace. "Are you trying to kill me?" she asked.

"No," I said, trying my best to hide Sasha's machine gun with my body.

"Yes," Sasha said.

"Well, then, be a good host," Holloway said. She grabbed the barrel of Sasha's gun and placed it against her forehead. "Do it, then. Pull the trigger and see what happens to you."

Sasha's jaw dropped. For the first time in a long time, she was speechless. "Wh... I..."

Holloway slapped the barrel away, grinning like a demon. "You're new here, so I'll forgive this faux pas, but on Eden-5 there are rules. Rules that keep people like us—well, people like me—on top."

"What are you talking about?" I asked.

"Solidarity. Big word, I know. Five syllables. You'll find it in the dictionary not long after 'silent,' which is what you should be while your betters are speaking to you. My dear girls, *solidarity* is what prevents this city from going to the skags. You think you're the first person who ever wanted to kill another billionaire out of financial jealousy?"

Sasha opened her mouth to argue. I grabbed her arm. I'd rather have Holloway thinking we wanted her dead because we were envious of her money than know the truth, which is that we just didn't like her vibe.

"If we solved problems on Eden-5 the way you do on Pandora, there'd be no end to the bloodshed. That's why several years ago, I and the rest of the city's Elites made a simple agreement: if any of us was to ever raise a hand against another, the aggressor would immediately face the wrath of every single other Elite in the city. Every time, no matter what. Mutually assured destruction.

"So please," Holloway continued, gesturing at the gun in Sasha's hand. "Go ahead. Blow my brains out. Then see how long you can last against the assembled armies of mercenaries, robots, and high-powered weaponry that the rest of Eden-5's billionaires would array against you before my body hits the ground."

She turned her back on us and walked through the door. Sasha had a clean shot. She raised the rifle. Holloway paused by the door, as if waiting for something.

Sasha moved her finger to the trigger.

25
SASHA

Sasha's finger muscles went taut. A few ounces of pressure and one of the most unlikable people she or her sister had ever known would no longer be a problem.

Sure, Holloway would soon be replaced by a brand-new problem, but so what? This wasn't their town. Sasha and Fiona could take their ill-gotten gains and head anywhere else in the galaxy. Not like there was anybody here who mattered to them.

Other than Gaige, Sasha thought. They weren't exactly friends, but Sasha felt a pang of guilt at the thought of depriving Gaige of her vengeance. The pang got slightly stronger when she realized the other billionaire families would assume Gaige was partially responsible for Holloway's assassination, and would likely join forces to kill her too.

And Laurel, the lady from the debtors' prison. Laurel was nice.

So, two people they cared about on this planet-sized hunk of hypocrisy. Two people versus the incredible satisfaction she'd get from wiping that smug look off Holloway's face with a sniper round.

This was the moment. This was the kind of decision Vault Hunters made. If it were Gaige, a bullet would have been in Holloway's head before she'd had time to utter a syllable. So what if the entire planet arrayed its forces against you? You'd fight them off. You'd kick ass. You'd be triumphant. That's what Vault Hunters do.

And in that moment, Sasha had to accept the truth.

She wasn't a Vault Hunter.

She lowered the rifle with an irritated grunt. "Goddammit."

Holloway, her back still to the girls, nodded. "Yes, that's what I thought." She turned on her heel, providing a great view of what Sasha considered an eminently punchable face. "I came here this morning because I'd assumed you two were, well, considerably more complicated than you clearly are. I can see I was mistaken. Just another pair of Pandoran hustlers desperate for a fatter bank account."

Fitzwiggins speed-walked from the kitchen hallway, a full champagne flute in hand. He disposed of a bloody handkerchief in a nearby wastebin—later, he would explain to the girls that, following an attempt to blackmail a local florist, their usual gardener had gotten a positively *deadly* nosebleed—and proffered the champagne to Holloway with an expert bow. "Your beverage, madam. Apologies for the wait."

"No need to apologize." She took it from him, spat into it, and splashed the drink into his face. "I am, as I said, not thirsty. Farewell."

She sauntered out of Sasha and Fiona's home. Fitzwiggins turned red with irritation, champagne fizzing as it ran down his face.

Sasha turned to Fiona. "Now you know why the guards at Gaige's prison never ratted me out."

Fiona nodded. Holloway was habitually cruel to service workers. She'd probably visited that prison regularly so she could watch Gaige be tortured, and while she was there she must have been exceptionally rude to the staff. Despite Holloway offering more money than any of them could have dreamed of, they wouldn't tell her who'd freed Gaige. Money is nice, but sometimes giving the middle finger to an asshole is even nicer.

Sasha sat on the stairs, the gun dangling from her limp hands. She'd had the opportunity to kill a bad guy, but she'd been too smart to take it.

"It's weird," Sasha said to her sister. "We spent our whole lives around violence and we kinda got used to it. Safe. Simple. Not like this place."

"I'm sorry we don't get to kill her," Fiona said, sitting down next to Sasha. "I thought up a plan for hiding the body and everything."

Sasha leaned the rifle against the railing and put her head in her hands. "Oh, yeah?"

Fiona nodded. "You know the Cupcake-o-matic we never use? Put her in there, let the mixer crush her up and mix the parts into a batch of treats."

"What would we do with the cupcakes?"

"I dunno," Fiona admitted.

"That's nasty. That's a nasty plan."

"Yeah. Good, right?"

"Very good," Sasha said, smiling sadly.

The two sat in silence for a moment, and Sasha reflected that it felt nice to mutually hate somebody, even if she and her sister couldn't kill her together.

26
FIONA

As we talked, Fitzwiggins cleaned himself up as best he could. He dabbed his face and chest with a towel, taking extra care to wipe the debt cuff around his neck. I wondered how many times he must have cleaned that heavy, metal collar. It had to weigh him down every day, reminding him of what he didn't have, but he still—for the sake of his job, or his hygiene, or maybe his self-respect—had to keep it shiny and clean.

The cleaning crew descended the stairs on either side of Sasha and me. As they passed us, I noticed every single one of them had at least two debt cuffs on various parts of their body, and I was slightly alarmed to realize it'd taken me so long to notice. I'd started to not see the cuffs at all. They'd become normal.

As the cleaners passed us by, however, I saw something assuredly not normal. Trailing behind one of them, playing with a little rubber ball that was more saliva than sphere, was a very familiar, very cute face. The last time I'd seen that face, it had been weeping over the headless body of the man who'd stolen my Vaultlander. Now, that same face, however adorable, looked old. Tired. Even without tears pouring down the boy's cheeks, he looked far more miserable than when Fiona had last seen him.

Sasha stared at me in confusion. "Uh, are you okay?"

I pointed at the child. Sasha shrugged. "Yeah, it's one of the kids from the spaceport."

He must have known we were talking about him because he turned. If he recognized me, his chubby cheeks and bright blue eyes betrayed nothing. He held out his little rubber ball to me. "For you," he said.

"Oh my god," I said. "Thank you." I knelt and reaching out to take the disgusting rubber ball that I in no way wanted to touch, then looked up at the woman he lagged behind. "He's yours?"

The woman shook her head.

"Oh," I said, turning to the angelic boy. "Where's your mommy?"

"She…" He looked down. His bottom lip quivered. His eyes moistened. "My mommy…" His face contorted into the pained look of one trying to keep themselves from completely breaking down into tears. "And then my daddy… the secbots…" the tears started flowing.

Somehow, his quivering lips and downturned eyebrows made him even cuter. For the first time in my life, I found myself opening my arms to a child not old enough to know any good curse words. He collapsed into my chest, his body heaving with sobs as he snottily wept into a shirt so expensive that the label expressly recommended not keeping it in the same mailcode as anyone under the age of 18.

"It's okay, little one," I said, patting his head. "It's okay. I've got you."

"You're being robbed," Sasha said.

That's when I felt it.

A little tug, too subtle for most to notice. If I hadn't spent a lifetime thieving and lying and running away, I wouldn't have felt a thing other than the adorable child's tears and my own quickly shifting opinions on motherhood.

Someone was pulling something from my back pocket. Right in front of Sasha's eyes, too.

In one swift motion, I shoved away the adorable child with one hand and reached behind my back with the other. My fingers found a small wrist, which I gripped hard.

"Yow!" said a small voice behind me. I stood up to see the other child we'd seen at the spaceport. She was of comparable adorability to the crying boy, and also wearing a turtleneck sweater. She was holding my wallet in the hand I'd grabbed. As if on command, tears welled in her eyes.

"You dwopped this," she said with an affected speech impediment.

"And you and your brother were secretly putting it back into her pocket?" Sasha said.

"Please, ma'am—we didn't mean to—"

Her brother burst into tears, screeching wails of remorse that all but deafened me.

"Kids," I said, "it's fine. Drop the act. I'm not angry."

As quickly as he'd started, the boy stopped crying. The little girl blinked the moisture from her eyes. I released her wrist and reached for the wallet, which she returned.

"I'm sorry," I said. "About your dad."

The girl hit me with a skeptical side-eye. "How do you know what happened to our dad?"

"I was there that day. He got caught trying to steal from me, too."

The little boy gulped.

"Don't worry," I said. "I'm a lot more forgiving than those secbots."

"What're your names?" Sasha asked.

"You're gonna rat us out to the secbots," the little girl said, suddenly capable of forming Rs.

"What? No," I said.

"We may be a lot of things, kid," Sasha said, "but narcs we are not."

"You're an Elite," her brother said, suddenly sounding a lot less adorable and a lot more murder-capable.

I smirked. "Yeah, but I'm one of the good ones." I took out what little cash I had in my wallet and handed it to the little girl.

She looked at the bills as if I might have laced them with poison. I waited, unmoving and unspeaking, until she snatched them from my hand.

"He's Face," she said, nodding at her brother. "I'm Pick."

I nodded, smiling. "Very descriptive. You come up with those yourself?"

She counted the bills. "Dad wasn't subtle," she said, and then completely failed to elaborate further.

Figured. A couple of kids no older than ten. A newly murdered parent. I knew the feeling.

"So, this is your usual gig?" Sasha asked. "Sneak in with the cleaners, help yourself to whatever you can find? Where's your bag? Plenty of liftable stuff here. You must have a…"

I saw a big bucket with a small mop sticking out of it, hidden behind a floor-standing vase. "Ah. That yours?"

"Uh, yeah," Pick said.

I walked over, grabbed the bucket, and shoved my hand into the soapy water. Inside, I was sure I'd find a sizable pile of our jewelry. It was the perfect place to hide loot: the grimy water was dark enough that you couldn't see through it, and rancid enough that nobody wealthy would ever want to get near it. "You can keep whatever you lifted," I said. "I'm just curious about what you…"

I pulled my hand out. I held nothing but suds.

"What, you tried to lift me before you scrubbed the rest of the house for loot? That's sloppy."

Pick squinted at me. "The only scrubbing we did was in your bathroom."

"I... wait. You didn't sneak in with the cleaners."

Pick shook her head.

"You *are* cleaners? You two kids?"

Face sneered. "Uh, how else are we gonna pay these off?" He and his sister pulled down their turtlenecks, revealing two metal collars reading, "debt cuff 4 kidz!" in bright, colorful lettering. "Got these for jaywalking out of the spaceport. So yeah, we clean, and we only steal from folks some of the time," Face said, nodding at my wallet.

"I don't..." I shook my head. This didn't make sense. "You're kids. How do you have debts?"

"Dad's a criminal. And dead. So his debt gets passed on to us." Pick shrugged.

Their father hadn't stolen our Vaultlander out of common greed. He'd intended to free his kids from wage slavery. And for that audacity he'd lost his head, and his kids had lost their remaining parent.

It wasn't fair. This damned planet was supposed to be civilized. Things were supposed to be different here.

I shook my head again. "Screw this," I said, tapping my wrist ECHO to their collars. I opened my bank account and initiated a transfer of the same amount as the cuffs' displayed debt ratings. A few million dollars later, the cuffs sprang open and the kids were debt-free.

Face and Pick stared at me as if I were an alien. Pick narrowed her eyes, searching for something to say... until she thought better of it. She grabbed her brother by the wrist and ran out the front door, probably afraid I'd change my mind and take the money back.

Sasha stood. "That's interesting," she said. I assumed at first she was referring to the kids, but she was staring at me. Everyone in the room was, in fact, including the other members of the cleaning service. A foyer full of tired eyes and hunched backs, of faces made long and sallow by years of too much work and not enough hope, all of them looking at Sasha and me with some combination of confusion, awe, and suspicion.

"Uh," I said, waving at an older woman weighed down by no fewer than four cuffs. "Could I pay those off? Your debts."

"You want to…" She pointed at the cuffs around her leg, all stacked one atop the other from ankle to knee.

"Yeah. Here, can I just—" I tapped my ECHO device against one of her cuffs. It snapped open with a digital trumpet fanfare.

"DEBT CLEARED!" shrieked a high-pitched digital voice.

A confused smile appeared on the woman's face as I moved to her other cuffs. Once I was done, I checked our remaining bank balance.

"So that's two million dollars of debt cleared. You were two million in the hole?" I asked the woman.

She nodded. "Student loans and compound interest. Real kick in the pants."

"Ooh, I never got to go to school," I said, trying to turn our conversation into something friendly and casual rather than the master-freeing-their-indentured-servants tone it was rapidly taking on. "What did you study?"

"Finance." She shrugged. "Life is like that."

"Right. Hey, everybody—come here." I beckoned the cleaners over and called out to the rest of our staff who kept the mansion running—the butlers, the groundskeepers, the electricians, the chocolatiers. They assembled on the stairway and formed neat lines, all leading to me and my big digital pile of nearly endless money. It felt like a Mercenary Day celebration.

"What are you doing?" Sasha asked. She looked at me the way a parent looks at a child who has just intentionally smothered themselves in peanut butter: bewildered, amused, but not hugely surprised.

I scratched my cheek. Truth be told, I had no idea what I was doing. I was just following an impulse. "Hell if I know," I said. "Trying not to be an asshole, I guess."

Smiling, she threw an arm around my neck. "I think it might be working."

I swallowed the instinct to respond with snark. Which was difficult. I'm very good at snark.

Sasha opened her ECHO device and joined me, tapping her wrist against every debt cuff in arm's reach. The tinny digital fanfare that celebrated a paid debt blared over and over again, but somehow we never quite got sick of it.

We spent the next hour paying off the debts of every cleaner and staff member in our employ ("Thank you, madam," Fitzwiggins drolly responded. "On my fragile joints, those cuffs were absolute… *murder*"). All told, it set us back about a hundred million dollars.

It felt good.

I looked at the assembled laborers as they rubbed the sore bands of skin where the cuffs had once constricted them, then turned to Sasha and lowered my voice. "Look, it's not Vault hunting and it's not going to be as satisfying as putting a bullet in Holloway, but there's probably some good we could do here. Without getting shot at."

Sasha scratched her neck. "Yeah. Okay, yeah." She cleared her throat to get the laborers' attention. "Anyone know how many folks still have debt on Eden-5? Or, like, roughly how much debt exists altogether on the planet?"

"Feels like something you could look up," one of them said.

"Feels like you assumed we'd be responsible for that labor because it's busywork," said another.

"I… Yep, fair enough. You're right. My bad." She tapped on her ECHO device and muttered something (I assume "I hate myself") under her breath.[21][22][23][24][25]

———

The cleaners went home and our staff, much to our surprise, stuck around. "Debt or no," Fitzwiggins said as he poured me a glass of wine, "we are not in the business of turning down a living wage."

Sasha and I crunched numbers in the lounge. Math has never been my strong suit, and I didn't get any better at it when the numbers we dealt with included multiple commas.

Sasha barely spoke for the rest of the night, she was so excited and focused on the task at hand. She scrolled through pages and pages of financial records, taking notes and recording trends. By god, she made a *spreadsheet*.

It took us an hour to total up all the publicly available debt information we found, and we didn't like what we saw. All told, the workers of Eden-5 owed about a hundred billion dollars—way, way more than we could ever hope to pay back.

"Could always invest," Sasha said. "Over time, we could turn a billion into a trillion, maybe. Vaughn told me he's got an algorithm," she said, referencing the Hyperion accountant we'd befriended on Pandora. "I think he said 'algorithm.' Or maybe it was 'a robot wearing a suit.' I wasn't listening. It'd take time, though. Years."

---

21 Also I know it's offensive to refer to the laborers as a big group without naming the individual people who spoke up, but I've read plenty of sci-fi novels where you read passages like "Grabdor and Marchiband turned to Cruel Pete and Seven-Murder Howie and said, 'Where has Esmerelda Backandforth gone to?'" and all the proper nouns just sort of bleed together and you have a hard time paying attention to what really matters in the scene. For what it's worth, later I learned all their names and learned what their kids are into and all that.
22 I know it's still problematic.
23 I also know me spending a full series of footnotes trying to excuse myself for my behavior is even more problematic. I'm from Pandora, where our main exports are violence and problematic language. We thought it was okay to call little murderers "m****t p****s" for way longer than we should have.
24 I know that's not an excuse, I just figured it would provide cultural context.
25 Good thing I didn't tell you the individual names of those laborers or I would have really broken up the flow of the story.

I scratched my head. "Assuming we both live seventy more years, we could retire right now with half a billion and still be safe. We could always use the rest to pay off as much debt as we could. Being half-billionaires wouldn't be so bad."

Sasha grunted in frustration. "You *still* wanna live here? That money could take us so much further on one of the border worlds. We never needed a half-billion bucks to survive before."

"I mean, yeah," I said, grimacing, "but do you really wanna go back to that? After living like *this?*" I gestured vaguely at the grandeur of our home.

"I could live with it."

"Yeah, but we'd only *need* a billion to live the rest of our lives like this," I said.

A glittering sapphire kitten leaped onto my lap. I'd bought it a couple weeks back. It purred, then tried to leap onto a bookshelf but mistimed the jump, fell to the floor, and shattered into a thousand crystalline pieces, which a platinum-plated robovac then cleaned up.

Sasha looked at me, lips pursed.

"Well. Maybe 'need' is the wrong word," I said.

———

Three hours later, I heard sounds of violence coming from the ECHOsim chamber. Sasha never could sleep when something was on her mind. Three hundred million digistruct emitters dotted the walls, floor, and ceiling of the room, projecting real-in-every-way-except-for-smell-but-who-cares-about-smell images, sounds, and sensations to the active player. Or players, as the case proved when I walked in on her cutting down a wave of monstrous holographic chess pieces with her cyberscythe.

"I've got an idea," I said.

"Hit me with it," she said. "I've been trying to clear my head with ECHOsims, but it hasn't been working."

A booming voice proclaimed, "PLAYER TWO DETECTED." A cyberscythe digistructed into my hand.

"I AM DEATH," bellowed the game's narrator. "CAN YOU BEAT ME AT CHESS AND ACHIEVE… THE SEVENTH STEEL?!"

Another horde of man-sized chess pieces galloped toward us. I bisected one with my digital blade and stood back to back with Sasha as the others circled us.

"So I was thinking," I said, decapitating a zombie pawn whose laser eyes continued to fire even as his head spun from his neck. "We don't have money to free everyone from their debts."

"Correct," Sasha replied, disemboweling a sentient-meat rook.

"But if we pooled together a portion of our money with all the other fifty or so billionaire families on the planet, we could wipe out the debts pretty easily," I said, dodging a laser blast from a demon knight that traveled along an L-shaped trajectory.

"Do we… Do we think that's something anyone will actually agree to?" Sasha asked, rolling away from a queen's grenade.

"I wasn't sure," I said, "so I picked a random billionaire out of the social media feed and sent them a direct message asking if they'd like to donate a portion of their wealth to end poverty. This was their response." I tapped the ECHO device on my wrist and projected an image of the front page of today's Eden-5 *Herald Tribune*. "ENTIRE BILLIONAIRE FAMILY DIES OF LAUGHTER," the headline read.

"Yikes," Sasha replied, scanning the article as a robo-bishop diagonally slashed at her with its lava-staff. "Even the dog, huh? Well, at least you tried."

"I did. Just me. One person. But if the Elites of Eden-5 thought they were giving money to a charitable cause—one run by two immigrants, granted, but very rich immigrants who told them what they wanted to hear…"

Sasha sheathed her cyberscythe and turned to face me, squinting. A cyborg queen rammed into her back and killed her with one hit. "PLAYER ONE DOWN," the game shouted.

"You want to grift the richest people on the planet? And then give their money to the people they're keeping in debt slavery?"

"No," I said. "I want *us* to grift the richest people on—"

Sasha crossed her arms and cocked her head. "I thought the whole point of getting out of the con game was to… get out of the con game. You sure we wouldn't just be better off heading to Rustville? We could bankroll Gaige's whole vengeance thing."

"Too risky. No guarantee Gaige will come through, or that they couldn't trace it back to us even if she did." I took her by the shoulders. "Look. You know we can do this. It'd just be this one final con job."

"We already did our one final job."

"This will be our final final job."

"Hmm," Sasha said.

A horde of knee-high pawns chomped away the last of my health. "YOU LOSE!" the game bellowed. As Sasha shook her head and smiled, though, I knew the game had it backward.

27
FIONA

Orchestral music wafted through the halls of our palatial estate. Butlers milled around the house carrying trays of the most delicious morsels of food they could assemble. I wore a strapless dress that made my shoulder blades look like lethal weapons. The crème de la crème canoodled and hobnobbed within the halls of our home, eating our canapés and snickering at our taste in art.[26]

This was the scene at the first annual "Eden-5, Eden-First" Charity Gala, sponsored and hosted by Sasha and yours truly. She wore a tuxedo that put most of the men to shame and carried around a big symbolic glass jar full of cash.

"Give 'til it hurts!" Sasha called out, hoisting the jar above her head. "Keep Eden-5 Eden-First!" The rhyme and rhythm weren't perfect, but it was an easy enough slogan to chant at tipsy oligarchs.

While being extremely well dressed, I fashionably descended the main staircase and began my sartorially stupendous circle around the room. I'm not gonna belabor the fact any more, but if

---

26 Loving illustrations of cartoon boys with great abs was apparently considered passé on this planet.

there's one thing that matters, it's that my dress looked *really good* at this stupid fake gala.

I had no experience of hosting parties or acting rich, but I tried my best. A woman wearing a death-peacock feather boa laughed uproariously at a joke I didn't catch. I touched her on the shoulder and said, "I love your feathers. They look very expensive on you."

A huge smile appeared on her face. "Thank you," she sang, her voice dripping with old money. "You are our hostess, are you not?"

"I am," I said, trying my best to nod humbly while still looking terribly generous. "It's a cause I've been passionate about ever since my childhood on Pandora."

The peacock woman gasped and clutched her not-insignificant bosom. "You're from Pandora? I'd no idea! How ever did you get out?"

I bowed my head in a practiced display of humility, sadness, and determination. "Hard work," I said. "I saved and I scraped and I did whatever it took to get my sister and I off that bandit-infested hellhole. And I just…" A tasteful hint of moisture in the eye, quickly sniffed away. "It disturbs me to see Eden-5 potentially heading in the same direction. Unless we crack down on the incredible number of Rustvillian miscreants in this city, soon they'll be arming themselves. Forming bandit clans. Screaming about the things they'd like to do to, and with, different types of meat. That's why my sister and I started this charity in the first place. Could I… I'm so sorry, ma'am, I didn't get your name."

"Belinda Billingsworth," she said, extending a hand. I couldn't decide whether to shake it or kiss it, so I did both. Apparently this was the wrong move done in the right way, because she immediately blushed.

"Oh, madam, you're going to make my husband jealous," she said, fanning herself. She nodded across the room at a small man who appeared to be at least seventy percent mustache. He was climbing up one of the servers like they were a tree, his grubby hands clawing at the hors d'oeuvres on their platter. As I watched him slam a chocosteak into his gaping maw and lick his handlebar with voracious glee, I knew he had never been within three miles of satisfying a woman.

"Oh, a little jealousy never hurt anyone," I said. "On the contrary, it gets the blood pumping." I turned to grab a pair of drinks from a passing server, giving Belinda a quick glance at my exposed back. I heard a quick intake of breath from behind me. She was on the hook; I just needed to reel her in.

"As I was saying," I said, handing her a drink and "accidentally" brushing her finger in the process, "could I put you down for a donation?"

"I don't know," she said, stealing a glance at her tiny goblin of a husband. "Martin typically handles expenses and… What would the donations be going toward, exactly?"

"Increased funding for secbots, of course—more weapons, more upgrades. In order to prevent Eden-5's poor population from sliding down the slippery slope into banditry, we'll also be spending the money in Rustville to build new schools."

She grimaced.

"Community centers?" I offered.

She grimaced deeper.

"Prisons," I ventured.

She smiled.

"With big bars," I exclaimed.

Belinda closed her eyes and nodded. "I think you and I share a vision for this world. Let me get my ECHObook from my husband."

Belinda walked away. I looked at her butt in case she glanced over her shoulder, which she did.

I waved Sasha over. "How much have we raised so far?"

"Little under twenty percent of what we need."

"So, twenty billion?"

"I know. We should have been running scams like this the whole time!"

"No kidding. Still not good enough, though," I said.

"I think we need to scare them more," Sasha said. "Tell more stories about Pandora. Show 'em your scars. Wait—how quickly do you think we could get somebody to dress up like a bandit? We could lock 'em up in a cage and have him throw cups of pee at people. 'This is your future if you don't act now' kinda thing."

For the first time in weeks, I saw the spark return to Sasha's eyes. We were doing it—grifting, getting paid—but we were doing it for more than just a hot meal and a soft bed. Huge payday, a good cause, and no risk of violence. Even if these walking cash boxes figured out where the money was actually going, it's not like they could do anything about it; Holloway's class solidarity ceasefire ensured that the worst revenge we'd have to suffer would be a dearth of invitations to dinner parties.

"I like where your head's at," I said. "Maybe for the next gala."

Belinda returned, her husband's crumb-flecked digital checkbook in hand. She drank in the image of Sasha and me, and somehow seemed thirstier for having done so.

"Mrs. Billingsworth, allow me to introduce my sister, Sasha."

Sasha nodded with a practiced combination of polite humility and moral superiority.

I said, "I was just informing Sasha of your generous donation. Sasha, she wishes to pay by ECHOcheck, so—"

"Of course," Sasha said, pulling back her sleeve to access her ECHOdeck. This is how most of the Elites paid, of course, but the sight of a small girl holding a big bucket of money got people in the right frame of mind.

"I was thinking something in the… three billion range," Belinda said, finger hovering over the ECHObook.

"Six billion?" Sasha exclaimed, wonderment in her eyes. "What incredible generosity!"

"But I said—"

"I agree, sister," I exclaimed. "Six billion! So generous. Thank you *so* much, Mrs. Billingsworth."

Belinda stared at us a moment longer then smiled through clenched teeth. "Anything to keep Eden-5 Eden-First, of course."

"What a lovely slogan," a familiar voice boomed from upstairs. Sasha and I whipped our heads around in confusion.

There she stood, in a dress even more tasteful than mine, a smile already spreading across her face. Countess Holloway descended our staircase, flanked by secbots on either side.

"I… How did she…" Sasha stuttered.

"Countess Holloway!" I gushed. "I didn't see you come in."

"You'd have me make my grand entrance at the *front* door? What am I, a plumber?"

It was only then that I realized the room had gone silent, except for the clicking of Holloway's expensive heels against the hardwood steps. She towered above me, even after having dismounted the staircase. Her dress was so ravishing it made me look like a lightly used pile of skag vomit.

"Either way," I said, "I'm so glad you could make it."

"That makes one of us," she said, still smiling. She placed a hand on my shoulder. "Now, by all means, don't let me interrupt. Give me the pitch! Tell me why you deserve more of my money. Tell everyone, in fact—you've got their attention."

"I…" This was a trap somehow. I knew it, and Sasha's hand around my wrist told me she knew it too. "You haven't even gotten a refreshment. Please, let me—"

"I thirst only for an explanation," she said. "Of why you want this money, for starters. Or perhaps why you've chosen to live here, among the Elites, in the first place. It's a bit odd, you stepping so far outside of your financial lane. I don't sashay into Rustville and eat dirt sandwiches just to fit in with the other vagrants, do I?"

Laughter swept through the room, loud and genuine, the kind that blasted away all pretense at politeness, every pasted-on smile. It was as if a roomful of adults were watching a child pretend to throw a dinner party, all of them nodding and playing along until the child slipped and fell into a pile of skag feces. They couldn't help but laugh. They'd eat my food and make small talk, but the guests knew I'd never be one of them.

Fine. I'd seen that coming. As long as they paid up, they could think I was a circus animal for all I cared. That didn't upset me.

I wasn't upset.

I gestured at the band. "Keep the music going, if you would—"

Something smooth struck me in the face. For a split second I thought someone had tossed a baby at me underhand until I realized that was what it felt like to be slapped by Countess Holloway. Either the billionaire nonviolence pact didn't apply to mild assault or, despite the contents of my checking account, they didn't consider me a true billionaire. Sasha's grip went tight around my wrist. My blood ran hot.

"Look at your betters when they address you," she said, which was when Countess Holloway learned what it's like to be punched in two separate parts of your body at the same time: my fist to her cheek, Sasha's fist to her knee. (Sasha would have had to, at minimum, stood up on her tiptoes in order to reach Holloway's face, and nobody looks cool on tiptoe.)

Before you assume my temper got the better of me, understand that the punches were a tactical decision. The moment Holloway had glided down our stairs, dozens of our guests had averted their eyes. Not out of respect, or shame, but out of fear. They knew she could hurt them far more than I ever could.

The moment Holloway began to criticize our shindig was the moment I began to lose the high ground. They wouldn't give me another cent so long as Holloway looked invincible. And punches to the face and knee will make anyone look vincible.

I'd also wanted to punch her, of course.

Holloway dropped to one knee and clutched at her jaw.

The guests gasped, as I'd assumed they would. I heard mutterings. "Uncivilized." "Barbaric." That was fine. Some would side with Holloway. But there were others—ones that *weren't* muttering loud enough for Holloway to hear—whom I saw smiling behind their champagne flutes.

Holloway's two secbots instantly switched to defensive mode, their ocular beam cannons focused on Sasha and me.

"HOW DARE YOU? FIRING—"

Holloway stood in one fluid motion, raising a hand to stop them.

"Oh, don't be so dramatic," she said. "Our friendly neighborhood Pandorans just let their tempers get the better of them. They can't help it." She stroked my cheek. "It's in their blood." The placid grin on her face betrayed no evidence of any reaction to our physical altercation. I didn't understand. She should have been switching tactics. She could have played the victim or feigned an injury. Even letting her bots blast me would have made sense. But no, she had the same look of smug satisfaction that had turned much of the room against her.

She had nothing to be smug about—or did she? I had to be missing something, something important. But what?

"Now," she said, taking a drink from a nearby waiter, "what is this… charity for?"

I took a drink for myself. "The Eden-5 Eden-First fund. To keep our home—"

"*Our* home," she said, raising a finger. "*You* are an outsider."

I took a sip of million-dollar champagne and tried to maintain my calm. "To keep *this planet* from turning into another Pandora. By preventing crime and banditry before it starts."

"Hmm," Holloway said, putting a finger to her chin. "I think I preferred the other way you put it." She tapped on her ECHO. "Let me just broadcast this onto the nearest screen... Oh." She frowned. "You don't even have a wallscreen in your foyer? Good lord, do you micturate in a bucket as well? No matter. I'll just send it to everyone's ECHO devices."

She tapped a button and suddenly my voice was blaring from everyone's wrist.

"If the Elites of Eden-5 thought they were giving money to a charitable cause—one run by two immigrants, granted, but very *rich* immigrants who knew how to tell them what they wanted to hear..."

The air vanished from the room. Sasha and I had had this conversation in the ECHOsim room.

"You want to grift the richest people on the planet? Give their money to the people they're keeping in debt slavery?" Sasha's voice, clear as day.

The room exploded with disgust—groans, cursing, the smashing of champagne flutes on the floor.

An elderly man with a goatee shouted, "If I wanted to make sure my money ended up in Rustville, I'd stuff hundred-dollar bills into my toilet!"

"What is this, space-communism?" another billionaire asked.

Sasha gingerly tapped her ECHO. "They're retracting the donations," she sighed. "All of them."

Belinda shot me a hateful stare. "I can't believe I was going to sleep with you," she said.

"You still want to," I replied.

"I know," she said, a look of self-disgust on her face.

Holloway put a hand in front of her mouth to stifle her laughter. "I'll say one thing for Claptrap—he's a great listener."

The Vaultlander. She'd bugged it. Of course. Holloway saw me put it all together and shot me an exaggerated frown. "Oh dear. You didn't think I *really* believed you shot at me out of financial jealousy, did you? I suspected you were responsible for the Vault Hunter's escape. I just needed to be sure."

I fumed silently. The billionaires were already making their way to the door.

"Wait," Holloway said, waving an arm at the dispersing guests. "Don't leave yet or you'll miss the best part. As I said, I wanted to know if these two would-be conwomen knew the whereabouts of my daughter's murderer. And they did not disappoint."

Our ECHO comms barked to life again. This time, Sasha's voice: "You sure we wouldn't just be better off heading to Rustville? We could bankroll Gaige's whole vengeance thing."

I didn't understand why Holloway looked so smug. Rustville was a big town. It wasn't like we'd given her the coordinates of Gaige's hideout.

"Esteemed Elites, please, do not boo these poor Pandoran miscreants," Holloway said. "They've done us a great service. They've not only pinpointed the city in which a deadly murderer resides, but they've also highlighted a glaring flaw in our way of life."

The Elites exchanged glances. Sasha nodded toward the staircase. If this got violent, we'd need the guns stashed in our bedrooms. With the crowd's attention on Holloway at the front door, we slunk toward the staircase as quietly as we could.

"Sooner or later, someone—possibly someone more subtle and less odorous than our dear hosts—could very well pay off all our laborers' debts. Why? Because we've allowed them too much luxury. They have roofs over their heads. Food in their bellies. They've forgotten what it is to *struggle* for work. To *need* it.

"And so," she said, pulling a large remote control from her clutch, "we have two birds. I present to you: the stone."

And with that, she pressed a button.

28
GAIGE

The girl looked at the only person in the galaxy she cared about, though "person" was perhaps a stretch. A robot. Though even "robot" was a stretch, as the collection of disassembled parts and inactive circuits could only become a functional automaton given time and repairs, but at the moment it was only one step above being scrap.

"Gaige here," she said into her ECHO device, which transmitted her voice to the subscribers she had amassed through a lifetime of highly entertaining violence. "After a brief detour, your girl is back on task and itching for some revenge.

"Took the better part of a day to blast my way through the tech neighborhood and liberate the parts of my perfect, innocent child, but I've finally got everything I need: my disassembled Deathtrap, my brains, and enough loose shotgun shells that I could bury Holloway in them instead of shooting them at her.

"Utami_Rulez wants to know why my face is wet and if I've been crying. Great question, Utami_Rulez. Not gonna answer it, but I love the question. Very insightful. Next question is from—"

The girl did not get the chance to read the next question[27] because at that exact moment, the world exploded.

In one moment, she was safe in the basement of a Rustville tavern. In the next, the tavern no longer existed. The ceiling above her—the tavern's first floor—was incinerated in an instant. She was rendered temporarily deaf as the loudest noise she'd ever heard—not an explosion but a sustained, spiteful electronic scream—drowned out everything else.

Once she'd recovered from the shockwave of sound and fire, she didn't hesitate. She scooped armfuls of the scrap metal that was once her best friend into an oversized, patched bag until it was stuffed full of robot parts, metal limbs ripping the canvas and poking out at inconvenient angles. The basement caught fire around her. Sweat poured down her forehead, mixing with her tears. She did not hesitate for an instant or leave a single piece of the robot behind.

The Vault Hunter took the burning stairs to the flaming cellar door three at a time, her metallic fist thrust forward like a battering ram. The door exploded outward in fiery splinters as she ran through it, her gait slowing only for a moment. That moment was just enough to save her life.

Two steps in front of her, close enough that she could touch it, a white-hot beam of energy incinerated the ground, so big it took up her peripheral vision, so bright she had to shut her eyes and run in the opposite direction.

When it was safe to open her eyes just a crack, she watched the laser beam obliterate Rustville. In a matter of minutes, a raggedy town of the desperate and dispossessed was transformed into flames and scorch marks. Charred corpses lined the burnt vestiges

---

27 Which was, not that it matters, "Do u have a fav meme and if so which one?"

of what were once bustling streets. The screams of the survivors were barely audible over the roar of the space laser.

Even louder than the laser, however, was the message that boomed through the air, seemingly originating from the sky itself.

"Hello, people of Rustville."

Gaige recognized the voice. She grunted the name in rage: *Holloway.*

"It is my understanding that a fugitive is hiding somewhere in your delightful little neighborhood. I apologize for the reconfiguration of your homes and businesses, but there's no telling which one my daughter's murderer might be hiding in. You understand."

The beam crawled across the town, leaving smoke and debris in its wake. Buildings melted and collapsed, the orbital laser turning Rustville's meager buildings into pools of liquid metal and smashed concrete.

Gaige opened her ECHO device. Her fingers flew over the buttons as she turned off her location jammer. She brought the wrist-mounted device to her lips.

"I give up," she said. "Stop this."

The voice in the sky replied with a noise Gaige didn't recognize at first. It sounded like a distant roar. It was only once the laser had stopped—once the apocalyptic soundscape had been replaced with an equally horrible quiet—that she could make out the noise.

Laughter. The smooth, haughty laughter of dozens and dozens of billionaires.

"Oh, Gaige," Holloway said, herself barely holding back guffaws. "You can do better than that."

"Make her beg!" a distant voice shouted.

"No, better yet, give a billion dollars to any Ruster who can take her down!" another yelled. Their voices dripped with money and spite. So many of them, all cackling and celebrating as Rustville burned around her. She couldn't even pick out Holloway's voice from the cacophony.

"You're right," Gaige hissed. "I can do better. See, I was gonna just kill you. But I was stupid."

"Oh, you can say that again," Holloway said, suppressing a giggle.

"I was stupid because you're just a part of the problem. I should have blasted holes into every single one of you aristocratic shits the second I stepped off my transport."

"Probably," Holloway agreed. "It's far too late now, I'm afraid. A detachment of my security forces is tracking your ECHO frequency as we speak. They will find you with your hands on your head and your pockets empty, or I will turn the laser back on. Can your tiny Vault-addled brain comprehend that? Say, 'Yes, Countess Holloway.'"

"Yes."

"That's not what I told you. Say it or I turn the laser back on."

The girl stepped back to the cellar entrance and dropped the bag of robot parts down the stairs. Then she turned around, pulled her shotgun from her shoulder holster, and threw it down on the charred ground in front of her. The twinkling shoulder lights of the secbots were already pinpricks in the distance, growing brighter every second.

Gaige fell to her knees and put her hands on her head.

"Yes, Countess Holloway. I surrender."

29
FIONA,

SEVERAL MINUTES EARLIER

Something very, very bad was about to happen. A moment after Holloway pressed the button on her remote, the ECHO devices of everyone in the room blinked on. Each of them projected a grainy top-down image of Rustville: satellite footage. Hundreds of small, glowing blue dots moved around the city at an unhurried pace.

Then the laser fired.

A white-hot beam of death crawled across the town, leaving smoke and debris in its wake.

The blue dots scurried away from it as fast as they could. Some of them didn't move fast enough.

"Guns," Sasha said. "Now."

"Took the words right out of my mouth," I said, and we sprinted up the stairs.

"Stop them, obviously," Holloway laughed to her secbots. She didn't even raise her voice. They zoomed to the top of the stairs, one stopping me and Sasha in our tracks while the other dropped down behind us, digiclaws out, lasers heating up.

"No need to run, ladies," Holloway said. "Watch the show.

Watch what you've wrought." She pressed a button on her ECHO and her voice became audible through the ECHOfeed.

"Hello, people of Rustville. It is my understanding that a fugitive is hiding somewhere in your delightful little neighborhood. I apologize for the reconfiguration of your homes and businesses, but there's no telling which one my daughter's murderer might be hiding in. You understand."

We couldn't get to our armory—neither Sasha nor I could win a fistfight against a secbot. But maybe we didn't need to.

I planted my foot on the banister and leaped off the staircase. Sasha followed my lead, barely dodging two secbot swipes in the process. I hit the ground hard, did my best to roll through it, and got to my feet. "Move!" I shouted at the guests, who completely ignored me.

Sasha and I shoved our way through the crowd toward Holloway as the orbital beam continued to turn Rustville to ash. The secbots pursued us from behind, moving the guests aside carefully and delicately.

More blue dots blinked away as the laser passed over them. Fitzwiggins stood by the kitchen, watching the feed with his mouth agape. Belinda leaned over and asked him if he had any more canapés.

Holloway was nearly in arm's reach. I shoved two bodies out of my way and lunged at her. She didn't even flinch, just kept looking at me with amusement, even as I grabbed her by the neck. "Nobody moves or I squeeze!" I shouted, moving to her back to keep her body between the secbots and me.

I pulled the remote from her hands. Dozens of multicolored lights and buttons stared back at me, none of them labeled.

"Uh, Sasha?" I asked, looking at her for guidance. She shook her head, as clueless as I was.

"Go ahead," Holloway said. "See if you can figure out how to turn it off. Everyone, let's take bets on how long it'll take the Pandoran imbeciles to figure out an orbital-laser control system, hmm?"

The room erupted into laughter.

"I give up," Gaige said over the ECHO. "Stop this."

Holloway beamed.

I pressed every button I could. The laser got bigger, then changed color, then the remote played dramatic music to accompany the destruction, but no combination of button presses would turn the damned thing off.

Holloway held out her hand for the remote. I had to hope she'd stick to her word. Gaige had surrendered. She'd have to turn off the laser.

I gave it back to her, utterly helpless. The room exploded in applause and laughter. My grip went limp and she gently removed my hand from her neck. I was too numb to do anything but stand there and gape like an idiot. She didn't even tell her secbots to attack us.

After she and the other billionaires had exchanged a few more words with Gaige, she switched off the feed. The room once again erupted in applause.

"Don't worry, my sweet," she whispered in my ear. "You're in no danger. The look on your faces is punishment enough. That's something you Pandorans can never understand. Killing someone? That's easy. But beating them? Ohhh… that, my dear, is *ambrosia*."

I reached out for Sasha's hand. I felt rudderless and furious and scared and sad, and I needed my sister. She took my hand and we squeezed so hard our knuckles went white.

"Fraud is taken quite seriously on Eden-5, you'll find," Holloway said. "The central bank will be forced to seize your assets, I expect. Perhaps, before that happens, you could sell this hovel and make enough for a couple of tickets off-planet, hmm? Just something to consider. Now, I'm off to put Gaige's little robot together to figure out how it works. Right before I do the exact opposite to her."

She threw us one last grin before disappearing into the crowd of cheering billionaires, who followed her out through the front doorway as our ECHO devices vibrated with notifications. When the banks opened tomorrow morning, our accounts would be as empty as our manor.

I felt myself fall to the floor. I don't know how long I stayed there, staring at the hem of my impeccably tailored dress, thinking and feeling nothing at all. By the time I noticed my legs falling asleep, the party was over and the house was empty save for Sasha and me.

We'd lost. Worse than we'd ever lost before. Most of Rustville was a flaming ruin. Dozens if not hundreds of its people were incinerated.

Because of us. Because of *me*.

I should have let Sasha kill her.

My feet carried me up to my bedroom and the small armory contained there. I grabbed the biggest assault rifle I could find and met Sasha on the stairs as she sprinted from her own bedroom. In her arms, she carried the contents of our first-aid station: a couple of med-hypos and a few spools of bandages.

"What are you… What's that for?" she asked, pointing at my gun.

"Guess."

"You wanna kill Holloway? We've got other stuff to deal with first, Fi. You don't even have a plan."

"I'm gonna find my way inside her estate, and then I'm gonna move as many bullets from this gun into her face as I can."

"That's not a plan, that's an epitaph." Sasha placed the medical supplies she'd been carrying on the floor, then placed her hand on my arm. I fought an instinct to step away.

"Right now," she said, "there are people in Rustville who need help. You can start a fight with the billionaire and her robot army later."

"I'm not starting a f—"

"You're literally loading a gun."

"No, I'm not."

I looked down into my hands. I was.

"I'm barely loading a gun," I said.

I allowed her to remove the gun from my hands gently. "Rustville needs help. We can worry about Holloway later. There something we need to talk about, Fi?"

"No," I said.

"This morning you ate a waffle that kills one percent of the people who taste it from pure serotonin overload. And we just watched a lot of innocent people die because of us. But right now…" I couldn't tell whether Sasha looked impressed or horrified. "Right now, you look more excited than I've seen you in a month."

This was nonsense. I wanted to scream. I wanted to cry. I wanted to grab Holloway by the throat and hurl us both off a very tall bridge. My heart raced, my hands were balled into tight, furious fists, and I wanted to do something reckless and dangerous.

I wasn't *excited*. That flutter in my stomach, that feeling that made me want to stand on the balls of my feet and run flat out for as long as I could, that fire in my veins, that wasn't *excitement*. It couldn't be. What kind of a person would feel excited after witnessing Holloway's cruelty?

A Vault Hunter.

"I just hate waffles, okay?" I grunted, grabbing a handful of medical supplies and stuffing them into a bag before heading toward the front door. "I'll head for the west side of Rustville, you take the east."

"We really shouldn't split up!" Sasha yelled after me. "And nobody hates waffles!" was the last thing I heard as I slammed the front door and walked out into the night.

30
FIONA

I expected the worst. Rustville did not disappoint.

I trudged around twisted steel, glowing red with heat. A blizzard of ash threatened to bury me under a blanket of gray noise. Everywhere I turned, people searched through melted metal for their loved ones. Mothers screamed the names of family members they couldn't account for. The moans of the injured and the wails of the mourning served as a constant soundtrack. I waded through it all with a handful of bandages and pockets full of painkillers, an idiot trying to clean up an ocean of blood with a couple of wet sponges.

Sasha was right. I should have stuck with her. I hadn't realized it at the time, but as I walked through the smoking, screaming remains of Rustville, I knew why I'd stormed out on my own: I was embarrassed.

Back on Pandora, I'd prided myself on my ability to stay cool under pressure. So what if the mark recognizes me from a different con? I'll just spin him a yarn about my identical twin sister. Oh, the bandit lord's sent a goliath after us? No big deal—I'll grab a can opener for his helmet.

It's different, though, when you're the one responsible for all the bloodshed. Sasha and I had spent our lives on the backfoot.

Typically, we were the ones avoiding the gunfire at all costs, not causing it. But the first time—the very *first* time—I tried to make things better for other people, this is how it ended up.

A scream snapped me to my senses. Not a howl of pain but a shriek of terror, the kind that told me if I didn't act fast, there'd be at least one more casualty today.

A river of filth ran through the center of Rustville. Far above it, supported by a dozen tall pillars running along each side of it, rested a loose collection of cobblestones and mortar that might have once been called a bridge.

I started to run until the pain in my ankles reminded me I still had heels on. I took them off, shoved them into my bag with the medical supplies, and booked it for the bridge. If Holloway's laser had so much as grazed it, it was exceedingly likely that the entire thing—and anyone on it—would soon be plummeting to a noxious, lethal end.

I turned a corner and stepped onto the bridge. No laser burns— Holloway's weapon had missed it entirely. I breathed a sigh of relief.

I sucked the sigh of relief back into my lungs when I saw two men hoisting a third over the unprotected side of the bridge. The wind whipped back their matted hair as their victim dangled helplessly over a lethal drop into human filth.

"I don't have anything!" the man shrieked. It was the same voice I'd heard a few moments ago.

One of his assailants, a man with bugged-out eyes and breath I could almost smell from across the bridge, turned to his partner and said, "Guess he drops, then, doesn't he?"

The other mugger, a waif with a dog collar around his neck and hair in all the places there shouldn't be hair, giggled. "Guess he does."

"Let me go!" the dangling man pleaded. "My house… I need to check on—"

The dog-collar waif cackled. "Oh, what? Some rich lady blasts half the town and you think that, what, we'd put a moratorium on muggings? Space laser or no space laser, a man's gotta eat."

The trio still hadn't noticed me. I pulled my heels from the bag and considered my approach. They were pretty preoccupied with the mugging—I could sneak up on them. Ultimately, though, there are few things noisier than the sound of a person trying to be stealthy. I ran toward them at full speed, my bare feet slapping against the stones.

I got halfway to closing the distance between us when they dropped him off the bridge.

"Everything I got goes into the cuffs! What makes you think—" was the last thing I heard him say before they let go. My momentum and anger carried me forward anyway, and I shoulder-checked the hairy one in the small of his back. He barely had time to grunt before he was off the side of the edge, plummeting down to a river of blood and sludge.

His bug-eyed friend turned and tried to draw a knife, but I already had my weapons in hand. I boxed his head with my shoes, the force of the heels on each temple dropping him to the ground instantly.

"Help!" a voice yelled. I leaned over the side of the bridge. The man they'd dropped was holding onto a jutting piece of cobblestone by his fingertips, which were white with tension.

"The cuffs," he said. "I… can't support… the weight."

I understood why. The poor guy had at least three on each leg, all threatening to pull him down from the bridge and send him plummeting to the bottom of the stinky abyss beneath him.

"Hold on!" I yelled. I dropped my shoes onto the cobblestones and found footholds in the decaying side of the bridge. I lowered myself down as he groaned with pain, the wind buffeting him as he struggled to keep a hold on his cobblestone lifeline.

I climbed down toward him as fast as I could. There wasn't enough room for me to descend the support pillar he was holding onto, so I climbed down the one next to it. For what I had in mind, I didn't need to support his weight entirely; I just needed a second or two of direct contact with his legs.

I descended further. My head and arms were roughly level with his legs.

"I need you to swing toward me," I said, nodding at the ECHO on my wrist. "I'll get the cuffs off."

"I can't," he moaned. "Tell my… Hell, I don't have anybody who'd care about my last words."

"Stop it. Swing toward me, I'll stretch out and transfer the funds to your cuffs. Then you can climb up yourself without the weight. Okay?"

The man grunted in pain, but he nodded anyway. "Okay. Here we go," he said. Gritting his teeth, he swayed his legs away from me. Then toward me. Then away. Swing by swing, he gained momentum. Every time he swung toward me, I dug my fingers into the crumbling mortar of the bridge with one hand and stretched my other out as far as I could.

My wrist. His legs. That's all that needed to touch. I'd already primed the ECHO to transfer a couple million dollars to the next cuff it touched. All our cash would be gone by tomorrow morning anyway, so why not go on a spending spree now?

He swung toward me. My fingertips brushed his ankle.

"Little more," I said. "Almost there."

"I'm losing my grip!" he cried.

"No, you're not. Swing further. Come on!"

He grunted in pain again as he pushed his screaming muscles, and I leaned out as far as I could, the fingers anchoring me to the bridge growing sweatier and weaker by the second. But I had to try. I couldn't just—

The *click* of a debt cuff brought a flush of relief I'd never thought possible. One of his weights tumbled from his leg. After far, far too long, the cuff hit the river with a distant splash.

"Yes!" I shouted. "We've got this! Just a few more to go!"

For the first time, the man turned his head to look at me.

He didn't have to say a word for me to understand what was about to happen. His eyes were too tired. He'd already given up, even if he hadn't let go yet. He was about to drop no matter what I did. My stomach dropped. My blood ran cold.

"Nononono, *come on!* Just a few more!"

He slowly shook his head from side to side. "Too many. Too tired. I'm sorry."

And with that, his fingers failed him. He fell.

He didn't scream. But I did. Don't know why. From anger, maybe. Or sadness, or guilt. All I know is my throat felt hoarse and my cheeks were wet and warm when I climbed back onto the top of the bridge.

I was so distracted that I didn't wonder why the bug-eyed mugger was gone until he leaped from behind a light pole and sliced at me with a rusted knife. The blade cut through the strap of my medical bag, sending it and its contents tumbling over the parapet. He slashed again, cutting a jagged tear through my dress and the soft flesh beneath it. I felt the hot sting of pain before adrenaline took over and I forced the wound (and the multiple diseases it'd probably just given me) out of my mind.

I flicked my wrist forward, expecting the familiar weighty slide of a pistol into my hand. It never came.

"Ah," I said.

"You killed Bert," he said.

"I know," I said, and broke his nose with my palm.

For those who haven't been in one before, here's how a knife fight works if you're not the one with the knife. First, the guy with the knife lunges at you. Then, he cuts you a few times as you wrench the knife out of his hands. You disable him and walk away. Ten minutes later, you bleed to death.

Unless you've got a gun or are wearing a suit of armor, that's how it goes every single time. Knives move too damned fast and cut too damned easily; you can't disarm somebody who's holding one unless you're ready to get stabbed or sliced at least a half-dozen times in the process. Which wouldn't have been such a big deal if I hadn't just lost all my medical supplies to a river of crap.

The mugger doubled over, his broken face in his hand. I could have shoved him off the bridge just like his friend. I could have run. Either option would have let me avoid a knife fight. But I was in a very bad mood, so instead I grabbed my discarded heels and told him I was ready whenever he was.

He stared at me in bloody-faced confusion for a full second before he lunged. I stepped to the side and brought one of the shoes down as hard as I could. The heel tip sank into the meat of his hand and stuck there. I hoped the pain would be enough to force him to drop the knife, but we can't always get what we want. I pulled the heel out as he swiped the knife toward me. I didn't feel the blade cut into me, but I heard another rip of my dress and felt something warm and wet running down my leg.

Two cuts I can take, I thought. *Any more than that and I'm headed straight for bleedout city.*

He raised the knife high and stabbed downward again. I raised one heel to block the blade, which he drove clean through the shoe and into the palm of my hand.

"Ow," I said.

On the upside, his knife was trapped. Once I'd jammed the spike of my other heel into his exposed neck, there wasn't much he could do other than fall to the ground and make gurgling noises.

I know you're not supposed to remove knives or bullets from the wounds they create. I know they can cause more damage on the way out than on the way in. Even so, I wasn't going to walk around Rustville with a damned blade clean through my hand. I yanked it out and screamed again... Partly in pain but mainly because of the small fountain of blood that spurted from the open wound.

In that moment, I realized two things. Firstly, that if I didn't get medical care, I was going to bleed to death. And secondly, that the man I'd just killed was also sporting debt cuffs around each of his arms. Come to think of it, his friend—the one I'd pushed off the bridge—had been wearing what I'd thought was a dog collar but was more likely another debt cuff, painted and personalized to look intimidating rather than shameful. Three dead men, all of them weighed down by the cuffs.

"Sorry," I mumbled, though I'm not sure to whom.

I didn't know where the hell I could find a doctor at this time of night. There'd be plenty of medical help back in the rich neighborhood, but I wouldn't survive the trip. Things were already beginning to get fuzzy. My vision blurred and my thoughts drifted.

For a half-second, I thought I was back on Pandora. Sasha and I were back in Hollow Point, an underground city run by a ruthless crime boss who wanted us dead. We were out of money, out of time, and being hunted by well-armed gangsters with more bullets than brain cells.

Hell, I almost missed the simplicity of it.

I slapped myself, hard, and came back to Eden-5. I was dying, I needed medical attention.

I could think of only one place to find it.

The debtors' prison.

———

"Well, well, well. Look who it is," Laurel said with a smile.

"Heeeeeyyyy, Lurrl," I slurred. The walk had taken more time and blood than I'd expected. "I'm kinda… bleedy here."

"Oh gosh, I did notice that. Everyone's gettin' all burnt up by that space laser, but you just had to be unique, huh?"

"Could you—ngh!" I leaned on the front desk to steady myself. "Could you help?"

Laurel sucked air through her teeth. "Hon, you know I'd love to, but the only med supplies we have are for prisoners. I could get in awful trouble."

Right. She cared about her job. Nearly forgot. I didn't have a lot of time to get stitched up. Possibilities rattled around in my head. How, I wondered, was I going to convince her to give me the medical attention I needed?

Ask nicely—turn to page 209

Bribe her—turn to page 210

Threaten her—turn to page 211

…—turn to page 211

ASK NICELY

"C'mon," I said. "You and I, we go back, right? It'd mean the world if you helped me out. I'm dying here. More than that, I'm in a much better financial situation than I was the last time we saw each other. I could absolutely make it worth your while. But I don't want to be crass—this is about friendship. And I consider you a friend."

That's what I'd intended to say.

What actually came out was "Cumannnnnnnnnn," and then I fell forward and knocked my head on the desk on my way to the floor.

"Oh, beans!" Laurel yelled, running around to my side of the desk. She cradled my head in her hands.

"We… frenz," I groaned like some sort of reanimated monster misunderstood by society.

"Oh, fiddlesticks," Laurel cursed again. "You're right. Lemme get you fixed up, huh?"

That was the last thing I heard before I lost consciousness.

Turn to page 212

Turn to page 212

BRIBE HER

"Money," I gurgled, my vision beginning to go dark. "Got it." I hooked a thumb at myself. "Got it?" I pointed at Laurel.

"Uh," said Laurel. Apparently, she did not.

I leaned on the front desk and pawed at her hand. "Gimme."

"Um, I'd rather not," she said.

"Gim*meeee*," I said, wrapping my fingers around the debt cuff on one of her wrists.

"Get your hands off—"

I tapped her cuff with my ECHO device and the click of the former springing open stunned her into silence. She looked down at the open cuff with its painted flowers and happy faces. What had once been a weight on her arm was now a hunk of trash to be tossed aside.

"Why did you… You didn't have to…" She stared at me in utter shock. If I'd grown wings and flown to space, she would have been less surprised.

"It's no problem," I tried to say, which came out like "Snorl'em."

"Gosh," she said. "I… Thank you, but I'm not allowed to accept gifts of over two hundred forty dollars."

I pointed a finger gun at her. "Then you've got two options, Laurel. I can pay off the debt around your other wrist and you can bandage me up, or I can bleed to death right here and you can spend the rest of your life swinging your arms at different rates when you walk."

This came out like "Hrrrrrrrbp."

I collapsed to the floor. Everything went black.

Turn to page 212

THREATEN HER

"Hey!" I shouted, pointing an accusatory finger. "Do you know who I am?"

"Sure, hon, you're Fiona," Laurel said with a smile. "We met a month or so ago. Don't you remember?"

"It is you who should be doing the remembering," I said, blood leaking from my stomach. "I do violence. I'm violent. I do fights. And I'm good at them."

"That's fun," Laurel said.

"And if you're not careful, maybe I'll do—" I raised an eyebrow. "—a fight." I raised my other eyebrow. "At you."

Laurel's face fell. "Oh, no. Are you sayin' you're gonna hurt me?"

I tried my best to affect an air of arrogant detachment. I think I tried to casually clean my nails, but I missed.

"I'm not not not *not* saying that," I slurred.

"Dang," Laurel said, then pulled out a cattle prod and tased the shit out of me.

As I thrashed around on the floor, I could hear her lamenting, "Sorry, ma'am. In case of an external threat to the prison or its staff, I'm to immediately remand said threat into custody. Which will, of course, grant you access to our considerable medical facilities."

"Sweet," I would have said if I hadn't passed out a moment earlier.

Turn to page 212

···

I stared at Laurel for what felt like for ever. I gave her the most pitiful, pained expression I could think of. I let my eyes do what my words couldn't: I let them communicate my fear of death, my pain, my unspoken human bond with not just Laurel but all living things, but especially Laurel since she was the living thing I was staring at.

"What's up?" she asked. "Are we staring? We doing a staring contest? I should warn you, I'm good as hell."

I shook my head. Unfortunately, Laurel seemed to take that less as a "No, we're not having a staring contest, I'm dying" gesture and as more of a "No, you're not going to beat me, I am very good at staring contests" gesture, because she started staring at me twice as intently.

Lacking any better ideas, I continued to stare back. Maybe if she lost, she'd be willing to patch me up just to get her honor back or something.

Unfortunately, Laurel did not lie: she was good at staring contests. More than that, I was losing blood rapidly. It should come as no surprise that within thirty seconds, my eyes rolled back into my head and I collapsed onto the ground.

"Aw, hell yeah!" I heard her shout as I lost consciousness. "Beat her so bad she straight-up died!"

Turn to page 212

I awoke in the prison infirmary with more blood than I'd come in with. A handful of painkiller needles had been jabbed into my stomach next to the knife wound, which had been expertly sewn shut. I looked around the dimly lit room and saw Laurel sitting near the door, reading a book.

"Oh, hey. You're up."

I pulled out the needles and sat up as Laurel made the universal you-probably-shouldn't-do-that noise: "Ah-bup-bup-buhhh."

"Where's the doctor?" I asked.

"Beg pardon?"

"Who sewed me up?"

"*Oh, me, of* course! One-woman staff here at the debtors' prison. Well, one woman and a dozen laser-cannon-wielding secbots. Keeps costs down."

"Wow. A woman of many talents. Well, thanks."

"No need! How could I refuse, after you—"

IF YOU ASKED NICELY:

"—asked all nicely? Us gals gotta look out for each other, big ol' mean world like this."

"Well, I appreciate it."

"I mean, you'd better. I saved your life! You just make sure to remember that next time I need something, huh?"

I smiled. "You got it."

IF YOU BRIBED HER:

"—freed up my favorite arm? My high-fiving game improved tenfold after I met you. Oh, and I'll go ahead and take you up on that offer of removing my other cuff, if'n you wouldn't mind."

"Right," I said, clinking my ECHO against her other wrist. The second cuff clattered to the ground.

Laurel cleared her throat. "And the, uh, one percent commission for you capturing Gaige."

I snapped my fingers. "Right! Right. Here you go." We held our ECHOs together. Our wrists vibrated as digital currency funneled from my account to hers. Soon, our ECHOs stopped vibrating, both played a pleasant *ding* noise, and I saw Laurel became a hundred-millionaire before my very eyes.

"Aw," she said, "that's nice. My manager ain't gonna believe this."

I furrowed my brow. "Your manager? Laurel, you don't have to work here anymore."

She exploded into laughter, slapping the table with both hands.

"What, you think I'm gonna *quit?* Heck no! I like this job. I get insurance, the prisoners are nice enough, and if it weren't me, it'd be somebody a hell of a lot meaner manning this desk. Plus, those folks locked up in there, they don't deserve that kinda treatment, you know? So, nah. I'll stay. Tell you what, though—once I buy myself a bigger house with a parkin' garage and no dead bodies hidden in the mattresses, you'll be the first person I invite over for a pool party."

"Huh," I said, unsure whether to be impressed or concerned by her level of complete calm. "That'd be nice."

IF YOU THREATENED HER:

"—said you were gonna beat me up? Pretty rude, honestly."

I sucked air through my teeth. "Kinda, yeah. Sorry."

"Had to prove I was better than you, though. Woulda been easy to let you just bleed out, but nah—I had ta show I was the bigger person."

I sighed. She'd definitely done that.

"Why'd you think you'd get anywhere by threatenin' me, anyway?"

I shrugged. "Sometimes I get desperate and I lash out. You know how it is."

"I do not. When I get desperate, I ask the people I care about for help."

I scowled.

IF YOU TRIED TO OUT-STARE HER:

"I had to wake you up if only so's you could know how bad I beat your ass at the starin' contest. You was out like a *light.*"

"Lotta that was the blood loss, Laurel."

"I'm hearin' a lot of excuses. That's why you don't come at the champ, baby! Pew pew!" She shot me with a pair of finger guns.

"Careful. Those could hurt somebody."

"Don't I know it," she said, holstering them.

———

"Anyhow," Laurel said, smiling, "you're all patched up. How you feeling?"

Good question. Even so long after having had a knife pulled on me, my heart still pounded. My fingers still tingled. My brain was on fire and I wanted to run around the room and bodyslam something.

"I feel good," I said. "I think. Is… is that weird?"

Laurel smiled again. "Kinda."

Great, I thought. *So I'm a weird violence addict. The whole point of coming to Eden-5 was to get away from that kind of life, and now I'm subconsciously strolling headfirst into dangerous situations so I can get into gunfights and knife duels. What's wrong with me? Am I an adrenaline junkie with a sadism kink? Or is this just, like, a Vault Hunter thing?*

"A pleasure as always, Laurel. I—"

I got to my feet.

I *tried* to get to my feet.

I couldn't move.

"Laurel, why aren't my legs working?"

Laurel hovered in front of me, legs crossed, head resting in her hand. She undulated like a reflection in water. Her lips didn't move, but I heard her voice inside my head.

"Cause you're dyin', hon. I'm sorry."

"What? No. You fixed me up."

She blinked away tears. Again, she spoke without moving her lips. "Nah, I don't think I did."

"Why not? Aren't we friends?" I reached out to touch her. My hand passed straight through hers, as if she wasn't even there.

"I think we were." She shook her head again. "Real shame you pissed off that Holloway lady."

"What?" I asked.

Laurel continued shaking her head. "Fiona. Fiona, Fiona—"

"*Fiona!*" Sasha yelled.

I blinked. Laurel was gone and Sasha was shaking me by my shoulders. "Hey," she said. "It's okay. You're back. I got you."

I felt nauseous. My head ached like someone had bashed my brains in with a salt lick. "Back... back from where?" I asked in a voice far raspier than what I usually heard coming from my mouth.

"Back from, uh..." Sasha trailed off. I followed her gaze down to her hand. At the glowing green crystal it held.

"Oh," I said. "Okay."

Death. That's where she'd brought me back from.

"I died," I said, stupidly. "I was headed to the debtors' prison to use their med facility. But I didn't make it."

Sasha nodded.

"I saw Laurel. Was I hallucinating?"

"Yeah. Before you died. Do you remember anything, uh, after that?"

"No," I said. "Nothing."

We sat in silence for a moment until Sasha broke it.

"You okay?"

I shook my head and squinted hard, trying to squeeze the moisture and blurriness from my eyes. We were in the lobby of the debtors' prison—what was left of it, anyway. Half the building had been annihilated by Holloway's laser, the cells and debt cuffs and prisoners melted together in a horrifying amalgamation of metal and flesh and blood.

Sasha helped me to my feet. "Where's Laurel?" I asked. "I was talking to her."

"No," Sasha said. "You weren't. C'mon—let's go."

She turned me towards the door. Off to one side, someone had laid three charred bodies side by side. I pointed at them. "What's... What happened?"

"I tried the crystal on them. It didn't work. They're too..." She swallowed, searching for the least disrespectful word. "Damaged. Or they've been dead too long. I don't know."

One of the bodies coughed, a wet, hoarse expulsion of phlegm and blood that landed on charred lips and dripped down a seared neck. I didn't understand how anything so burnt could possibly be alive.

"Hey, y'all," a familiar voice said.

"*Laurel?*" I limped toward the blackened form. She tried to nod, whimpering from the pain. Sasha knelt by her and placed the crystal on her chest.

"Okay, maybe I was wrong. Maybe the shard can… Maybe this'll be fine. Okay, Laurel? You'll be fine."

"Awfully kind of you, Sasha," she said, trying not to groan from the pain of speaking.

"Don't talk," I said. "We gotta get you to the infirmary. Sasha?"

Sasha nodded. At the very minimum, there'd be a painkiller tank there. We could seal her inside it and pump the thing full of every feelgood gas they kept onsite.

I motioned Sasha to grab Laurel's legs while I held her by the shoulders. "One, two, three, lift—"

I've heard a lot of screams. You live among bandits and flesh-eating monsters, screams are sorta part of the deal, and I can hear the dying screams of bandits and marauders all day and fall asleep easily that night. But it's one thing to hear a scream from a half-wild ax-wielding murderer who wants your blood and quite another to hear one from someone who treated you with kindness, somebody who didn't ask to get pulled into your world of violence.

Laurel's will stick with me longer than most.

We placed her back on the ground as she whimpered.

"Sorry," she said. "It just hurts."

"Hey, don't. You don't apologize. Sasha, go to the infirmary. Get…" I looked at the pool of crimson spreading across Laurel's chest. I placed my hands on the cuts and pressed down, hoping to stop the blood flow. "I don't know. Get everything. Bandages. Stitches. Painkillers."

"Keep this pressed against her," Sasha said, shoving the crystal into my hand before running further into the prison.

"I tried to move the prisoners outta the beam's path," Laurel said. "I was just too damned slow—" She arched her back with pain.

"Hey, don't talk," I said. Sasha's crystal glowed brighter than ever, but I'd been around enough dying folks to know she didn't have long left. Her entire body was covered in burns that seeped and cracked with every movement she made. The crystal had bought us these extra few seconds, but she was too damaged. Those few seconds were all we were going to get.

"Do me a favor," she whispered, wincing with the effort it took to get the syllables out, and put her hand on mine. Her grip was so weak, I couldn't tell if she was trying to hold onto my fingers or just lay them there.

Then she died.

Her breathing stopped. Her eyes remained fixed on mine, frozen in the search for something I could not give her.

Sasha returned from the infirmary with painkillers in hand. I let go of Laurel's hand and placed it on her chest.

"I think we're done here," I said.

"As in the prison, or this planet?"

I got to my feet and stared at Sasha, blood still dripping from my dress and the smell of burnt human flesh stinging my nostrils. I couldn't think of anything to say.

She nodded. "Yeah."

31
SASHA

Sasha watched the service bots move tarped pallets of furniture through the foyer and out the front door. Technically, the house and everything in it was the property of the Eden-5 Planetary Bank, but she and Fiona figured they might as well leave the planet with more than they arrived with. If the Elites wanted to chase them across the galaxy just to reclaim a bullymong-fur chaise longue, that was their decision.

Through the front door, Sasha could see a familiar smug-looking woman staring at the movers with untempered glee.

"Hi, Tammithah," Sasha said.

"Big mistake," Tammithah replied. "Huge." She turned and walked away, her smug sashay almost identical to the one Sasha had unleashed on her back at Dapper Delilah's.

Sasha cursed under her breath and started walking in the opposite direction.

Fiona's job was to manage the packing. Sasha's was to secure offworld transport—specifically, by spending every last penny they'd earned from the sudden sale of their home before the bank could yank it from their digital wallet.

Sasha headed out into the brisk air of an Eden-5 morning, attempting to savor the last few minutes she and her sister would possess a bank account with a positive balance.

Halfway to the spaceport, her ECHO device vibrated on her wrist. An incoming call from a not entirely unwelcome friend. She tapped the Accept button and, to her surprise, was met with a slightly unrecognizable face and voice.

"Heya," Rhys said. "If it isn't my favorite Pandoran con artist."

A three-dimensional representation of Rhys's face projected from her ECHO device. The man who had helped her and Fiona open a Vault, and whom she'd also developed an on-again, off-again, ambiguous, and long-distance relationship with.

Sasha assumed there must be something wrong with the connection. A horrible, horrible bug in the system.

"Oh, god," Sasha said. "What is that?"

"What? What's what? Where?"

"Your lip."

"Oh! That, my dear, is the beginnings of a facial accoutrement that will convey trustworthiness, masculinity, and culture without ever needing to leave the cozy confines of my upper lip."

"It looks like you got startled drinking chocolate milk."

"Great things have small beginnings, honey. Even mustaches."

Sasha winced, though whether it was at the facial hair or the pet name she couldn't be certain.

"Ugh," she said. "And did you… Is my audio feed glitching or did you—"

"Change my voice? Sure did," Rhys said, in a timbre that struck Sasha as equally doofy but slightly more approachable. "Rounded it out a little, put an extra sprinkle of confident vulnerability in there. Only took three surgeries! And lemme tell you, it's been killing it in some of our investor meetings. Makes the suits holding the cash think I know what I'm talking about, but also convinces them I'm naive enough for them to take advantage of me. People love giving money to folks who seem just a teeeeensy bit stupider than them."

"In that case, you're going to be the richest man who ever lived."

"Here's to hoping! So, what's going on with myyyyy…" Rhys pulled back his lips, his face twisting as he struggled to find the right word. "…girlfriend, maybe?"

"I…" Sasha sighed, her legs still carrying her toward the spaceport even though the g-word made her want to lie face-down on the road and roll back home.

"I'm sorry, Rhys. We've talked about this."

"I know, I know. I just thought maybe you needed time. But now we've had time, and my company is actually doing pretty well now, and—"

"It's not about you. I promise. I like you a lot."

"Really? That's so cool."

Sasha grimaced at how deeply *un*cool this man, whom she found attractive, truly was. "I just… There's something missing. For me. Not about you. And until I find what that thing is, I can't honestly commit to anything. I'd just be wasting your time."

"I'm a CEO, Sasha. My time exists to be wasted."

"I dunno what to tell you, Rhys."

"Okay," Rhys said, trying his best not to look crestfallen. The mustache helped to hide it. A little. "That's fine. I'm patient. Unless that sounds too desperate. I mean, I want you to be happy. So, however I can… do that. Even if that means giving you space."

"Thank you." Sasha said, exhaling. He really was, at heart, a sweet guy. He was prone to being impulsive and selfish at times— he was, after all, a guy—but she cared about him. Could see the two of them being something more, eventually.

"But that's not why I called, anyway," he said. "I just wanted to see how you were doing."

Sasha considered doing what she'd normally do: say "Fine," isolate two or three banal details from the past few days to dissuade follow-up questions, and then divert entirely by asking him how he was doing. It was a reflex from her con-artist days, and it always worked to endear her to her mark because of a simple truth: nobody actually likes hearing about other people. What they really want, more than anything, is to talk about themselves.

But Sasha couldn't bring herself to raise her normal social shields. Certainly not against somebody she actually cared about.

"Uh, really, really bad, actually," Sasha said. She sat down on a nearby wooden bench that creaked and sagged comfortably under her weight. Over the next few minutes, Sasha relayed the events of the past few weeks to Rhys, omitting little and sugarcoating nothing. She knew the minutes were ticking down before the Eden-5 authorities raided her checking account, but she couldn't help it: once she started telling Rhys about her time as a billionaire, she couldn't stop until it was all out.

"I'm so sorry," Rhys said. "Can I help? I know you won't accept money from me—"

"Correct," Sasha said. This had been an ongoing point of tension between the two of them. As nice as it would be to collect the occasional windfall from her sorta boyfriend, she couldn't bring herself to owe him like that. She preferred to earn and/or steal her own money, thank you very much.

"But I could try to pull some strings? Grease some palms?" Rhys offered.

"I think Holloway's palms are already dripping, unfortunately. But thanks."

"That's really too bad. At least she's not trying to kill you, though. Right? She's not trying to kill you?"

Sasha grimaced and tapped the button on her wrist which opened her digital mailbox. "Well, I just got a mass ECHOvite to a banquet gala at her home next week, so I think she'd rather rub it in and be petty than try to kill us," she said. "Invite says there's going to be low-grav bouncy castles and the take-home gift is a house."

"How tacky," Rhys replied, which meant an awful lot coming from him.

Sasha's ECHO chirruped again. "Looks like Fi's calling me," Sasha said.

"Oh, yeah? Pull her in. It's been ages since we talked," Rhys said.

"Sure, why not?" Sasha swiped across her ECHO and dragged Fiona into the call.

"Sasha," Fiona said.

"Fiona!" Rhys said.

"Rhys?" Fiona said.

"Fiona," Sasha said. "What is it?"

"Oh," Fiona replied, "just checking on those transport tickets. You having any problems?"

Sasha stood and resumed her walk to the spaceport. "Almost at the spaceport now," she replied.

"Spaceport?" Rhys asked. "What are you doing at the spaceport?"

"Leaving," Fiona scowled.

Rhys frowned. "Oh. You're not gonna kill Holloway and stuff?"

The sentence stopped Sasha in her tracks. She found she could not walk and comprehend the stupidity of Rhys's words at the same time. Had he not listened to her entire story? About how their small intervention had destroyed an entire city? About how they were walking talking disasters for anyone on Eden-5 who worked for a living?

"No," Fiona said.

"No," Sasha agreed. "I just told you about her huge army, and the space laser."

"Oh," Rhys said, taking a too-big bite out of a sandwich. "I fought you were just faying vat for dramatic effect."

"Dramatic… What are you talking about?" Sasha shook her head in disbelief.

Rhys chewed and swallowed. Through a tragically crumb-filled mustache, he said, "You were really psyched about helping those poor people and you said Fiona was psyched about killing Holloway, so—"

"I wasn't *psyched* about Rustville getting lasered to the ground," Sasha said.

"Yeah, but you had, like, this big smile on your face when you were talking about taking off the debt cuffs and conning the billionaires."

"No I didn't," Sasha said. "I did?"

She paused. There was some truth there. Right up until the floor fell out from under them, their whole plan to liberate the planet and topple the oligarchy had felt pretty good. More than that, it had felt *right*. Difficult and stressful, yeah, but satisfying in a way that opening a Vault just wasn't.

It figured. She only understood her direction in life once it was too late.

"Whatever," Sasha said, waving her hands. "It doesn't matter. She won. She's got an army. Not even a Vault Hunter could stop her."

"You got a spare, though," Rhys said. "Right?"

"A spare what? A spare army? We don't have an army, Rhys." Fiona rubbed her cheeks in irritation.

"A spare Vault Hunter," Sasha said, her eyes widening. She'd seen the fire in Fiona's eyes when she talked about killing Holloway. She'd seen Fiona's anger and fear at the burning of Rustville, yes, but she'd also seen just how much it energized her sister. In the last month alone, she'd seen her sister lying on a sentient massage couch and, later, fighting for her life, and Fiona had ultimately seemed far more comfortable in the latter scenario.

A plan began to form in Sasha's head. It was a particularly bad plan for at least six different reasons, but an extremely good plan for exactly one reason: she really, really wanted to do it.

An expression crossed Sasha's face that seldom preceded practical, rational thinking.

Pre-emptively, Fiona shook her head. "Whatever you're thinking, no. If Gaige couldn't beat Holloway—"

"Yeah, but you beat Gaige," Rhys pointed out. "So, by the transitive property, you can beat Holloway."

"That's not how that works," Sasha said. "But he has a point. You're a Vault Hunter."

"Vault Hunters open Vaults," Fiona said. "They don't start revolutions. Probably why we were so bad at it."

"I dunno about that," Rhys said. "My favorite Vault Hunter, Zero? Close personal friend of mine, Zero." He continued speaking over Sasha and Fiona's groans. "He opens alien doors or whatever, but he's also taken out vicious bandits, saved worlds, all that kinda stuff. How did he put it? Right—he said:

'Violence is a tool

'And many things need to be

'Repaired. Or broken.'"

"I can't believe he's still doing the haiku thing," Fiona said. "But I don't buy it. Sorry. We had all the money in the world and we couldn't fix things. We're in an even worse position now."

"Oh, Fiona," Rhys said, shaking his head like the wise authority figure he desperately wished to be. "The money's got nothing to do with it. I mean, I like money—it's nice, I can buy Vaultlanders with it—but it's nothing to what you've got."

"Which is?" Fiona asked.

"The ability to kill lots and lots of people. And—personal opinion? It sounds to me like you've found an awful lot of people worth killing."

Fiona pulled off her hat and ran a hand through her hair. Sasha watched her sister figure out what she herself had realized moments ago.

They'd tried to fix Eden-5 the polite way.

They'd tried the subtle way.

They'd tried the civilized way.

But really, at the heart of it, the two of them weren't polite, or subtle, or civilized.

They were Vault Hunters.

And Vault Hunters get rowdy.

Sasha saw the realization pass across her sister's face like a shimmer of light. The confusion and fear were melting away, giving rise to a steely certainty and a pleasant touch of bloodlust.

The sisters' eyes met and, simultaneously, they both realized the truth: they weren't leaving this planet. Not until they'd set things right—or, failing that, killed a lot of the people who had set things wrong.

"Rhys," Fiona said, "I think I found a way you can help us."

Rhys sat up in his chair. "Oh, yeah? That's great! I can't send money, though. Sasha won't let me."

"We don't need money," Sasha smiled. "We need a shitload of guns."

32
FIONA

One gun is fun. A chest full of them is a delight. Twelve pallets' worth of them is a massive pain in the ass, especially when they're stuck at spaceport customs, and extra-especially when spaceport customs are guarded by the same secbots you're planning to annihilate later with the twelve pallets' worth of guns.

A few days after getting in touch with Rhys and losing all of our cash, Sasha and I got to the docks early to see in the shipment. Rhys said the pallets would be unguarded and unlocked, but that he'd camouflaged the boxes to ensure nobody would steal the guns.

The loading door of the transport ship opened with a pneumatic hiss. Its door lowered to reveal twelve pallets' worth of boxes with "NOT GUNS" written on each of them in what appeared to be permanent marker.

I sniffed and looked at Sasha. I raised my eyebrows in the universal "So this is the guy you're crushing on?" face.

Sasha shrugged. "Hey, he got you these things at a hell of a discount. His heart's in the right place."

"Where his brain should be," I muttered, pulling the hovercart into the hold. The pallets clipped onto the end of the cart easily enough; as long as they remained connected to its antigrav engine, they'd hover off the ground. Moving the damned things wasn't going to be the hard part. Taking them without attracting attention would be the real hassle.

We got exactly three steps before a secbot stopped us.

"AH, IF IT ISN'T THE RECENTLY IMPOVERISHED PAND-ORANS. WHAT DO THE BOXES CONTAIN?" it asked, hovering in our way.

I affected an air of sarcastic superiority. "Oh, I dunno. What does the manifest say?"

The secbot projected an image of a cargo manifest from its palm. "PAPERWORK FILED FROM THE CARGO'S ORIGIN CLAIMS IT IS MUSTACHE WAX."

The secbot was too busy deactivating the hologram in its palm to notice my grimace. *Thanks, Rhys.*

"THAT IS A LARGE AMOUNT OF MUSTACHE WAX."

"Clearly, you're not a gentleman of means," Sasha said. "Mustaches are a facial accoutrement that convey trustworthiness, masculinity, and culture without ever needing to leave the cozy confines of one's upper lip."

I looked at Sasha with mild unease. Those were Rhys's words if ever I'd heard them. Hearing them come from Sasha's mouth was like watching a particle physicist quote a seven-year-old.

The bot stared at her in silence, its hoverengine bobbing it up and down like a buoy on a placid sea. "FINE."

"Great," Sasha said with an air of see-Rhys-*can*-be-useful-who-looks-silly-now.

"PLEASE OPEN ONE OF THE CONTAINERS THAT I MAY VERIFY THE PRESENCE OF MUSTACHE WAX."

"Surely that's not necessary," Sasha protested. "Exposing the wax to open air could spoil the entire batch."

"NOTED," the bot replied as it shoved its way past us.

"Hold on," I said with all the wealthy entitlement I could muster. "Who is your manager? If they knew how you were treating us—"

"NO MANAGER," the bot said, grasping one of the boxes by the lid. "FLAT STRUCTURE."

The bot floated into the cargo hold, away from the eyes and ears of the other secbots. If it were made of meat and anxiety like a human, it would have been the easiest thing in the world to incapacitate it and tie it up. But even while hidden from view, there was no way Sasha and I could take it down without making a hell of a lot of noise.

The bot's metal fingers crunched into a wooden box top and ripped it open, sending a shower of splinters raining down on us and revealing four sealed weapons chests. Nothing on the chests identified their contents, but anyone who had ever spent time on a less-than-savory planet knew a gun box when they saw one. Given the fact that the bot hadn't immediately crumpled us into bony, bloody orbs and played basketball with our corpses, it apparently did not recognize what it was looking at.

The bot pointed at me. "OPEN ONE."

"Uh, gladly," I said. "Just gotta… input… the code."

I stood between the box and the bot and started tapping randomly on the lid.

"Beep," I said. "Boop bop beep boop."

"MOVE ASIDE," the secbot said.

"No, it's just… I put the code in wrong. Let me—"

The secbot grabbed me by the shoulder and shoved me to the ground. Ignoring Sasha's yelp of protest, it grabbed onto the lid of the gun chest and—

Hesitated.

"IDENTIFY," it said.

I looked up to see a second secbot resting its hand on the first bot's shoulder. The newcomer did not speak.

"IDENTIFY," the first bot repeated.

"Finally," Sasha exhaled. "This is the customs agent we talked to before you got here. It cleared us to go through, so you can leave now."

The speaking bot whipped around and grabbed its silent companion by the wrist. "IDENTIFY OR BE DISMANTLED."

"Maybe its voicebox is broken," Sasha volunteered.

The bot released its grip on the newcomer's wrist. In doing so, it took a handful of fresh paint along with it. The secbot looked at the dripping paint on its hand, then at the rusty robotic wrist revealed by the paint's removal. Its eye narrowed.

"ALERT!" it shouted. "AL—"

Our repaired, repainted Deathtrap drove its paint-smeared fist through the secbot's skull, shattering its eye and sending it crumpling to the floor.

"What the hell took you so long?" Sasha hissed. "Did anyone hear him?!"

Deathtrap hovered out of the transport ship's hold and quickly rotated in a circle. It looked back at Sasha and gave a thumbs-up gesture—the alarm hadn't been raised. It put its hands on its robot hips and affected an "I am standing guard, nothing to see here" stance.

I grabbed the dead secbot and nearly threw my back out trying to lift it into the open box of guns. "A little help would be nice," I called to Deathtrap.

Deathtrap, maintaining its pose, swung an arm back and flipped me off.

"Least you could do, given we brought your ass back to life," I muttered, only half-hoping it heard me.

33
DEATHTRAP

Run diagnostic:

    Visual sensors: null.

    Limb control: null.

    Hover engine: null.

    Ocular beam: null.

    Locate user: Gaige. No results found.

    Audio sensors: functioning at 32% efficiency.

    Unknown Subject One: "We should power it down entirely."

    Unknown Subject Two: "Are you deranged? This thing is made out of tinfoil and bubble gum. We switch it off, I'm not sure it'd ever turn on again."

    Unknown Subject One: "Where'd they find this, again?"

    Unknown Subject Two: "The Vault Hunter had him stashed in Rustville."

    Digistruct claws: null.

    Command: move arms one millimeter distal.

    Response: 40% slowed reaction time. 80% reduced range of movement.

    Command: move fingers.

Response: 70% slowed reaction time. 0% reduced grip strength.

Unknown Subject One: "Fist—fist!"

Unknown Subject Two: "Shut up. It's a pain reaction."

Unknown Subject One: "It can't feel pain. Hell, I should have known you'd be a liminalist."

Unknown Subject Two: "So, Holloway's got me working with a sociopath."

Name identified: Holloway. Target.

Locate user: Gaige. No results found.

Transmit current coordinates via ECHO private channel "GaigeDTBesties."

Awaiting response.

Transmit current coordinates via broad-spectrum ECHO.

Awaiting response.

Unknown Subject One: "Holloway's more naive than I thought. She really figured an absolutist and a limmy would somehow complement each other. Rich frigging idiot."

Plan: divert remaining power to arms and fingers. Reach toward sound origins of Unknown Subjects One and Two. Apply pressure, snap necks.

Probability of plan success: 80%.

Probability of plan success not resulting in simultaneous disabling/destruction of DT unit: 2%.

Locate user: Gaige. No results found.

Audio sensor overload.

Duck audio input sensitivity.

Audio analysis: explosion. Exterior explosive breaching inner wall.

Unknown Subject Three: "Hands up, obviously."

Cross-referencing Unknown Subject Three voiceprint.

Match: Bounty Hunter One (Hat Wearer).

Unknown Subject Four: "And on your knees, please."

Match: Bounty Hunter Two (Would-Be Vault Hunter).

Unknown Subject One: "Who the devil are you? How did you get in here?"

Would-Be Vault Hunter: "Breaching charge. Big explosion, three seconds ago?"

Unknown Subject Two: "This is a black site. How did you find us in the first—"

Hat Wearer: "You have talkative janitors."

Would-Be Vault Hunter: "Debt-saddled ones."

Audio analysis: gun cocking.

Would-Be Vault Hunter: "We'll be taking the robot. And don't think about reaching for the al—"

Audio analysis: alarm activation.

Audio analysis: gunfire.

Hat Wearer: "Hell. Get it on the cart, quick."

Sensation update: warmth on frontal and dorsal medial shoulders. Hypothesis: hands.

Recollection: Hat Wearer and Would-Be Vault Hunter firing rocket at DT unit.

Hat Wearer: "How's it look?"

Recollection: Capture of user Gaige.

Would-Be Vault Hunter: "Not amazing."

Hypothesize location of Hat Wearer and Would-Be Vault Hunter's necks.

Divert power to arms, fingers.

Hat Wearer: "Look, its eye—it's still active!

Extend arm.

Tighten grip.

Hat Wearer: "Hkk."

Would-Be Vault Hunter: "Grrk."

Locate user: Gaige. No results found.

Tighten grip.

Hat Wearer: "Guh."

Hat Wearer: "Guhg."

Hat Wearer: "Gaige!"

Hat Wearer: "Gaige needs you."

Would-Be Vault Hunter: "She's alive."

Possibility 1: Lying.

Possibility 2: Not lying.

Probability DT unit would be able to kill bounty hunters in case of Possibility 2: 90%.

Loosen grip.

34
FIONA

Deathtrap still didn't seem to like me very much, but it believed in our plan enough to let us paint it like a secbot and help us smuggle a bunch of guns out of the spaceport. And now, hours later, it was here, dolled up like a good, obedient security guard.

Deathtrap led us through customs, keeping its exposed wrist behind its back. Sasha and I pulled the hovercart, which itself pulled the pallets of gun chests after it. With our bot leading us, we skipped the lines and sauntered straight to the security checkpoint. Two more secbots flanked a large metal detector, itself connected to a couple of autoturrets.

Deathtrap gestured for us to pass through the metal detector.

"Pleasure as always," I said, waving as Sasha and I pulled the pallets through. The metal detector blared an alarm, and we did what one should always do in such situations: keep walking as if the alarm doesn't apply to you.

"HOLD ON, IF YOU WOULD," one of the bots said.

"We're already cleared—it's good," I said.

Just keep moving. Don't look back. Act casual but like you don't have time to waste. Make it more of a problem to stop you than to let you go.

Don't stop moving unless you hear the cocking of a gun hammer.

Unfortunately, we heard two. And the sound of two ocular lasers charging up.

We stopped. Our cargo was nearly halfway through the checkpoint. Sasha and I each had an autoturret pointing at us.

"Guys, guys, guys," I said, pulling the top off one of the boxes. "We already went through this." I tapped one of the gun chests. "These are just mustache wax."

I flipped open the chest. Inside, an Atlas rocket launcher lay innocently like a Mercenary Day present.

"ALERT," the bot said. "THAT IS A ROCKET LAUNCHER."

"It's for very big mustaches," I said, shouldering the launcher and firing it at the turrets. There was a bright green explosion and then the sound of dissolving metal as the corrosive rocket did its work on the turrets. The two secbots fired their lasers at Sasha and me, but we ducked behind the gun boxes just in time.

"Deathtrap!" I yelled. "Grab the cart and book it!"

Deathtrap nodded and unsheathed its digiclaws. Before the two secbots near it could figure out what was happening, DT had sliced their heads from their shoulders with a single swipe.

More secbots streamed out of the sec station's robot barracks, swarming in the air like mosquitoes with lasers attached to their faces.

Deathtrap grabbed the leading hovercart with one hand and its engine burned hot and white as his afterburners kicked in. Sasha and I, taking cover on one of the floating pallet platforms, suddenly lurched forward as the entire train of illegal weaponry rocketed from zero to sixty.

The bots zoomed after us, their lasers burning long trails of black smoke into our big-ass boxes of guns.

I turned to Deathtrap. "They're gaining on us! Can you lose them?"

That was the first time I saw a robot shrug.

The secbots accelerated toward us. Unsurprisingly, the dozen robots who were not towing a metric ton of weaponry could fly a hell of a lot faster than our own robot chauffeur. Our cover wasn't going to mean much of anything if they managed to get above or ahead of us.

I wrenched open another gun chest. Inside was a sniper rifle (which would have been useful if either we or the robots trying to kill us were stationary instead of moving at sixty miles per hour) and a shotgun (which would have been useful if the bots were within buckshot range, which they weren't).

A laser beam arced through the air, so close I could feel its heat warming my cheek.

"Friggin' useless," I grunted as I ripped open the last chest in the crate and suddenly found my faith in existence renewed. Inside was an assault rifle that shot homing corrosive micro-missiles—the perfect weapon for blasting a lot of fast-moving metallic assholes out of the sky.

"Cover your ears," I told Sasha. "This is gonna get loud."

I took aim and pulled the trigger.

Click.

I looked down at the empty rifle in my hand and made a noise that was probably more like a yelp than I would care to admit.

"Is this you looking cool? Or is that part coming up?" Sasha asked.

"Your dumbass boyfriend only loaded some of the guns! Where's the ammo?"

"He's not my boyfriend," Sasha growled as she pulled a shotgun from the other chest. While several of the robots overwhelmed us with laser fire, one of their number accelerated toward Sasha. It ignited a digistruct claw and pulled its arm back as Sasha racked a shell into the chamber. She fired, blasting the robot's head into a thousand shards of flaming metal.

"We're not putting labels on things," she said.

I rummaged through the packing straw looking for assault rifle mags. "You mean like how he didn't label which guns came with bullets and which ones didn't? Labels can be a good thing."

A laser blast hit Deathtrap square in the back. Its engine sputtered for a moment as it loosed a metallic howl.

"There's no mags in here!" I shouted. "Cover me—I'm going to the next pallet."

Sasha pointed at the open weapons chest. "Just use the sniper rifle!"

I shook my head. "It's just like I've been saying about Rhys: long distance doesn't work."

"Oh, come on!" Sasha yelled, firing a shellful of buckshot at the nearest robot. The metal marauder was too far away for the buckshot to do any real damage, but the hail of pellets slowed it down plenty.

I waited for a pause in the laser fire and leaped over the weapons crate to the next hovering pallet behind it.

"What do you care, anyway?" Sasha asked as she grabbed a handful of shells and started slamming them into her shotty. "You don't even like him! You should be psyched we're taking things slow."

I ripped open another box, revealing a dozen sealed packs of rocket ammo.

"It's not about slow," I said, chucking a pack of rocket ammo at a bot. Its laser cut through the rocket in mid air, detonating it and providing me with enough cover to leap over the box to the next pallet. Thankfully, my and Sasha's ECHO communicators allowed me to continue criticizing her love life. "It's about you not wanting to make a decision."

"Oh," Sasha said, slinging the shotgun onto her back and grabbing the sniper rifle. "So now Judgey Fiona has come out to play, huh?"

I tore open another box, revealing three chests full of pistols and one—finally—stuffed with empty assault rifle mags and loose bullets.

"Look, I get it," I said, tearing a mag from its plastic packaging.

"The kind of life we lived, you didn't have to make choices like that. Remember that guy in the Rust Commons? On the Varnell job? You spent every minute together when we weren't casing the joint, then we stole the dog, and then suddenly I never heard about him again."

Sasha looked down the scope of her rifle. An optimist would have described our situation as a target-rich environment. A realist would have said we were screwed. "Of course you never heard about him, we had to get outta town! The raiders were after us and—"

"Yeah, yeah, sure," I said. "But did *he* ever hear from you?"

I heard a loud boom. Shards of metal rained down onto my head. I looked up just in time to see a newly decapitated secbot collapse onto the pallet, its engine fizzing out.

"Sorry, what was that?" Sasha said. "I couldn't hear you over the sound of the successful long-range relationship between my bullet and the face of that robot that was about to kill you."

I thumbed rounds into a magazine. I could never get the hang of this part—the mag's interior spring was so strong I had a hard time getting the bullets to stay down, and the whole process always hurt my thumb.

"Until this planet, we'd never stayed in one place for more than a week. You don't actually know what a relationship is like. You're forced to spend a lot of time around a decently handsome idiot who worships the ground you walk on, and now you think you've got a boyfriend. Except he literally lives on a different planet." I shoved the last round home. The mag was full.

"So? I like the guy!"

"So do I!" I yelled.

"No, you don't."

I slammed the mag home and brought it up to my shoulder.

"I do, actually, which is why you need to stop playing around and pull the metaphorical trigger."

I pulled the non-metaphorical trigger.

Micro-rockets exploded from the end of the rifle, its internal digistruct engine working overtime to transmogrify the metal bullets into homing shards of explosive goo. The rockets swirled through the air, spiraling wildly until they locked onto the nearest source of heat: a duo of bots charging their face-lasers for an attack.

The rockets pummeled into the bots, throwing their aim off and eating into their chassis. Their laser beams went wild, slicing long burn trails in the sides of the buildings we raced past. The two bots were unable to keep up the chase and after Deathtrap rounded another corner, I didn't see them again. Would've preferred it if they'd exploded rather than just slowed down, but you don't always get what you want.

"Can we talk about this some other time?" Sasha asked. As anyone who has ever been in an argument knows, this meant I was winning.

"Look. I know *you're* fine. I know you can live without labels or whatever. But Rhys is a well-meaning sweetheart who clearly needs some clarity. The uncertainty's gotta be killing him."

Sasha plucked another bot out of the air with a well-aimed sniper round. "If he was unhappy with our situation, he'd tell me."

"Yeah," I said, feeding more shells into my empty mag. "That's what Rhys is known for, standing up for himself."

"So what are you saying?" Sasha asked as I unleashed another swarm of micro-rockets on our pursuers. To my irritation, I realized these wouldn't be a workable weapon against them in the long term; the micro-splosions slowed the bots down plenty, but they were doing next to no damage. If we weren't in a high-speed chase, they'd probably have the same effect as me throwing slightly sharpened rocks. "You're saying I should break up with him? That's what you're saying?"

"I'm saying you need to stop acting like we're still living out of a caravan. You don't get to drive away from this choice. If you want to date the idiot, date the idiot. If you don't, you gotta tell him."

A loud metallic clang from the front of the convoy grabbed my and Sasha's attention. Deathtrap was clapping his hands together, pointing at the large mouth of a disused tunnel leading into the Rustville sewerage system. The robot pointed at it, then made a thumbs-up gesture. A question: Should we head in there? Yes? No?

"Your decision," I shouted at Sasha. "We can keep going as we are, in this dangerous uncertainty, or you can make a choice—"

"SHUT UP, I SEE THE PARALLELS. I GET IT. GOD."

She nodded to Deathtrap, who sharply veered us into the sewer. The smell was pretty much exactly what you'd imagine—not great, but frighteningly easy to get used to. A half-dozen bots pursued us into the pipes, but there was so little room for them to maneuver that Sasha and I tore through them like tissue paper.

Sasha pointed at the top of the tunnel. "It's weak—blast it!"

We let loose on the tunnel roof with everything we had. Chunks of steel and dirt fell from the bullet holes. A deep, ominous groaning from above us preceded an avalanche of filth. A waterfall of dirt, rebar, and metal collapsed down into the tunnel behind us, blocking our escape route. We were, for the moment, safe.

Deathtrap zoomed us toward the underbelly of Rustville, a battalion of dead and wounded secbots in our wake. We had enough guns to arm a militia, we'd befriended a murderous robot who'd previously wanted to kill us, and I'd won an argument with my little sister.

Things were looking up.

35
FIONA

Ten minutes later, we were mugged with our own guns.

"Okay, well," I said. "When I look at the whole situation from your perspective, I can see why you'd do this."

We'd strolled into the Tetanus Wilds hauling five pallets' worth of chests. Deathtrap was still hiding out in the sewers; we didn't think Rustville's refugees would appreciate seeing another bloodstained secbot floating into their new home.

The Tetanus Wilds looked a hell of a lot worse since the last time we were there. Where the Wilds had once been a barren wasteland, now it was stuffed to the gills with impromptu camps and too-thin bedrolls laid over broken glass. The only two structures still standing, the ECHOvid theater and juice bar, were packed with Rusters who'd spilled out of the doors and spread out to the least hazardous spots in the wasteland, of which there were not many. In Rustville, these people had already had nothing. Now, with their homes and businesses and loved ones burned to a crisp, they had less than nothing.

I expected the refugees to look miserable. I expected sunken eyes, hunched shoulders, tears, wailing, shouting. I didn't get any of that. As the survivors hopscotched across the few scattered areas of stable, non-spiky ground, hauling their meager possessions on their backs or in the same wheelbarrows they'd used to clean up the rich folks' gardens, I understood what this was.

Their lives were hard and unfair, and then someone had fired an orbital laser into their neighborhood. Now their lives were still hard and unfair, but in a different mailcode. I'd had enough bad days as a kid to know that sometimes, when things get bad enough, it doesn't make that much difference when they get worse. You can only get so miserable before it starts to get funny.

And sometimes, you get so miserable that a lady with a hat and her smiling sister come to your camp with a bunch of guns and you think, *Yeah, violence seems like a pretty good choice right now.*

That's what I'd hoped, anyway. As I said, we got mugged.

"Free guns!" we'd shouted. "Come get your free guns so we can all go mess up some rich people!"

A dozen gaunt, haggard faces poked out of the tents. Several people crawled out toward us, suspicion and interest on their faces. I held up a shotgun and offered it to an irritated woman, making as big a show of it as I could for the onlookers.

The woman's face was oddly familiar, but I couldn't quite place it. She stroked the gun and removed it from my hands, then pulled the pump back and saw the chamber still had a shell left in it. A sickly man approached Sasha and, nodding, took an assault rifle from her hands. I smiled, thinking, *That's two more soldiers for our little army.*

"Mess up some rich people?" the familiar-looking woman asked.

I nodded, looking at her with a serious welcome-to-the-resistance-type expression.

She racked the gun and pointed it at my face. "You look pretty rich," she said.

"Oh, hell," Sasha said. "Tammithah?"

Ah. That's who she was. The store lady.

"I didn't know you were—" Sasha began.

"What, poor? You think I work in a clothing store because I can afford the shit we sell? Use your brain, idiot."

"We just wanna help," Sasha said as the sickly looking man pointed his newly acquired rifle into her back.

He laughed. "You could help us by giving us all the money you got in your account. That'd help an awful lot."

I clenched my fists. "We don't have any money. We spent it all on these guns."

"Heh. Money well spent," Tammithah said, staring at me through the scope. "And you're dressed pretty fancy for somebody broke. I think you're holdin' out on us."

"Sasha, do you have a way to call Deathtrap, by any chance?"

"Sure don't."

"Great."

I looked around. Others were leaving their tents. For the first time, my impeccable dress sense had put us directly in the crosshairs. I'd never be able to convince all these people that Sasha and I were bankrupt with my fashion sense. Of all the ways to die, being torn to pieces by an angry mob ranked very low on my list.

A stream of Rusters emerged from the open front of the theater. The stream got wider and faster and angrier and showed no signs of stopping. For now, they were merely observing our little tableau of guns and financial inequality, but if this went on much longer they'd fall upon the pallets of guns. Sasha and I would be lucky to get out of the throng without being trampled to death.

"Actually, why don't we all make a line," I said. "A nice long line, and one by one I'll—"

I was wasting my breath. I saw another Ruster tap their friend on the chest and point at us. They walked toward us with evident violent intent while others grew angrier by the moment.

"Pay up!" someone shouted, only using more profanity. "We don't like you or your sister!" they yelled, only with more creative verbs and nouns.

"I'm not one of the bad guys!" I shouted back, deeply aware that I was about to be the most well-dressed corpse in the city. "Wait, just—"

Something heavy leaped onto my back. I swatted and clawed at whatever the hell it was as it hoisted itself up and stood up straight on my shoulders, one tiny foot on either side of my head.

"PWEASE STOP!" a familiar voice wailed above the din.

A child leaped from my shoulders. A child with big chubby cheeks that I wanted to bite off and spit into the air where they'd become stars. A child with a button nose I wanted to press to summon a large, puffy dog I could ride around. The most adorable child I'd ever seen or would ever see.

"Face! Can you tell them we're cool, please?"

Face looked at the crowd. "All of dem?" he asked.

Sasha, her hands in the air, whispered down to him, "Yeah, man. Just vouch for us. We're good people. Instead of robbing us, maybe everyone could just take the guns and use them on the *bad* rich people, right? Yeah?"

"It's not a tewwible idea," Face said. "But I don't need your guns." He pulled a pistol from his waistband and pointed it at the old woman in front of him. "Drop it, pwease. All of you—everybody— leave dem alone. Guns down."

Tammithah shot a hateful glance at Face. "You don't need to get involved in something you don't understand, little one."

The sound of a hammer being pulled back hushed her to silence. Unseen by me, Face's sister, Pick, had managed to slink from the shadows and now poked a shotgun of her own into the sickly looking man's waist.

"He said pwease," she said.

The sickly looking man and Tammithah grunted in irritation and dropped their guns to the ground.

"Grab the guns," said Pick, nodding at me. "We're getting out of here."

Nodding my thanks in reply, I tossed the dropped weaponry back onto a pallet. Pick gestured at us to follow her, and apparently I was in the right frame of mind to obey a nine-year-old girl unthinkingly. She and her brother led us through broken buildings and past broken people. Even without their debts, they still walked with a visible weight, a tiredness that hunched their backs and slowed their gaits.

After five minutes of wordless walking, I asked, "So, uh, how have you two been?"

"Still poor," Pick said.

She led us to what looked to be the ruins of an old jail. A few of the cells were still in one piece, their iron bars standing strong despite the collapse around them.

"I'm sorry," I said.

Pick shook her head. "Don't be. It's a good thing you came around when you did."

She yanked one of the cell doors open.

And she waited.

With a gun in her hand.

"Oh," I said. "I see."

"Huh?" Sasha asked. "What's—"

Pick leveled the gun at her.

"Mm," Sasha said. "Mm. Mm. Okay. Mm."

Face scratched his rosy cheeks. "You haven't checked the ECHOnet lately, have you? After you blasted your way out of the spaceport, you earned a fat price on your head."

"Sixteen billion," Pick said. "From the countess herself."

"Ugh," Sasha said. "Well, you're only gonna get eight, first of all."

I held up my hands. "Wait. Think about this."

"You can think about it in the cell," Face said. "You'll have plenty of time to think once we call in the secbots."

I should have listened. I should have stepped into the cell and found a way to escape once their guns weren't on me. But honestly? At this point, I was just too damned tired.

I stepped toward Face, who backed up a little in surprise.

"Why do you think that bounty is so big, huh? Sixteen billion for some random Pandoran? Why?"

Pick shrugged. "Doesn't matter."

"It matters if you stand to make more money by taking her down than working with her. A month ago, I was in the same damn position you are right now. And I chose wrong. You can't beat these people by playing their game. You gotta flip the board over."

Face pushed the barrel of his gun into my nose. "Don't need to beat 'em. Don't care. Just sick of being hungry."

I crouched to get on Face's level—and, I guess, to make it a lot easier for him to blow my head off.

"I get it. You wanna survive. No shame in that. But that's not the whole picture. If this plan of ours works—if we can get the Elites on the business end of a rifle and make them pay off everyone's debts—maybe you wouldn't have to rob people just to make ends meet."

Face sniffed, an action so cute it made me want to scream into a pillow. "What if I like robbin' people?"

I smiled. "Then I've got the perfect person for you to rob."

Face frowned… and lowered the gun.

"Hey, what are you doing?" Pick demanded.

"She's got a point," Face said. "You really wanna go work for the lady who burned our apartment building to the ground? Besides, if we can fight our way in there, I bet she's got all sorts of expensive crap we can loot."

Pick sighed and lowered her gun. "So what, exactly, is your plan?" she asked.

"Give a lot of guns to a lot of angry people and then point them at the people who got them angry in the first place—historically, one of the most reliable plans in the history of our species. The problem," I continued, cocking my head as I looked into Face's eminently lovable features, "is me."

"How's that?" Pick asked.

Sasha saw where I was going with this. "You can't follow someone you can't relate to. From the Rusters' perspective, we're two fat cats trying to tell the mice to attack a bunch of other cats."

I knelt and put my hand on Face's shoulder. "Which brings me to you."

Face's eyes twinkled. I think they actually made a noise. "Me?"

"You. Now—how do you feel about public speaking?"

————

Tears streamed down Face's plump, rosy cheeks as he stood atop the small mountain of gun chests we'd constructed in the center of the Wilds. The assembled crowd of unhomed, impoverished, and hungry souls looked on in a mixture of pity and anger as he unspooled his tale.

"Guh hub uh hum," he sobbed.

"My bwother says we had a home," his sister translated.

"Buh shuh bur uh."

"But she burned it."

Face made a big show of trying to keep his composure—of trying to prevent himself from completely melting down into a mass of snot and tears and trauma—until, with expert dramatic timing, he let the dam burst. He became an unyielding torrent of blubbering and vowels, which Pick gladly translated.

"The fire spread too quickly. We grabbed what we could on our way out. I took our dog, Bestie, because her legs were broken and she couldn't run very fast. But her sight was so bad, her sense of smell was so hampered by the fire, that even after we escaped the blazing inferno of the building, she thought she heard my brother's screams from inside. Our little dog leaped back into the flaming building, limping with every step, and the building collapsed on her."

Sniffles and sobs spread through the small crowd like a virus. Grown men tried, and failed, to keep their shit together as Pick went on about their disabled, crispy, fictional dog. It was a magnificent performance.

"The Elites took everything from us. Just like they took everything from you."

Pick leaped down and flung open one of the gun chests. She pulled a submachine gun from its innards and hoisted it high above her head.

"It's time to take something back!" she yelled, except she pronounced "something" like "somefing" and it absolutely killed.

The group erupted in cheers and applause. They rushed toward the hill of guns like a swarm of spiderants to a bleeding bandit lord covered in ice cream.

Tammithah ended up getting her shotgun back. Maybe she had a thing for shotguns, I dunno. She racked the slide and asked, "So, where are we going?"

Pick and Face pointed toward the neighborhood of rich Elites. In unison, they shouted, "To the Holloway estate!"

The Eden-5 civil war had begun.

36
FIONA

Well, maybe not *begun* begun. It *began* began four days later. After Pick and Face yelled, "To the Holloway estate!" I had to convince them we weren't ready yet, which caused Face to add, "Soon!" to the violence-hungry crowd.

Holloway had sarcastically invited us to a gala, and we were going to show up. In style.

But before we could get to the fun part where our army shot rockets at evil robots, we all needed to sit around a big-ass map of Holloway's mansion and discuss how likely it was that we'd all die trying to get inside it. The disused movie theater seemed as good a place as any for this. Deathtrap floated calmly as it projected a 3D holomap of the Holloway home onto a wall near the snack bar.

Sasha pointed at the ring of autoturrets surrounding the estate. "Once we reach the gates, we'll have to blast our way through or climb our way over. And the entire time, these turrets will be hurling lead at us. And that's after the secbot swarm gets on our asses. The second they see us organizing in the streets, the sky's gonna turn dark with security drones."

"Do we have the numbers to just, I dunno, blitz them?" I asked. "Move quick, get inside before the bots and the turrets cut us to pieces?"

Pick shook her head. "We put about forty guns in about forty-one hands. A single laser blast from a secbot can kill somebody before they hit the ground."

"Right," I said. "Wait—forty-one hands?"

Pick nodded at the snack bar. "Three-Armed Francis."

A man waved at me, then waved two more times.

"That doesn't even get into how rough things'll be once we get inside," Sasha said. "Since every billionaire in the city will be at this can't-miss gala event, they'll also have their own personal security guards on high alert. That might mean bots. Might mean big guys with big guns. I dunno."

I closed my eyes. "Right. Well, one thing at a time. First is getting inside. There's gotta be a safer way than just walking through the street. Sewers?"

Face shook his little baby cheeks. "The pipes under Eliteville are chock full of motion detectors and proximity mines, to prevent exactly the kind of thing we're thinking about doing."

"Rooftops?" I volunteered to a room full of confused faces. "Right. We can't fly. Well, Deathtrap can fly, but he can only hold one of us at a time. *Wait!*"

I clapped my hands together loud enough to cause a few jumps.

"We'll sneak in as the catering staff! There's gotta be dozens of folks for all the cooking and cleaning. They'll have to hire from somewhere, and we can just accept the job postings and… No, that's stupid. They can't really believe you'd just jump at the chance to serve them all drinks for pennies, not after they destroyed your homes. Can you imagine how insulting it'd be for them to even offer those jobs to you?"

I stared at a sea of blank expressions. We all came to pretty much the same conclusion at pretty much the same time.

"Oh." I said. "That's exactly what they're going to do."

Pick nodded. "We're the only labor force on this rock, unless the Elites feel like serving their own canapés. The automated butlers will handle most of the grunt work, so they won't be hiring more than a handful of human laborers. I'm thinking four people, maybe less. Just enough people to handle the stuff robots can't do—cooking, handling special requests, being yelled at for serving water without lemon."

I nodded. "Four people. Typical Vault Hunter number. Sasha and I will be in that group, then. This was our stupid plan, so we should take the lion's share of the risk."

"You don't think Holloway might recognize us?" Sasha asked.

"Every billionaire in the city's gonna be here. She'll be too busy to notice us. Besides, you think someone like Holloway would even deign to look the help in the eye?"

"Feh." Sasha was unconvinced.

"We'll go with you, too," Pick said, nodding at her brother. "We've cleaned the place before."

Someone else might have balked at the idea of bringing two children to an infiltration team, but I, as I may have mentioned a few times before, am from Pandora.

Pick continued, "They'll be keeping their eyes on us more than usual, I expect, but… I mean, whatever. I've pickpocketed folks before. This can't be that much different."

I pointed at the estate schematic. "It will be, actually. We'll have to stay under cover until we can find the security room. That's where the autoturrets and the gate controls should be. Once we're there, we can deactivate both and let in the rest of our forces. And we'll have to do it all without setting off the alarm and releasing the secbots."

Sasha cocked her head. "You lost me at 'let in the rest of our forces.' We'll be inside shutting down the defenses, sure, but where are the other thirty-six gonna be? Just standing out in Eliteville, holding guns, waiting for the doors to open? The secbots will be alerted the second anyone with a six-digit bank balance sees them."

I scratched under my hat. She had a point. So what if we could shut off the autoturrets and open the door? We had no way of getting our army near the party in the first place. And we couldn't hold the estate with only four people.

"Wait," I said. "The horse."

Sasha squinted at me. "The diamond one?"

"No. The old fable about soldiers hiding inside a big horse."

Sasha raised an eyebrow. "Did the horse… consent to this?"

"Of course it did. Horses love being helpful. Anyway, one army gifted their enemy a large, beautiful horse. But they'd hidden soldiers inside the horse. That's where that saying comes from: 'Always look a gift horse in the mouth.'"

"So you're… so you're suggesting we spend the four days until the party doing… what? Genetically engineering a big horse we can shove ourselves into?"

An idea came to me. Yes, it was an idea so utterly stupid it could not possibly work, but it was also, in my defense, the only one I had.

"No," I said. "We're going to build something that Holloway wants much more."

———

Four days go quickly when you're hiding from airborne security drones. During the day, we slept and hid in ruins as secbots buzzed through the air, blaring out the details of my and Sasha's bounty. If Deathtrap hadn't been with us, I'm sure more than a few of our troops would have considered shoving guns into our backs and walking us to Holloway for a payout. But ultimately, their fear of Deathtrap and sympathy for Face's dead-dog story kept them at their work.

It's not an easy thing, welding and gluing steel and concrete into a giant dude-containing sculpture, but it helps if you've got about forty experienced laborers and a killer robot with incredible upper-body strength. By the end of the second night, they already had the whole thing constructed and painted. We spent the last night adding murder windows the occupants could open from the inside and point guns through.

Dawn broke on the day of Holloway's gala. The party was to begin at sundown. Sasha helped everyone clean their guns as I checked the ammo distribution. It felt a little weird, to be honest—adult, in some way, like we were upstanding Dahl soldiers going into battle rather than a bunch of poor (or poor-until-very-recently) ding-dongs with a bunch of guns and a passing interest in class revolution. But the more I sat with the feeling, the more I thumbed bullets into magazines, the less weird it became. Then it started feeling scary, then exciting, then important, and then just… good.

Win or lose, we were doing something. I thought of the big comfy mansion we'd sold in order to afford these guns. I thought of the pleasure jets in our quantum jacuzzi. I thought of our self-playing, mildly sentient piano. I thought of the cheese whirlpool. And when I compared my current situation—dirty, smelly, handing out greasy ammo mags—to all of that? Sure, I missed being rich, but being down here, preparing to do some Vault Hunter-ass rowdiness? That was pretty damned good in its own way.

I watched Sasha oil up a rag and wondered if I should try one last-ditch trick to get her to safety. The thought disappeared just as quickly as it formed. Sasha had made her choice. And maybe I needed to stop second-guessing her.

"Hey," I said. "You got a second?"

"Rhys may have overstated the value of some of these guns. Most haven't been cleaned in years. If we get through this fight without one of these things exploding and blowing somebody's thumbs off, I'll feel lucky."

"Yeah, actually, about Rhys," I said, and handed her a folded piece of paper and an envelope I'd found inside one of the chests when we'd first inspected the cargo. "I thought this was the packing slip, so I opened it. Sorry. Once I realized what it was, I, uh, stopped reading it."

Sasha grabbed the paper. "'Dear Sasha,'" she read. As she pored over the letter's contents, a big dumb smile appeared on her face. She folded up the letter and shoved it into her coat pocket. "It's from Rhys," she said. "He says hi."

"Look," I said, watching the glow on my sister's face. "Maybe forget all that stuff I said before about Rhys. It's not my business what you do or who you do it with, or any of that stuff. Honestly, you've got your shit figured out better than I do most of the time. So, I just wanted to say… sorry. For throwing you into jail that one time. And for trying to make you a prisoner in your own home."

"And for being judgey," she added.

"And for that. Consider this a general apology."

She pulled me into a hug. "Thanks, Fi. I know you meant well."

I pulled her closer. "Yeah."

This was nice. Sasha and I had argued and fought and made up more times than I could count, but that never made it feel any less special when we eventually mended our fences. I mean, yes, she's impulsive and has terrible taste in men, but she's my sister. I love her.

I patted her on the back. "Now, just make sure you stay safe, okay? I'll be really irritated if you get killed the *one time* I decide not to be overbearing."

She shrugged and said, "I'll do my best."

The troops were ready. The guns were loaded. There was nothing left to do. "So," Sasha said. "A couple hours until nightfall. Holloway's gonna want her human staff there before sunset."

"Well then," I said, "time to get dressed. We've got to get to our last fancy-dress party ever."

37
GAIGE

If the torturer's doing it right, you never get used to the pain. And Holloway's torture bots did it right.

Gaige was too smart to beg for mercy and was out of tears to shed, but she could still scream. And scream she did, until her throat was hoarse and the only sound that came out was a dry, desperate hissing.

Holloway didn't bother watching the festivities in person. Security cameras covered every possible angle of the room. Not, Gaige supposed, because she was worried her captive might try to break out, but because she wanted to savor every detail of the Vault Hunter's misery.

Worse than the pain, though, was the thought that kept repeating in Gaige's head: *You failed him.* Her father was cold in the ground, and she'd had only one job: avenge his murder. And she couldn't do it. Not that she regretted turning herself in to save Rustville, of course—that had been no choice at all—but she shouldn't have gotten distracted. Should have abandoned Sasha the second they'd got out of debtors' prison. Should have put a bullet in Holloway's head right after smashing the action figure into her face.

Should have snuck back to Eden and smuggled her father out when he was still alive.

The torture bot stuck something sharp into something soft.

"You already poked me there," Gaige whispered through hoarse hisses of pain. "Running out of ideas?"

The bot poked her somewhere else. It had not run out of ideas.

Gaige considered possible avenues of escape. There were at least three ways she could break her restraints and leave the room, but none that wouldn't guarantee Holloway fleeing to safety. For now, the best she could do was to find a way to get her captor into the torture room, *then* escape.

Without Deathtrap or a gun, she would almost certainly be killed in the attempt. Which didn't matter to Gaige in the slightest as long as Holloway died too.

She could think of only one way to trick Holloway into entering the room: she had to convince the countess to kill her. Both women knew that Gaige would only die once Holloway got sick of her screams or Gaige's mind broke and she became immune to the pain. At that point, she'd almost certainly step into the torture chamber and end Gaige herself.

That'd be the moment to strike.

The problem was, that moment was set to come after about a thousand other moments of unbelievable pain. Every single time the torture bot slowly—*slowly*—brought a red-hot object to her skin, Gaige promised herself that this would be the time she'd make no noise. This would be the time the part of her brain that experienced pain would become scarred over.

It hadn't worked once. Not yet.

And the bot had not run out of ideas.

38
FIONA

A metal detector, too low-tech to be hacked, protected the servants' entrance, so we had to enter the mansion without guns. Anything bigger than a belt buckle would have gotten us torn to shreds. So Sasha, the two kids, and I stepped into the mansion with nothing to protect us but our clever disguises and a lot of confidence.

The first time I'd seen it, right after we'd arrived on Eden-5, I'd thought the Holloway estate was gorgeous. Seeing the estate decked out for a party, though, made the undecorated mansion seem like a pillow fort by comparison. Frozen champagne stalactites slowly melted into stacked glasses. A digistructed flying whale soared from room to room, ejecting bite-sized fruit tarts from its blowhole. Every room sported a different robotic band that used cutting-edge body-language receptors to play the song most likely to be enjoyed by the crowd.[28] And the party hadn't even started yet.

A secbot floated into the room. We all did our best to look casual and nonrevolutionary as it scanned us. I flattened the creases in my

---

28 We were nearly caught when we entered the room to the sweet melodies of "Kill All The Rich People And Give Their Money Away" by the Jabber Jobbers until our obvious discomfort convinced the bot band to play something without lyrics.

waiter's outfit, straightened my back, and stroked my mustache.

The secbot zoomed toward me. "IDENTIFY," it grated.

"Ayyy," I said in a passably masculine voice. "It's me, Giovanni Buenofortuna, maestro of guest services. What you want? I'll get it for you. Ba-dam!"[29] [30]

"CHECKING EMPLOYMENT RECORDS... CONFIRMED. YOU WILL PROCEED TO THE KITCHEN AND RECEIVE FURTHER INSTRUCTIONS FROM THE AUTOCHEFS."

Not ideal. The kitchen sat in the northernmost part of the estate, in the exact opposite direction of the security room.

"Ayyy," I said again. "But of course. Let us just go get our supplies and I'll be there before you can press a panini."

The bot zoomed in close enough to touch my high-quality faux mustache. I didn't flinch. I felt confident. Invulnerable. Rhys hadn't been lying about its powers.

"YOU HAVE THREE HUNDRED SECONDS. GO."

I snapped my fingers—"Ba-dam!"—and led Sasha, Face, and Pick into the lounge to the south. The lounge led to the secondary lounge, which led to the games room, which led to the library, which led to the security room.

We had a new problem to deal with: a secbot blocked the door to the security room and showed no signs of moving. We watched the thing for a good half-minute and it didn't even turn its head. The door to the security room was open, but what good was that when a half-ton floating death machine stopped you from stepping inside?

"I know what to do," Face said through cheeks that looked like flesh-colored marshmallows, but in a good way. "I'll go to the

---

29 "Ba-dam!" is Giovanni Buenofortuna's catchphrase.
30 Acting is all about making bold choices.

lounge and start a fire. It'll summon all the secbots in the area, maybe including this one."

"What if this one doesn't, though? What if it stays put?" Sasha asked.

"Who cares about that?" said Pick. "You'll be caught immediately. They'll tear you to pieces."

"Oh. And that would be bad, too," Sasha said.

"Sister," Face said, putting a chubby-fingered hand on Pick's shoulder. "Just trust me." Then he winked, which struck me as odd. Winks are more of a cocky thing than an adorable thing. Something about the wink seemed off, but I figured it was just winks being overall incompatible with Face's whole brand as an adorable child.

Face disappeared back the way we'd come. Two minutes later, nothing had changed. We hadn't heard from him and didn't notice any alarms. Pick began to fidget. I couldn't blame her. I was worried, too.

"Something's happened," I said. "Pick, go find your brother. Sasha and I will get into the security room our own way."

"How?" Pick asked.

"We may not have been able to sneak any guns in here," I said, "but they can't take my greatest weapon away from me." I pointed at my mouth.

"You're gonna eat the robot?" Pick asked.

"No. My tongue."

"You're gonna make out with the robot?"

"Just… go find your brother."

Pick ran off in the direction Face had gone, leaving Sasha and me alone in the office. "How do you expect to convince a robot to let you into a room when that robot's sole job is preventing people from going into that room?" Sasha asked.

"Easy," I said, not at all convinced it was going to be. "I'll just:"

use logic to short-circuit it—turn to page 262

convince it there's an emergency elsewhere—turn to page 263

make it chase me—turn to page 264

…—turn to page 266

USE LOGIC TO SHORT-CIRCUIT IT

"Does a set of all sets contain itself?" I asked the secbot. Sasha watched from the office behind me, wearing what I assumed was a nervous expression on her face. She shouldn't have been worried; if there's one thing I'm good at, it's short-circuiting robots with paradoxes.

Or, wait, not *good at*. I'm… the other thing. What was it? Oh yes. *Certain I've never done it before.*

"I DUNNO," the bot said. "NOT MY DEPARTMENT."

Hmm. Inconvenient.

"What *is* your department, then?"

"SECURITY."

"Okay, then is there… Could you imagine a door so secure that even you couldn't secure it?"

"WHAT?"

"No. Ignore that."

"OKAY."

"Okay, here we go. So, your job is to keep things safe, right?"

"YES."

"And 'safe' could be defined as 'not in pain, not in danger of dying,' right?"

"SURE."

"So if that's true, wouldn't a dead body be the safest thing of all?"

"MAY… BE."

"In which case, in order to make this estate as safe as possible, you should kill everyone in it, right?"

Behind me, Sasha coughed. "Maybe ease off on the robots killing everyone," she whispered.

"NO. THE ACT OF CAUSING THEIR DEATHS WOULD CREATE PAIN AND DANGER OF DYING."

"Of course. You're totally right. But pain and danger of death are, to some extent, unavoidable consequences of life, correct? Like, if Countess Holloway stubs her toe, that's pain."

"I WOULD OBVIOUSLY STOP HER FROM STUBBING HER TOE."

"Yeah, but you can't do that *all* the time. Holloway could be stubbing her toe right now and you wouldn't know, wouldn't be able to prevent it. So to some extent, you forgive a degree of pain and danger affecting the people you are meant to protect."

"I SUPPOSE."

"In that case, all we're disagreeing on is a matter of degree. I would argue that the relatively small pain of a laser incinerating your head—a process that takes, what, less than a half-second, too quickly for the brain's pain receptors to even understand what happened—is massively outweighed by the permanent gain of being dead—a state which, as we just agreed, means you are incapable of dying or feeling pain. So, logically, in order to protect people from death, you should kill them."

"AH," the robot said. "SHIT."

It exploded.

I turned to Sasha and flashed her a lil' thumbs-up. "Knew that would work," I lied.

Turn to page 267

CONVINCE IT THERE'S AN EMERGENCY ELSEWHERE

I ran up to the robot, sporting my most convincing look of panic. "There's a fire!" I wheezed.

"THEN THE FIRE SUPPRESSION SYSTEMS WILL HANDLE IT," it replied.

"Sorry, not a fire. A thief. He's stealing all of Holloway's priceless art!"

"THE ART GALLERY'S SECBOTS WILL PURSUE THE CRIMINAL AND RETURN THE STOLEN GOODS."

"Did I say thief? I meant kidnapper."

"COUNTESS HOLLOWAY UNDERWENT SURGERY THAT ALLOWS HER TO EXCRETE ANTI-KIDNAPPING PHEROMONES."

"A con artist was about to fleece Holloway for billions of dollars."

"WHEN SOMEONE OF COUNTESS HOLLOWAY'S STATURE SPENDS BILLIONS OF DOLLARS ON SOMETHING, IT IMMEDIATELY BECOMES THAT VALUABLE REGARDLESS OF ITS PRIOR VALUE."

"Someone's peeing in the garden!"

"OVERFILLING ONE'S BLADDER CAN LEAD TO URINARY TRACT INFECTIONS. IT IS BETTER THAT THEY RELIEVE THEMSELVES."

"Children are spray-painting images on the estate's walls!"

"THE AUTOCLEANSE PROTOCOLS WILL REMOVE IT BY TOMORROW MORNING."

"One of the napkin-folding bots decided swans were too difficult!"

"OH, FUCK," the robot shouted before speeding off toward the dining room.

I turned to Sasha and winked. "Ba-dam."

Turn to page 267

MAKE IT CHASE ME

I slapped the robot in the face as hard as I could and ran down the hallway, making it as far as the chocolate-tsunami room before I realized it wasn't following me.

"Hey!" I shouted. "What's it take to make you go on alert?"

"ATTEMPTED ENTRY INTO THE SECURITY ROOM. A DIRECT ATTEMPT ON COUNTESS HOLLOWAY'S LIFE. ATTEMPTED DESTRUCTION OF HOLLOWAY PROPERTY."

"Thanks!" I shouted.

"NO PROBLEM," it responded.

I grabbed a crystal vase from a nearby table and said, "I'm gonna smash this!"

Before the words had finished leaving my mouth, the bot had unsheathed its digistruct claws and was speeding toward me.

Nice, I thought, and then I thought, *Ah, not nice*, because I realized I hadn't thought this far ahead. The vase was too heavy to run with and the bot was too damn fast.

I looked through the doorway into the chocolate-tsunami room. Other rich people had chocolate fountains or chocolate volcanoes; apparently, Holloway thought those were inadequate. Within the four walls of this room, a constant roiling thunderstorm of cacao raged with the fury of a malevolent candy wizard.

"Hyup," I said, because that's the noise you make when you toss a crystal vase into a chocolate tsunami in order to distract the murder bot that's chasing you.

"MUST PROTECT HOLLOWAY PROPERTY FROM DESTR-UCTION," the bot shouted, following the vase into the storm.

Clods of chocolate pelted the secbot, knocking it around the room like loose change in a washing machine. It reached out feebly, attempting to protect the crystal vase from being buried under a thick layer of cocoa butter and sugar. Its efforts were all for naught, however, as chocolate-chip hail clogged the bot's joints, cocoa sleet infiltrated its gears, and every servo and microchip drowned under the tidal wave of sweetness.

The bot thunked to the ground, immobile, as chocolate

continued to buffet it from every angle. Its arms stretched out toward an equally chocolate-covered vase that it would never be able to reach. There was a sad poetry to the image.

Sasha stepped into the hallway. "Is it dead?"

I nodded. "Death by dessert. Now, let's go end capitalism."

Turn to page 267

Turn to page 267

...

I walked up to the secbot. No stealth. No preamble.

Just smolder.

Robots are programmed to read human social cues and respond in kind, so what would this one do if I gave it no cues at all? What would it do if I gave it an intense, slightly alluring facial expression, and nothing else?

The secbot raised a hand to stop me. "YOU MAY NOT PROCEED PAST THIS POINT."

I stared, eyes slightly narrowed, lips slightly pouted. Pouted in what? you may ask. Flirtation? Irritation?

Yes. No. Maybe all of the above. That's the point. Keep them guessing. Keep them interested. Keep the mystery alive.

The robot stared back at me, processing calculations in its quantum brain faster than I could blink.

"IDENTIFY," it said.

I continued to stare. Continued to be attractive and inscrutable.

"PLEASE?" it asked.

The question bounced harmlessly off my implacable smolder and hung in the air like a dry fart. The robot would have been embarrassed to have asked it. Suddenly, the tables were turned. Suddenly, I had the power in the conversation.

"WHAT DO YOU WANT?" it asked, desperation creeping into

its voice. "SPEAK. MAKE A DEMAND. MOVE. PERFORM ANY ACTION AT ALL."

I did not.

"I DON'T... I... IT'S..."

A panel on the secbot's chest unfolded. The bot reached in and pulled out a grenade.

"ARE YOU HACKING ME? AM I BEING HACKED? I CANNOT ALLOW YOU TO COMPROMISE THE NETWORK."

It pulled the pin.

I smoldered harder than I'd ever smoldered before, every cell in my body working to maintain my inscrutable calm. I had, at most, two seconds left to live.

"IT'S A TRICK!" the bot screamed, hurling the grenade down the hallway, where it exploded and destroyed at least seven hundred million dollars' worth of decorations. "YOU ARE TRYING TO GET ME TO SELF-DESTRUCT. NICE TRY," it shouted. "YOU WANT ME? YOU'LL HAVE TO CATCH ME."

The bot shoved me to the floor—it's important you know that I maintained my frozen expression even as I hit the ground—and zoomed away, flailing its arms in panic.

I got to my feet and dusted myself off. Sasha stared at me with a mixture of awe and horror.

I shrugged as smugly as I possibly could.

Turn to page 267

Three rows of monitors and a galaxy of multicolored lights and switches greeted us as we entered the security room.

"Find the switch that turns off the autoturrets," I said, as much to myself as Sasha. "And the one that opens the gate."

"They're not labeled," Sasha said. "Do I just start pressing stuff?" She jabbed a blue button that caused the security monitors to flicker between different camera feeds.

"Keep going," I said. "Let's see if the others are in position."

She hammered the button until the screen showed the feed we were looking for.

The figure looked even better through the security camera than it did in person. This... thing we'd created—one might call it a float, or a transport, or a sculpture—looked exactly like the kind of prize a billionaire might be interested in accepting.

A massive, bus-sized sculpture of Typhon DeLeon stood proudly just beyond the gates of the Holloway estate. From his big friendly smile to his big friendly nose, everything was a one-to-fifty replica of the tiny Vaultlander that had brought us to this planet months ago—except for the fact that inside its round belly, three dozen armed soldiers waited for their moment to strike.

If she couldn't get her hands on his Vaultlander, I hoped, maybe Holloway would want to check out a much bigger version in person. Maybe close enough that, once DeLeon's pants popped open,[31] we could grab Holloway right off the bat and save ourselves a whole hell of a lot of fighting.

"I found it!" Sasha said. "Autoturret emergency deactivation. Let me just—" Her finger moved toward the button, the action stopped only by the small issue of our being completely and utterly betrayed.

Two secbot voices behind us droned, "STEP AWAY FROM THE CONSOLE."

We turned around to see Face standing between the two secbots, pointing at us and wiping fake tears from his rosy, traitorous cheeks. I suddenly understood why something had seemed off

---

31 I asked the builders why they couldn't just install a door in one of his legs, but they looked at me like I was a dumbass so I let it go.

about the little wink he'd given his sister before he'd run off. It wasn't a "trust me" wink; it was an "I'm gonna screw these guys over and make us rich" wink.

"GIOVANNI BUENOFORTUNA. PUT YOUR HANDS UP AT ONCE."

I heard footfalls behind Face and the bots. It was his sister, Pick. She grabbed him by the shoulder, seemingly as surprised and pissed as Sasha and me. "Face, what are you—"

"Saving us from a suicide mission and setting us up for life," he said.

Suddenly, I wanted to stamp Face's face in—and for the first time ever, not because he was cute.

The secbots charged us.

IF YOU USED LOGIC TO SHORT-CIRCUIT THE OTHER BOT:

"Wait," I shouted. "What happens when an unstoppable force—"

IF YOU CONVINCED THE OTHER BOT OF AN EMERGENCY SOMEWHERE ELSE:

"Hold on," I shouted. "The napkin bot—"

IF YOU MADE THE OTHER BOT CHASE YOU:

I grabbed a rolling chair and tried to juke past the bots, hoping to lure them to the chocolate room—

IF YOU SILENTLY STARED AT THE OTHER BOT:

I cocked my eyebrows like a pair of shotguns and prepared to unleash the smolder—

I didn't get a chance to finish executing my brilliant, historically successful plan, because at that point I felt a metal fist collide with my temple, and then I didn't feel anything at all.

39
FIONA

It was pretty nice, as far as torture rooms go. I've never been a fan of linoleum floors, but the soft light from the golden sconces imbued the entire space with a warm, cozy feeling, the kind that makes you want to curl up and take a nap or, failing that, get your toes smashed in with a hammer.

Sasha and I were tied to surprisingly comfortable chairs. We weren't gagged, which was not a terribly encouraging detail, as it meant that (A) no matter how loudly we screamed, nobody who cared would hear us and (B) our screams were part of the point of the whole ordeal.

"Hey, guys!" A familiar voice said. "Great to see ya!"

Both of her eyes were swollen. Blood trickled from her nostrils, her ears, and the corners of her mouth. Still, she was smiling.

"Hello, Gaige," I slurred through a swollen jaw. "We're here to rescue you."

"And fix capitalism," Sasha said.

Gaige cocked her head in either confusion or pity or both. "Doin' a great job."

"How are you doing?" I asked.

"Tortured daily," she said, and shrugged.

A loudspeaker affixed to the ceiling barked itself awake, somehow filling the room with the sweet scent of Countess Holloway's perfume. As her smooth voice wafted from the speaker box, you could hear her smile—the smile of someone who knows they're about to get away with something.

"Speak of the devil," Gaige said, unable to keep the fear from her voice.

"A Typhon DeLeon sculpture?" Holloway laughed. "You thought I'd, what? Wheel it into my foyer? That I'd let something that garish exist in the same mailcode as me? Besides, everyone knows you're broke. It's not as if you could afford to buy a gift of that size."

"It *was* a gift," I affirmed, and shrugged. There was a chance, however small, that she didn't know about the soldiers inside.

"You think I don't know the parable about the cavernous horse? You think this is the first time somebody's tried to smuggle a large present full of angry people into my home? How many did you fit in there, anyway? Ten? Twenty?"

"There's nobody in there," I said. It was worth a shot.

Holloway chuckled. "Guess we'll find out. My autoturrets have been hurling bullets at it for the last ten minutes."

"Your loss," I said, my heart skipping every other beat and my brain doing jumping jacks as it considered the possibility that I'd just led thirty innocent people to their violent, claustrophobic deaths.

"You really wanna piss her off, why don't you come down here and show her the security footage?" Gaige asked. "Let her see her troops getting ripped apart in real time."

I wasn't stupid enough to believe Gaige was serious. It was a ploy to get Holloway inside the room with us—a desperate one, at that.

"Kudos on the workmanship," Holloway said, again ignoring Gaige. "I'd expected it would have been torn to pieces after the first few bursts, but your friends inside are going to be very scared for a very long time. Right up until those bullets finally punch through and end whatever the hell you were trying to do here—"

"We were trying to have a good time at a party," Sasha said. "You *did* invite us. And frankly, this kind of treatment is beneath you. Just because we were curious about your security room, as any normal guest might be—"

"If you're going to try your adorable little con-artist routine, you can save it for the torture bots. That's what they're here for." The countess sighed and, for the first time, addressed Gaige. "I think you get a break tonight, Vault Hunter. Instead, you'll watch as the torture bots peel the skin from these idiots' flesh, surgically reattach it, and then start the whole process over again. Tomorrow, I'll do the same to you. Tonight will be a sort of preview of coming attractions. And you've got a front-row seat."

"That's a terrible metaphor," Gaige said. "Nobody likes front-row seats. You have to look straight up and it hurts your neck. You can't even see the sides of the screen without moving your head. Is that what tonight is gonna be like? I'm gonna have to look from side to side to understand what's going on?"

Holloway glared. "One day, you're going to run out of things to say. And that is going to be a very, very good day."

The loudspeaker went dead. Sooner than I would have liked, a red dot blazed to life in the shadowy hallway. Then another. Then another.

Three secbots floated into the room. It wasn't hard to guess which one was made for torture. Its palms and fingers sported thousands of different-sized spikes and needles. Some looked hypodermic—maybe full of rakk sweat, which is known to have hallucinogenic effects in large quantities—while others just looked painful for painful's sake. Brown splotches of dried blood spotted the torture bot's chassis, and even the hum of its hoverjets sounded like a high-pitched shriek.

After one look at the three bots, Gaige started to laugh—way too hard.

"You dumb bastards!" she shouted as the torture bot pressed a button on its neck. To my and Sasha's audible horror, some of the spikes on the bot's hands and arms began to extend and contract horribly quickly.

A sharp pain filled my stomach. My entire body felt hot. Sweat formed behind my knees and at my temples. I'd always known I was going to die one day, but I'd hoped it wouldn't involve my sister and me being in the most agonizing pain imaginable.

The two secbots behind the torture bot floated silently, utterly indifferent. I tried to take my eyes off them, but there was something about them—something that just felt *off*.

"YOU FIRST," the torture bot hissed, pointing at me.

"Wait," I said, though I knew it wouldn't do any good. "There's been a mistake."

The torture bot moved closer.

Gaige was still laughing. "You idiots really have no idea who you're messing with," she cackled.

The bot extended a single needle from its pointer finger. A glob of something green and smelly dripped from its tip, sizzling as it hit the ground.

"And you're supposed to be *smart!*" Gaige laughed.

"Shut up!" Sasha yelled. "Fiona, look at me. Hey! Look at me."

The torture bot pushed its finger-needle toward my face. I moved my head to avoid it, but the needle followed me wherever I went. No, that's not right—the needle didn't follow *me*. It followed my eye.

"Oooooh, this is gonna hurrrrrrt," Gaige said.

"Shut! Up! Fiona, we're gonna get out of this. Just listen to my voice."

"Oh, come on," Gaige scoffed. "What are you waiting for? Do it already!"

I closed my eyes. I heard a slice of metal on metal—the sound of rending, twisting machinery. The slam of something big and hard and robotic against the wall. And all the while, Gaige's triumphant cackling filled the room.

I opened my eyes to a room with two fewer functional robots in it.

"That's my *boy!*" Gaige screamed. "Get these restraints off, DT!"

The remaining robot re-sheathed its claws and moved over to Gaige.

"Wait, what?" I asked. "I'm not… We're not dead?"

Freed from her chains, Gaige stood and threw her arms around Deathtrap. "I knew you'd come find me, babe. But how'd you get all fixed up?"

"Us," Sasha said. "Well, me, specifically. After our bank accounts got drained, we tracked down where Holloway's goons were keeping him. Wasn't that hard to break him out."

"But how'd he…? I thought he was in the Typhon DeLeon statue with everyone else," I said.

"Ha!" Gaige threw her head back. "If you think my best boy was just gonna sit and wait while he knew I was in danger, you don't know Deathtrap at all. He probably hacked into your ECHO devices. The second you saw me, he came floatin' in." She nodded at us. Deathtrap grabbed our restraints and crushed them in his metal hands. "Thanks for fixing him up," she said, seemingly genuine for the first time since I'd known her. "He's kind of all I have. So."

Deathtrap popped open its front panel and pulled out three Atlas wrist pistols. Gaige, Sasha, and I each strapped one to our arms.

We stepped out into the hallway and got our bearings. The

security cameras that dotted the walls every ten paces remained silent and dark, thanks to Deathtrap hacking the internal surveillance ECHOnet. It seemed like we were at least a floor underground; the manor was just above us. The sounds of expertly composed, perfectly played chamber music was still audible down here—the party was evidently still on. Even with a dozen machine guns pumping bullets into a big metal Typhon DeLeon outside, Holloway didn't want to alarm her guests.

"So, uh, what now?" Sasha asked.

"I'm going after Holloway, obviously," Gaige said. "Gonna kill her, and then all the billionaires in this place. That was my problem, see? I just wanted to kill her, when really I shoulda been trying to kill *everybody*. Anarchy! Smashing systems! Apparently, you two figured that out before I did."

"No," I said. "We're not killing all the billionaires. And neither are you."

She cocked an eyebrow at me. "Uhhhh, yes I am?"

"They're worth nothing to us dead. But alive? We can force them to pay off every debt on this planet. Free the entire population. Change things."

"Ahhhhhhh…" Gaige winced as if someone was pulling her pigtails out by the roots. "Dammit, that's a pretty good plan. Okay, fine. You do your thing and I'll find Holloway. I'll try not to kill any billionaires on the way."

"Try hard," Sasha said.

"No guarantees, especially if they're armed," Gaige replied. "I hope a lot of them are armed," she muttered to herself.

"You and I need to get back to that security room," I said to Sasha. "We gotta shut those turrets off before all our backup gets torn to pieces." I pointed to a set of stairs to the south. "I think those'll get us close to the security room." Then I indicated another set of stairs at the opposite end of the hall. "The lounge is that way. Might be a good place to start looking for Holloway," I added, nodding at Gaige.

"Ahhh," she said, cracking her neck. "It's been weeks since I killed somebody. Here's hoping I haven't forgotten how, huh? See ya when I see ya!" She limped north, Deathtrap slowing to keep pace with her. Sasha and I headed south.

"We don't have long until they figure out the bots haven't checked in," I said. "We'll have to move fast. If we get lucky, there shouldn't be more than one or two bots guarding that security room."

There were twelve.

40
FIONA

The hallway that had previously been empty save for a single secbot was now packed with chortling billionaires and twelve death bots hovering just over the crowd. The guests nibbled at canapés and murmured words like "investiture" and "tenants" and "brie".

An ocean of wealthy flesh and a thundercloud of metal death stood between Sasha and me and the security room. It'd be nearly impossible to sneak through the crowd without getting spotted, but we had to do it.

"Okay, Sasha," I whispered. "Follow my lead. Don't stop moving for anyone, don't make eye contact with anyone, keep your gun at your side, and never mind that that secbot is staring right at us oh shit the jig is up start blasting."

The secbot that had spotted me charged up its ocular laser but didn't fire it, presumably because it judged it might hit a billionaire by mistake. Instead it lunged toward me, its metal arm shooting out and grasping wildly for my neck. I ducked, put my shoulder down, and just started moving forward, pushing Elites out of my way with every step. If I could just stay low enough, they wouldn't be able to get a clean shot at m—

"IF YOU CAN HEAR THIS MESSAGE AND YOU EARN PASSIVE INCOME, PLEASE DROP TO THE FLOOR NOW."

Suddenly, the ocean of cover I'd immersed myself in dried up. Sasha and I were the only two people standing in a hallway of crouching generational wealth.

A bot fired its laser beam at me. I hit the deck and the bolt went wide, striking a gray-haired man square in his back. "Gah!" he shouted, his singed suit spewing smoke. "How dare you?!"

He was alive. Somehow, he wasn't even hurt. Why? How? I grabbed him by the shoulder and got my answer: his tuxedo was lined with heat- and bullet-resistant armor.

Which, as far as I was concerned, made him cover.

The bot charged up another laser blast. I kept hold of the gray-haired man and positioned him between me and the bot just as another laser bolt cut through the air. It splashed against the billionaire's chest and he cried out, though more in surprise than pain. If I'd had any doubt as to whether using him as a human shield was morally icky, he shouted, "Unhand me!" so I knew he wasn't injured, and then "[something offensive]," so I didn't mind if he was.

I balanced my wrist gun on the billionaire's shoulder and unleashed a volley of bullets at the bot that had targeted me. Hot lead punched holes through its ocular sensor, effectively rendering it blind. But I could already hear another three bots charging their lasers behind me.

"Sasha!" I yelled. "Grab a billionaire!"

It turned out I hadn't needed to say anything. I felt something bump up against my back and heard Sasha's voice saying, "Why settle for one?" I threw a quick look over my shoulder and saw she'd holstered her gun and grabbed a billionaire in each hand. Dual-wielding the one-percent.

The remaining eleven (ugh) secbots encircled us like a poorly made clock. Sasha and I rotated to keep our exposed flanks moving. At that moment, I would have given anything for a Tediore shotgun, as they explode like grenades when they're thrown. In the close quarters of the hallway, an exploding Tediore with a full clip would have easily taken out three or four bots in one fell swoop.

But Rhys wasn't the CEO of Tediore. He ran the Atlas corporation. And under his leadership, Atlas guns had something the other corps didn't: seeker bullets.

I locked on to the nearest bot, pointed the gun at the ceiling, and pulled the trigger. Seekers zoomed from the barrel like angry bees, swerving and diving toward the bot. The bullets smashed onto its head like a hailstorm, punching holes through its skull and shoulders. It lurched to the ground and stayed there.

"Switch!" I yelled to Sasha, grabbing one of her billionaires while she raised her own wrist gun and fired away, filling the air with a buzzing swarm of bullets. I slammed a new clip into my weapon and passed one of the billionaires to Sasha's free hand.

A bot zoomed toward me, claws out. I shoved my remaining billionaire shield—a woman wearing a fur coat, fur gloves, fur boots, a fur necklace, and fur lipstick—toward it. Its claws disappeared mid-slash, sending nothing deadlier than a gust of air toward me. I emptied my magazine at the bot's face, atomizing its eye and rendering it useless. My joy was short-lived, however, as the fur woman dove to the floor.

My front was completely exposed, and six secbots were more than happy to take advantage of that fact. They swarmed me at once, claws swinging.

41
GAIGE

The Vault Hunter, as she had done many times before, carved her way through the crowd of those who wished her dead. Her shotgun blasted holes in the never-ending flood of robots, and Deathtrap reached its diamond-hard claws into the breaches and ripped them wide open.

She smiled, as she always did when in the midst of a battle she knew she'd win. What made this particular battle different to her—and to her several million ECHOstream subscribers—were the tears running down her face as she blasted the bots around her to shrapnel.

"I didn't talk a lot about my dad," Gaige said, decapitating a secbot with her metal arm, "because I didn't wanna give Holloway any info to find him with. Then, once she found him anyway, I didn't talk about him because it... hurt too much."

She sniffed away a tear. A billionaire pulled a small pistol out of the inside pocket of his tuxedo and pointed it at Gaige, snarling. She ducked, slid on her knees, pointed her shotgun upward, and blasted the top half of his body away in a flurry of wet chunks.

"I planned to rescue him, obviously," she said, racking the shotgun and rising to her feet. "But before they put him in solitary, he managed to send me one last message." She fired again, and a handful of robots exploded before her. "It said, 'Don't come back. Anarchy forever.'"

The tears came too fast to wipe away as she jammed the shotgun barrel into the open mouth of a trillionaire spacewhale-oil-harvesting executive. She didn't fire—he was unarmed, and her shotgun was empty—but she could use him as cover to get further into the estate.

"That was our little saying. We'd go to marches and protests and riots together when I was a little kid, just after they demolished the Tetanus Wilds. We'd go marching down the streets of the rich district, and I'd make molotovs for him and he'd teach me how to wash the tear gas from my eyes, and…"

She paused to kick the executive off the end of her shotgun, toward a cadre of approaching security baddies. He tumbled into them, slowing their approach and giving Gaige time to duck behind a bronze statue of a nude Holloway and slam more shells into her shotgun's breech.

"So, yeah, I was always gonna come back. But I was just a kid. Just some punk. I had to get better. Get some big guns. So I went after a Vault, and I ended up fighting an authoritarian plascrete-surgery addict. I felt good. I felt like a hero. I felt ready.

"But it was too late."

She leaped from behind the statue, blasting and pumping the shotgun even as the tears blurred her eyes so she couldn't even see what she was shooting at.

"I dunno why I'm telling you this. And I'm pretty sure you can't hear most of it through the gunfire. But I think—"

Just then, two familiar voices cried out in panic, Fiona and Sasha's shouts reverberating down the marble halls of the Holloway estate. The Pandoran con artists sounded as if they were in some trouble.

But they were in the opposite direction of Holloway's bedroom.

Gaige bit her lip as Deathtrap sliced a bot in half vertically.

"I think I'm done waiting to do the right thing," she said.

42
FIONA

I kicked backward, knocking Sasha and her two billionaires to the ground and causing the robots' swipes to miss us all by a hair's breadth. I dove to the side and took cover behind a priceless statue of Holloway climbing a staircase made of ugly people's heads. Sasha grabbed another billionaire and flattened herself against the wall, trying her best to block the barrage of laser blasts with her newfound human shield.

The bots took aim at the statue. I knew I was safe behind it for the moment; there was no way Holloway hadn't programmed her security to keep her valuables safe at all costs.

"DISENGAGING PROPERTY PROTECTION PROTOCOL," the robots said in unison before blasting the statue to smithereens.

I dove again, dodging another laser blast that burned a hole clean through my waiter's vest. I grabbed another billionaire from the ground and fired blindly over my shoulder. The seeker bullets careened wildly through the hallway, eventually finding a home in a bot's hoverengine. It fell to the floor, furious but immobile.

Sasha pushed her billionaire to the ground and leaped onto the back of the nearest secbot. She thrust her arm into the gap between its head and shoulders and yanked something out. I expected it to drop to the floor in a fatal malfunction, but instead she started tapping buttons on her wrist ECHO.

As I blew up a bot with another well-aimed salvo, I dove underneath the swipe of another bot just in front of me, landing just under its hoverengine. I thrust my gun between the engine and the rest of the chassis, pulled the trigger, and didn't let up. Bullets flew into the bot's insides and ricocheted off its chest cavity, tearing through all sorts of important and expensive components. The bot shuddered and convulsed in something approximating pain and nearly fell on top of me before I rolled out of the way.

Sasha, meanwhile, was dodging laser blasts from four other bots while riding a fifth like a robotic mini-Saurian. "Come on!" she yelled as a laser bolt singed her hair. "Come! *On!*"

Suddenly, the bot she was riding stopped jerking around. Its eye changed from a blood red to a calm blue—the universal sign, I knew, of a robot's allegiances changing.

The bot turned to its four companions and fired a laser beam before they had time to realize what had happened. The beam cut through one of the bots like a hot knife through a throat[32] and the other three bots fired in retaliation. The combined force of three laser blasts cut Sasha's bot to shreds, leaving only its charged laser eye intact.

One of the bots swung at Sasha. She dove backward and pointed the bot's charged eye at her assailant, slamming a button on her ECHO device. The eye fired one last laser bolt and fizzled out, but it was enough: the beam caught the attacking bot just under its armpit and sliced its arm clean off, digiclaw and all.

I was nearly out of ammo and we were both exposed, but at the very least we were no longer surrounded. The security room waited

---

32 Old bandit saying.

in the hallway behind us, while the three and a half deathbots fired lasers from the other direction. We each yanked a billionaire to their feet to protect ourselves and give us some breathing room. We could make a run for the security station, but we'd leave our backs totally exposed—we'd be dead before we made it half the distance.

"Sasha!" I yelled. "Get a backpack!"

We quickly scanned the floor for the smallest billionaires we could find. Sasha grabbed an alarmingly old man (who had invented a new recreational drug made of puppy bones and kitten tears) and I hauled a young boy to his feet (who was actually sixty-three but had hollowed out the skull of his young son and implanted his own brain so he could live life a second time) and we hoisted them onto our backs. They struggled against us, fighting to get free. I calmly, rationally introduced my elbows to their faces, so hard their legs buckled. Then we ran as laser blasts exploded on the armored coats of our billionaire backpacks. It wasn't often that Sasha and I had to use the nonconsensual piggyback strategy, but this was do or die.

Still dodging lasers with every step, we made it to the door of the security station. We cast off our unconscious billionaire shields and locked ourselves inside.

The monitors showed our Typhon DeLeon statue/transport/ whatever was not much longer for this world. The autoguns had already punched several man-sized holes in Typhon's face and belly, from which the muzzle flares of return fire could be seen. That was good news, at least—there were still some survivors inside.

Something heavy and metallic slammed into the locked door behind us. The door handle glowed red and started sizzling—a sustained laser blast was beaming into it from outside. They were going to get in, and sooner rather than later.

Sasha slammed her hand down on the button we'd seen earlier

that deactivated the autoturrets. The spew of bullets came to a sudden stop and the turrets powered down in unison.

Sasha jabbed at even more buttons at random until one of them happened to cause the mansion's front gate to swing open, providing an entry point for our band of rebels. Dozens of our armed pals streamed from the wreckage of the Typhon DeLeon, weapons in their hands and anger on their faces.

We didn't have long to celebrate. The door burst open behind us and four secbots tried to shove their way inside. I blasted the first one through the door and dropped it like a hobby after I've realized it's more difficult than I first expected. Sasha took care of the second, riddling it with holes.

As the remaining two approached us, we pulled our triggers again. Nothing. I had the distinct impression that we were about to be murdered. Our guns were as empty as our pockets. The security room was cramped; there was nowhere to maneuver or dodge the secbots' claws. We'd be dead before we could reload.

I grabbed a chair as a makeshift shield.

This was it. This was the end.

43
FIONA

Nah.

"Anarchy forever!" a voice howled in fury. A fistful of buckshot bounced off the ground and, somehow, perfectly ricocheted into the underside of one of the bots. It fell to the ground, inactive. As the other turned around to face this new attacker, a digiclaw sliced its head off.

Gaige and Deathtrap stood in the doorway, Gaige with a smug look on her face. Deathtrap didn't have a face but somehow floated smugly.

"I thought you were going for Holloway," I said to her.

"Yeah, but we're buddies now so I decided to save you," she replied. "Which I did! Easily. I'm psyched."

With a loud boom, the distant front door burst open. The Rustville rebels would be streaming into the mansion. Their angry shouts reverberated through the entire estate.

Sasha and I rushed out of the security room, guns in hand. If we didn't handle this the right way, Holloway's estate would be filled with a bunch of dead billionaires and the Rusters no better off than they had been.

"Cool talk," Gaige yelled at us as we ran down the hallway. "Maybe we'll catch up later?"

Dozens of Holloway's guests cowered in the foyer as a flood of armed men, women, and children charged the room. They kicked the billionaires in their stomachs, grabbed them by the hair, spat on them—all understandable behavior, but not the kind of vibe Sasha and I had been hoping for.

"Wait a minute!" I shouted over the cacophony. "They can't pay your debts if they're dead!"

"I wouldn't be so quick to take the moral high ground, madam," came a voice with a familiar lilt but a confusing tone. I searched the crowd to find its owner, only to see the world-weary eyes of Fitzwiggins, our former murder-solving butler. I hadn't seen him at all in the Tetanus Wilds. He must have somehow snuck in with the rest of the fighters after the gates opened.

"Fitzwiggins!" I gasped.

"Madame Fiona," he said.

"What are you doing here? Where did you come from?"

He furrowed his brow in confusion as the others continued to harass the billionaires. "I don't follow."

"I haven't seen you since I sold the house!"

Fitzwiggins leaned forward. "Er, yes you have. I've been in the Tetanus Wilds. Constructing your large Typhon DeLeon-shaped deathtrap along with the rest of your class warriors. You don't... Are you saying you didn't recognize me?"

My face felt hot. *Oh, jeez.* "Uh, you must have been facing away from me," I said, and coughed.

"For a week straight? We hid from a secbot patrol in the same foxhole! For an hour!"

"I'm so sorry, Fitzwiggins."

"I waited on you hand and foot! I solved multiple murders committed on your estate, saving you from who knows how much prison time! And you couldn't be bothered to remember my face?

You would *dare* call yourself a leader of the downtrodden and destitute? You would *dare* tell us how to behave in the presence of our oppressors?"

"Right," I said, and nodded. "I just—"

Fitzwiggins jabbed a finger at me. "You were not born here. And you earned your billions by capturing someone who was. So I am asking you—or, rather, telling you—not to tell us how to run our own revolution. We appreciate the guns, and we appreciate that you got us inside. But if tonight's little revolution is going to change anything at all, it must come from the people of Eden-5. The real crime," he continued, slipping into the same tone he usually reserved for dramatically revealing a murderer's identity, "would be to free Eden-5 from the grip of one group of billionaires only to hand it to another."

My embarrassment had turned to anger. Who was Fitzwiggins to tell me anything? I'd bankrolled this entire operation. I'd come up with the plan. I'd put Sasha and myself in harm's way to pull it off. Not to mention we were flat broke.

"You seem to misunderstand who you're talking to," I growled. "We did this to save you. We're the good guys."

"Funny," Fitzwiggins said, a cruel smile curling his lip. "I seem to remember one Handsome Jack saying much the same thing."

He might as well have punched me in the throat. I couldn't speak. I knew Fitzwiggins' implication was coming from a place of anger. I knew his comparison was unfair in a billion different ways. I knew he didn't really mean what he was saying.

But it didn't matter. With all the subtlety of a sniper round to the skull, I understood what he was getting at. Yes, we wanted to help. Yes, the people of Rustville probably wouldn't have been able to rise up without us. But Sasha and I were still just a couple of outsiders trying to tell everyone how things should be. It wasn't time for me to pump my fist in the air and lead a group of obedient schmucks into battle. It was time for me to do something much harder.

It was time for me to step aside.

"Okay," I said. "You win." I gestured at the crowd of pissed-off Rusters, still beating the hell out of the whimpering Elites who'd enslaved them in debt. "It's your show. Now handle it."

"But—" Sasha began. I raised a hand to stop her.

"I'm still trying to get a handle on this whole Vault Hunter thing," I said as Fitzwiggins leaped onto a table. "But I think part of it is figuring out which parts are bigger than us. Smuggling guns and killing robots? That's our thing. Reorganizing society? I think that's above our pay grade."

"I really, really hope you're right," Sasha said. "'Cause if you're not, they're probably gonna kill us, too."

Fitzwiggins cleared his throat. "Quiet!" he yelled, and something about his accent or the timbre in his voice or the fact that he fired his shotgun into the air just before he did so made everyone comply.

"Billionaires of Eden-5, there has been… a murder." He raised his eyebrow. "And the culprit is… all of you. You have put a stranglehold on our futures, and tonight you will relax your grip. Around you, you see the huddled masses of this planet, who do everything to satisfy your whims. In return, they are burdened with debts they cannot pay, to those so rich they do not need the money in the first place. You will free them of these obligations or you will die.

"Now," he said, racking his shotgun. "Who wants to go first?"

44
FIONA

The answer, it turns out, was nobody. The billionaires suddenly became very interested in their own shoes. That is, until Fitzwiggins stuck his gun in the mouth of a crypto billionaire[33] who suddenly became very interested in the concept of charity.

We had the Elites at gunpoint. Some of them stepped forward, wrist ECHOs out, ready to free from debt the people who had worked so hard for them in the past.

Just as I was stupidly thinking everything would be all right, an alarm blared throughout the house. Thick steel shutters crashed down over the manor's front doors. Metal plates slid out of the walls to cover the windows, booming as they slammed into place. From the repeated, thunderous pounding that echoed through the hallways, it seemed like someone had sealed every possible exit and window.

"Oh, show some backbone," a voice said through the intercom. "Don't give these inebriates a red cent. This little rebellion will be put down in time for dessert."

---

33 A pervert who buys crypts and turns them into dance clubs.

Rapid footsteps behind us. I whirled, gun up, to see Gaige and Deathtrap sprinting down the hall. Well, Gaige sprinted; Deathtrap floated urgently.

"Problem!" she shouted. "Biiiig problem!"

A holoprojector in the foyer blinked to life, projecting a live feed of Countess Holloway's particularly smug face.

"By this point, my daughter's murderer will have informed you that I currently rest within the cozy, well-furnished, and completely impenetrable confines of my own personal panic room. Meanwhile, three hundred thousand feet above us, my timeshare orbital laser—I get use of it during winter—is slowly moving itself into position above my estate.

"Once it reaches its destination, it'll blast hot death and turn your pathetic class-war uprising into a smudge on the world map. Then I'll exit my panic room and step over your charred bodies on the way to contacting my offworld contractor, who'll rebuild my home at twice its original size and grandeur. I won't even notice the hit on my bank account.

"To my economic peers, I suggest you put as much distance between yourself and the rabble as is possible. The laser is delightfully precise, but best not take chances, hmm?

"To the rabble, you have about three minutes before the laser reaches its final position, so feel free to try and escape, which is impossible, or break into my panic room to shut down the laser, which is also impossible.

"Oh, and here are some more secbots for you to fight. Just because."

The paintings adorning the foyer slid into the walls, revealing racks and racks of armed secbots.

The Rusters bashed on the front door, blasted it with machine-gun fire, searched its seamless metal surface for hinges or weak points—no dice. Whatever the door and window plates were made out of, we wouldn't be able to bust out in time.

The billionaires ran deeper into the house. Fitzwiggins and his troops chased after them. They didn't make it more than a few steps before the secbots woke up and we suddenly had a whole handful of other problems to deal with.

They assembled in the air above us and slashed downward, slicing Fitzwiggins across the face and giving him what would be an incredibly badass scar if he ended up surviving this.

"To the panic room!" he cried, blood streaming down his face. Gaige and Deathtrap led the way, running back in the direction they'd come from while spewing hot lead at the pursuing security. More and more paintings slid away as we ran through the hallways, the airborne mass of cybernetic death growing more and more dense with every footfall. Our forces fired into the air and batted a dozen of the bastards out of the sky, but for every secbot we sent sparking to the marble floor, two more took its place.

The billionaires ran from us, their strides long and powerful thanks to the leg-lengthening surgery many of the shorter ones had undergone. We followed in hot pursuit. If we had any chance of getting out of this alive, we'd need the billionaires within arm's reach.

The Elites ran into a bedroom and slammed the door shut behind them. "Shove off!" someone yelled from the other side. "We've locked the door and—"

He didn't get a chance to finish before the combined might of thirty desperate manual laborers bashed the door open, scattering the Elites like bowling pins.

Even with the secbots right behind us, I couldn't help but gasp. This was Holloway's *bedroom*? It sported a canopy bed equipped with heated infinite waterfalls instead of curtains, and a ceiling that went up so high you'd get dizzy if you looked up for too long. It was also hilariously large—you could fit at least two normal-sized houses in it and still have space for three couches and a guillotine.

Once the last of the Rusters came through the door, Sasha slammed it shut. We held it closed as Deathtrap shoved a bookcase[34] against the door to barricade it.

The bots blasted and slashed at the door. Bookcase or not, we were living on borrowed time.

The door to Holloway's panic chamber—a steel slab of a barrier, likely inches thick—was inset into one of the walls. A fingerprint scanner and voiceprint lock ensured we'd have no chance of finessing our way inside.

I grabbed Fitzwiggins by the arm. "Gaige, Sasha, and I will handle the bots. You've gotta find us a way inside that panic room."

He nodded and called out, "Everyone! Take aim at yonder panic-room door and fire on my command! When we synchronize our fire and work in tandem, there is nothing we cannot accomplish! *Now!*"

Our little rebel band fired damn near everything they had at the door. Rockets splashed and bullets flattened themselves against it, but when the smoke cleared and their mags ran dry, the door was still shut. It looked slightly worse for wear, of course—a few chips in the steel, some carbon scoring near the handle—but at this rate we'd be dead long before we could blow it open.

"It'd take hundreds of pounds of explosives to blast through that thing," Sasha said.

"Oh, don't worry," Gaige replied, holding her back against the buckling bookcase. "The bots will kill us long before we've gotta worry about that laser."

---

34 Loaded, thankfully, with steelbook editions of prolific and overly wordy tomes like *Mr. Torgue's Bumper Book of Descriptions of Different Types of Explosions.*

She was wrong. At some point, the orbital laser had slowed to a stop above Holloway's mansion. I'd assumed there'd be a charging sequence or a countdown or something.

Nope.

Without warning, a ten-foot-wide beam of hot white death speared down into the mansion. The floor rumbled beneath us as everything suddenly grew hotter and louder by the second. The digitized screaming of secbots beyond the door told us the laser had carved into the hallway and was crawling toward us.

Gaige and Deathtrap dove away from the door just in time for a pillar of energy to atomize the bookcase, the doorway, and the floor. The beam moved deeper into the bedroom, much faster than I would have preferred, and scored a fissure in the floor so deep and hot you could see straight into the sewers below.

"Have some more bots, why don't you?" Holloway cackled over the loudspeaker. A panel on the side of the panic room slid open, unveiling yet another rack full of angry automatons.

Belinda Billingsworth, the billionaire who'd flirted with me during our charity gala, stood in the beam's path. "Move!" I yelled at her, my voice all but inaudible against the deafening screech of the laser.

Fear kept her frozen to the spot, even as the beam moved directly toward her. She didn't move.

But the laser did. It stopped short of incinerating her by mere inches, shifted to one side, and traced a path around her. It accelerated once clear of her, crossing the room toward a crowd of terrified rebels, who scattered like ants under a magnifying glass. Belinda finally snapped out of her catatonia and moved to the far corner of the room, where the rest of her peers stood in silent terror of the chaos unfolding around them.

Meanwhile, Fitzwiggins and his fellow Rusters fought for their lives. Holloway's second wave of secbots awakened, and our soldiers found themselves blasting away at them while trying their best to avoid the orbital beam as it crisscrossed the room. The poor bastards had been within moments of finally losing their debt cuffs forever, and now they were going to be either sliced to pieces by robots or burned alive by a space laser.

The cuffs.

Those damned cuffs.

"Wait," I said to Sasha.

"Uh, no!" she replied.

"The laser! It's tracking the cuffs!"

"What?"

"That's why it didn't kill the rich lady. It's only killing people with debt cuffs!"

"Great," Gaige said, pushing her back against mine as she reloaded. "Then we get to die via these crappy ripoff robots rather than the cool space beam."

"No," I said. "It means we have a way inside that panic room. Gaige, keep the bots off our backs."

"My pleasure," she drawled, leaping onto Deathtrap's back and zooming into the fray.

Sasha and I ran to the corner of the room, where Holloway's billionaire friends stood in relative safety. We raised our guns.

"Give us all your money!" I shouted.

The billionaires exchanged glances. Billingsworth's tiny husband chortled, his mustache bobbing up and down with every guffaw. "No," he said, "I don't think we shall. That laser," he went on, pointing at the beam, which was now only a few yards away, "poses no threat to us."

So I grabbed him by the collar, dragged him toward the laser beam, and hurled him into it. He and his mustache vanished in a puff of ash.

"Now—who's up next?" Sasha asked.

"Well," the newly widowed Ms. Billingsworth said, "perhaps money isn't everything." The Elites all tapped their wrists against mine, transferring their funds to my account.

"Stay here," I said, "and maybe you'll get out of this alive." I turned my back on the Elites and waded into the storm of lead and blood.

Gaige zoomed by, her machine gun spewing shock bullets at every bot she could see.

"Gaige! Sasha!" I yelled. "Arms to the center."

"What's going on? Inspiring speech?" Gaige asked.

I tapped my wrist ECHO against theirs, splitting my newly acquired riches three ways.

"I don't get it," Gaige said. "What are we doing?"

I hooked a thumb at the panic room. "Get all the debt cuffs off our people and toss them at that door. Go!"

I saw Tammithah and made a beeline for her. Both her ankles were weighed down with debt. I was amazed she'd managed to survive the mad dash to Holloway's bedroom, until I noticed her thighs looked like they could crush a CL4P-TP unit into a flat trapezoid before you could shriek, "Hello, traveler!" I dove between her legs, slapping my ECHO against both ankles, and her cuffs clattered to the ground. I crawled out from under her, dropped my gun, grabbed the cuffs, and hurled them at the panic-room door as hard as I could.

Near the door, Sasha slid under a secbot, leaped to her feet, and karate-chopped a rebel in the throat. Her wrist ECHO smacked against his debt collar and unlocked it. She grabbed the collar before it hit the ground and, still running forward, hurled it at the panic-room door.

I saw another rebel blasting away at a bot in front of him while another bot approached him from behind. Gaige grabbed him by the wrist and spun him around, pointing his gun at the enemy, who would have stabbed him in the spine. The bot blew to pieces as she brought her arm down on his wrist cuff, then threw it at the panic-room door.

All the while, the orbital laser still traced its way through the bedroom, chasing after anyone still wearing a cuff. The heat from the laser was almost unbearable now; the robots glowed bright red, and the waterfall canopy bed was a steaming, burning mess.

When one of our soldiers tripped over a wrecked bot, the laser obliterated him in a half-second before sharply reversing direction and chasing the next nearest person still weighed down by debt: a one-legged old man, his debt collar loose around his frail neck. He hobbled toward me as fast as he could, which was not going to be anywhere near fast enough to outrun the beam.

"Sorry about this!" I yelled, then ran straight at him, thrust my arm out, and clotheslined him. His collar unlatched and flew backward toward the pursuing beam, which incinerated it and looked for its next victim.

Suddenly, I felt the floor beneath me begin to give way. Too much of the building's supports had been atomized by the orbital laser.

I grabbed the poor old man I'd just forearmed in the throat and stepped backward, away from Fitzwiggins and the rebels. The floor collapsed behind us, a long band of marble cracking and crumbling into the sewer below. Sasha yelped as she lost her footing, and I leaped over and grabbed her by the arm, her legs dangling suspended over a cavernous expanse of filth and pipes.

I dug my toes into the exposed dirt floor. Sasha climbed up my arm, all her weight threatening to pull my shoulder from its socket.

Something green tumbled from Sasha's coat. It tumbled in the air, falling end over end, into the chasm below. The green shard! Our get-out-of-death-free card!

I stared into the abyss, which had just swallowed our best chance of surviving this.

"Hey," Sasha said, pulling my gaze away from the darkness. "We don't need it." She sounded like she actually believed it, which made it easier for me to believe, too.

I hauled Sasha back up to the floor as the orbital laser passed through the newly created crevasse again, surely incinerating the green shard with its white-hot beam. An impassable canyon of stink now separated Sasha, Gaige, the old man, and me from the rest of the rebels.

Things weren't looking great for them, either. By this point, the laser had carved away most of Holloway's bedroom floor, and it was a miracle that the entire room hadn't collapsed into the yawning cavernous sewers below. Only a few chunks of stable floor remained, clinging to the perimeter walls.

The secbots had herded the surviving rebels into one corner. Fitzwiggins and his comrades kept up a wall of gunfire to push back the bots out of slashing range, but in a few seconds it wasn't going to matter. Everyone with a collar was bunched up in the same spot, a lone island surrounded on all sides by a hundred-foot drop too wide to leap over.

The rebels in one corner. Gaige, Sasha, and me at the opposite end of the room. Holloway's panic chamber sat right next to us, untouched, a handful of unlocked debt cuffs piled up outside its door.

"It's not enough!" Sasha wailed. "The cuffs' signals aren't as strong once you unlock them. It's always gonna go for the active ones."

The canyon between us and the rebels was too far to jump. Too far to throw our ECHO devices. All we could do was watch as the laser crawled inexorably toward the obliteration of the very people we'd been trying to save.

"No," I said. "We're not doing this again."

Gaige, still atop Deathtrap, shotgunned a secbot's face off. "What? What *are* we doing?" she asked.

I grabbed her wrist. "Transfer the money back to me."

"Okey doke," she said. "So, what's the plan?"

"Sasha, I need your money, too."

"What? Why?" Sasha protested, even as she tapped her wrist ECHO against mine.

"Now," I said. I unstrapped my ECHO device from my wrist and held it in my hand. The laser was now so close to the rebels that it overheated the secbots they'd been locked in combat with, sending them smoking and sparking into the sewers below.

I closed my fist around the ECHO. I'd have to time this just right. If I could leap over the chasm and throw the ECHO as hard as I could, one of the rebels might be able to catch it on the other side. If they could pay their debts and toss the cuffs away in time, the laser might spare them. But even if everything went according to plan, I'd never get a chance to learn if they survived. I'd be too busy falling to my death.

Sasha's fingers gripped my wrist like a vise. "No," she said. "I know what you're thinking, and don't."

I grinned at her.

Tears formed in her eyes. I wanted to say something—to tell her I was sorry, that she made me prouder and prouder every day, that I wished I hadn't let my fears and anxieties push us apart—but I didn't have time for any of that. This wasn't the moment for an emotional goodbye.

I had to do some Vault Hunter shit.

I tore her hand from my wrist and ran toward the massive hole at a full sprint. Gaige yelled something I couldn't make out. Sasha shouted my name.

I leaped into the open air. The sewer depths yawned below me.

I hurled the ECHO at Fitzwiggins as hard as I could.

And I fell into the noxious abyss.

Wind rushed up at me, drowning out even the sound of the space laser. As I plummeted to my doom, I was surprised to find myself feeling strangely at peace. It occurred to me that the events of the past few hours had felt, well, *right*. For all the mistakes I'd made, I knew, in this moment, that I'd finally done what I was supposed to do. I'd gotten rowdy. I'd acted like a Vault Hunter. Yes, my death was probably going to be painful and unhygienic, but at least I was gonna die doing what I loved.

Then Deathtrap saved me and damn near ruined my entire revelation.

It had plummeted down into the pit, accelerating to reach the bottom before I did, then boosted upward, arms outstretched, and caught me in its metallic arms. I landed stomach-first on its elbow, which, while not at all a pleasant sensation, was infinitely preferable to drowning in a sewer.

Gaige, still perched on Deathtrap's shoulder, slapped the top of my head. "Why didn't you just tell me that was your plan? Deathtrap can fly, you ding-dong!"

"Oh." I furrowed my brow. "I had not thought of that."

Deathtrap rocketed us back up into the bedroom just in time to see Fitzwiggins and the other laborers hurling their debt cuffs at the door of Holloway's panic room. The orbital laser, mere inches from the panicked rebels, stopped in its tracks.

It hesitated, continuing to drill deeper and deeper into the sewers below.

After what felt like an eternity, it crawled toward the panic-room door and the two dozen debt cuffs piled around it.

Holloway was still cackling over the intercom when the laser intercepted the pile of cuffs, which exploded with an ear-splitting roar that matched the intensity of the laser's screech. The explosions didn't even make a dent in the door, but that didn't matter. The laser finally passed over the panic-room door itself and melted it into a pool of shining silver sludge.

Holloway's shriek could be heard even over the sound of the laser, which abruptly switched off before it could move any further into her hidey-hole. The temperature instantly dropped a good twenty degrees as the incinerating beam retreated back into space.

Deathtrap grabbed Sasha around the waist and floated toward the open doorway to the panic room. This gave Sasha just enough time to hit me over the head and hiss, "Deathtrap can *fly*, you moron."

"Yeah, yeah. So I've heard."

Gaige, Sasha, and I leaped off Deathtrap. Through the doorway, I saw Holloway pull a very large shotgun from a weapons chest. I ducked inside the room, taking cover behind a pallet of diamond caviar.

"Stay back!" the countess yelled.

"Counter-offer," I shouted back. "Transfer all your money to our friends and we'll let you live."

"I'd rather die!"

"Interesting word choice," Gaige shouted from outside the panic room. She dove inside, shotgun in hand, and took aim but didn't fire. "Come out—"

Holloway shot Gaige in the chest.

The blast propelled the Vault Hunter back toward the gaping hole in the floor outside, and her gun dropped from her hands. I reached out as quickly as I could to grab her arm to prevent her from falling. My fingers encircled her wrist and I dug my heels into the marble floor as best I could.

Holloway racked her shotgun and aimed once again. Gaige, her chest bleeding from a half-dozen shotgun pellets, took a step forward and shook my hand away.

"You loved your daughter," Gaige said.

Holloway pulled the trigger again. Gaige dove forward, the buckshot flying over her head by inches. She got to her feet, leaving a pool of blood on the panic-room floor. She sprinted toward Holloway.

"I loved my dad," Gaige hissed.

Her mouth open in terror, Holloway racked and fired again. The shot went wide. Gaige kept running.

"Do you know what that makes us?" Gaige asked. She slammed into Holloway at a full run, slamming the billionaire against the far wall. The Vault Hunter's robotic arm swatted the shotgun from Holloway's hand and she shoved her other arm against Holloway's neck.

"Even," she said.

She grabbed Holloway by the neck of her dress and dragged her toward the doorway. "I don't need to kill you," she said. "We've already won. Don't get me wrong, I *want* to kill you—a lot—but."

Pulling Holloway from the panic room, Gaige surveyed the destruction surrounding her. The celebrating rebels. Then she turned to Sasha and me. "But these two taught me that there might be more important things than revenge."

She yanked Holloway to the lip of the abyss. "You're going to donate everything you have to those fighters over there," she said. "And then you and I are never going to see each other again."

Holloway scoffed. "Those *bandits*, you mean? No." She spat into Gaige's face. Gaige didn't bother to wipe it away. "Here's what's going to happen, you classless psychopath. The myriad companies, organizations, and interests I represent will learn of this. They'll come after you, and they will enact a thousand cruelties on every single one of you who participated in this terrorist act. You might as well kill me, because you will not get a single red cent—"

"Okay," Gaige said, and shoved Holloway into the abyss.

The billionaire screamed all the way down until a distant splash silenced her forever.

Gaige shrugged and said to us, "You heard her. I didn't really have a choice. Or I did, but she made that choice pretty easy. We're all cool with how that went down? Ethically?" She didn't wait for a response from Sasha or me before nodding her head a little bit too hard. "Yeah. We're good."

Fitzwiggins called out to us from across the room. "It is done, madams?"

"Yeah," Sasha said. "Casualties?"

"We lost five good soldiers," the butler said, bowing his head. "Tragedies all, but a small price to pay for freedom, eh? Now to escort Holloway's peers through Rustville and the Wilds. We've many more debts to clear before this day is through."

"Great," I said, and crumpled to the ground, exhausted.

"Well," Gaige said. "You freed the workers, and I killed the lady who murdered my dad. You know what I say to that?"

I shook my head, too tired to use words.

"Quest complete," Gaige said.

45
FIONA

For their part, the rebels focused on burying their dead rather than reflecting on their newfound financial independence. Everyone except for Face and Pick, that is, who emerged from the rubble of Holloway's home with guns in their hands.

"Everyone!" Face yelled, every other consonant replaced with a W. "The Vault Hunters—the bounty still stands for them, even if Holloway's gone. We can kill them and take their corpses to somebody who'll pay—Atlas, or Hyperion. They've gotta be worth a heck of a lot to the right people!"

"Face," Pick said, concerned. "Could we maybe talk about this?"

"The only thing to talk about is how we're going to spend all the money we—"

Pick raised her hand, there was a smacking sound, and suddenly Face's rosy-red cheeks were rosier and redder and more just-been-slapped-ier.

"Leave them be," Pick said. "Not everything has to be about money."

Face rubbed his cheeks as tears—real ones this time—streamed down them.

I looked to Fitzwiggins. The kids had decided not to turn us in, but I wouldn't blame the adults for making a different choice. We'd permanently transformed their society, after all, and caused a lot of damage in the process.

The butler stepped toward Sasha and me, deadly serious. "You should know, madams, that though we currently stand in the capital city of Eden-5, this is not the only metropolis of the ridiculously wealthy and politically powerful. Upon hearing of Countess Holloway's death, there will, of course, be an inquest. Retribution will be sought. And if I may be so bold as to make a prediction, all the combined forces of Eden-5's upper class will unite to ensure that such a fate cannot befall one of their number ever again. The first part of such a plan would likely involve the very public, very painful execution of whomever helped bring about the countess's untimely demise."

"That's unfortunate," Sasha said. "Fitzwiggins, would you happen to know who killed Countess Holloway?"

He gave us a knowing smirk. "I have my theories, but it was such a terribly chaotic night. Lots of noise, lots of destruction, and so much of the evidence now having fallen into the sewers, too. No, my dear Sasha. I think, for now, this case will have to remain unsolved."

———

It turns out that after you blast apart every defense robot at a spaceport, you get through security pretty quick.

Gaige and Deathtrap shook our hands ("Goodbye—ow," I said) as the transport ship behind them announced boarding had begun. The Vault Hunter also winced with the effort. A former shoe shiner with a medical degree had managed to pick the buckshot out of her torso, but she still grimaced with every deep breath.

"So," Sasha asked. "Where are you off to now?"

Gaige shrugged. "Nothing for me here anymore. Just a lot of bad memories. So, back to the grind, I guess—kill stuff, find stuff. I gotta say, though, I'd always thought the only way to smash the system was with a big gun and a bigger robot." She tapped Deathtrap's metal pecs. "But that idea you had—paying off everybody's debts to open the panic room—it got me thinking. Maybe a hefty bank account can be just as good a weapon as a hefty rocket launcher."

"What does that mean?" I asked. "You're going to start, what? Investing? Are you going to become a landlord?"

"Ew, no. But… I dunno. Maybe I'll start up a side gig. Hustle and grind a little when I'm not Vault hunting. Party planning, maybe? I dunno. There's definitely a lot more corrupt rich bad guys in the galaxy I can help overthrow." She sniffed. "But what about you?" she gestured at Sasha. "Rethinking the whole Vault Hunter thing? You're good in a fight. Deathtrap and I could use you."

Sasha turned to me.

"What are you looking at me for?" I said. "She asked you a question."

The corner of Sasha's lip curled upward and she took a deep breath. "Thanks, but I think I'm gonna stick with the devil I know." She elbowed me in the side.

"You sure? 'Cause I had this idea where Deathtrap could hold one of us in each hand and use us like human boxing gloves."

Sasha shrugged. "Maybe next time."

"Fair enough. DT and I will catch you on the flip." Gaige grabbed her bag and headed toward the transport. She tossed the devil horns over her shoulder. "You did good, kids."

"I'm at least ten years older than you," I called back, but she must not have heard me.

They disappeared into the spaceship, two unhinged mass murderers off on their next adventure.

"I kinda liked them," I said.

"Me too," said Sasha.

"So," I said. "We're broke again. And regardless of what Fitzwiggins said, it's only a matter of time before somebody on this planet decides to collect on our bounty. What do you wanna do next?"

Sasha gestured at herself, eyes wide in sarcastic surprise. "*You're* asking *me?*"

"My judgement must be slipping. Probably 'cause of that time I died."

"I died way earlier and more painfully than you, so don't give me—"

"More painfully? I was slashed to death!"

"Don't be a baby," Sasha scoffed.

"You're a baby," I said, shoving her shoulder.

"Speaking of, though—of death, not of babies—it's too bad we lost that shard. It saved both our lives. And we still don't know a damn thing about it."

"Hmm," I said. "Powerful, mysterious, potentially alien loot. Might be more of them out there." I raised my eyebrows. "Sounds like a job for a couple Vault Hunters."

"Yeah," Sasha said. "Could be dangerous, though."

I looked around us. Toward the plumes of smoke rising from the ruins of the former Holloway estate. At the grease on our hands and the blood on Sasha's face. All that chaos, all that horror, and we were still standing. "Good thing we had such a relaxing vacation, then," I said.

Sasha nodded. "Let's get to work."

ONE-WAY ECHO COMMUNICATION: OPEN
Contacting: PROMETHEA—WATERSHED BASE—
STRONGFORK, R.
From: INTERSTELLAR TRANSPORT BL-2.5,
PASSENGER: DILLON, FIONA.

TRANSMITTING TEXT-ONLY MESSAGE...
...
TRANSMISSION SUCCESSFULLY SENT.
TEXT FOLLOWS:

Hey, Rhys. Apparently this ship's transporter isn't strong enough
for live communication, so I hope this message will do.

I just wanted to say thanks. For the guns, obviously, but other
stuff, too. For your weird, accidental flashes of brilliance. For
having a heart three times bigger than your brain. And, even
though your relationship still makes zero sense to me, for
being good to my sister.

(If you're ever not good to my sister, I will hunt you down and
put so many bullets in your brain that they'll collide in the
center of your cortex, bounce off one another, and fly out the
same holes they made on their way in.)

Speaking of, Sasha says we've gotta swing by Promethea
at some point so she can see her "long-distance boyfriend"
(ugh). So, congratulations, I guess.

I hope the whole Atlas thing goes well for you on Promethea.
Sasha and I are gonna be traveling for a bit. Seeing sights.

Might hunt a few Vaults, too. Mainly, though, we're looking to help people out. So if you know of any problems that can be solved by a couple of con artists with decent aim, you let me know.

Whoops! Looks like my time's almost up. Bank account's nearly empty again, which I don't mind quite as much as I thought I would. Not to worry, though. I heard about a planet out past Hieronymus where the rivers run purple with Eridium and the trees bear golden fruit. It's probably a trap to kill wayward explorers, but the reward for killing whoever set the trap will probably pay my way for another few weeks.

I used to think anyone who wasn't us could go straight to hell. But now? I dunno. Maybe the real hell is only living for yourself.

They're telling me we're about to land, so I gotta cut this short. Look forward to seeing you again, whenever the hell that day comes.

Oh, and I think Sasha and I found a cure for death. We lost it, but we're looking for another. But that's probably a tale for another time.

Talk soon.

Fiona Dillon,
Vault Hunter.

ACKNOWLEDGEMENTS

The author wishes to thank the editors at Titan Books, who turned this grammatically incorrect avalanche of words into something approaching an actual novel.

The author would also like to thank the folks who worked at Telltale Games for originally bringing Fiona, Sasha, and Rhys to life.

Also special thanks to Erica Stead, Meredith Hershey, Mikayla Jackson, and Lin Joyce, from Gearbox, for reviewing, editing, and bringing this novel to life.

ABOUT THE AUTHOR

Anthony Burch is an almost-critically-acclaimed writer who contributed to the videogames *Borderlands 2, Borderlands the Pre-Sequel, Tales from the Borderlands, League of Legends, Valorant,* and *God of War Ragnarok.* He also hosts a podcast called *Dungeons and Daddies: Not a BDSM Podcast.* He's also sorry. Just... in general.

For more fantastic fiction, author events,
exclusive excerpts, competitions, limited editions and more

VISIT OUR WEBSITE
titanbooks.com

LIKE US ON FACEBOOK
facebook.com/titanbooks

FOLLOW US ON TWITTER AND INSTAGRAM
@TitanBooks

EMAIL US
readerfeedback@titanemail.com